GILDA JOYCE
and the Ladies of the Lake

JENNIFER ALLISON

To my students, with appreciation for all they taught me

First published in the USA in 2006
by Dutton Children's Books
A division of Penguin Young Readers' Group

This edition published in 2007 by Hodder Children's Books
a division of Hachette Children's Books

1

A Catalogue record for this book is available from the British Library

ISBN-13: 978 0 340 91137 2

Typeset in Bembo by Avon DataSet Ltd,
Bidford on Avon, Warwickshire

Printed in the UK by CPI Bookmarque, Croydon, CR0 4TD

The paper and board used in this paperback by Hodder Children's
Books are natural recyclable products made from wood grown in
sustainable forests. The manufacturing processes conform to the
environmental regulations of the country of origin.

Hodder Children's Books
a division of Hachette Children's Books
338 Euston Road, London NW1 3BH
An Hachette Livre UK company

Acknowledgments

I am grateful to executive editor Maureen Sullivan and Dutton Children's Books president and publisher, Stephanie Owens Lurie, for providing a wonderfully helpful and supportive publishing environment for Gilda's adventures. Many thank-yous to outstanding literary agent and friend Doug Stewart, whose ability to do fifteen things at once while keeping his desk neat constantly amazes me. Thank you also to the very talented Greg Swearingen for capturing Gilda's world with his fine cover art.

Several friends and family members contributed their professional expertise: Captain John Phillips of the Pittsfield Township Police Department; Valerie Bijur Carlson, who teaches English and theatre at Connelly School of the Holy Child; author Carolyn Parkhurst; and Professor Kenneth Brostrom, who shared his keen eye for detail in reading the final draft of the manuscript. I would also like to thank the relatives and dear friends who helped me look after baby Max during his first year: my husband, Michael (who made 'Daddy and Max days' a routine); Eleonore Boussoukou (who is secretly an angel); Harry and Ariadne Magoulias ('Papou' and 'Neh Neh'); Paula Allison-England ('Grammie Paula'), Barry England, and 'Grandpa Ken.' Finally, a thank-you to some friends who use their boundless creative energy to help and encourage others: Nancy Finley, Diane McFarland, Martha Daly, Sean Smith, Matt Howe, and my aunt Nancy Pegg.

Contents

Prologue

by Gilda Joyce, Psychic Investigator

If you think a school for girls is simply a place to wear ribbons in your hair and expose your dimpled knees, you've never been to Our Lady of Sorrows.

When I first entered the school, I was all set to tie my hair in a ponytail, get a fake tan, and write my homework assignments in pink gel ink. I was prepared to hear girls bragging nonchalantly about the BMWs and diamond earrings they received for their birthdays. I almost looked forward to hearing the flashlight-wielding nuns tell me to 'leave room for the holy ghost' when I danced lowdly with mossy haired prep school boys.

What I didn't expect was the ominous warning: 'Keep your voice down around the dead.'

I didn't expect the broken sculptures that

1

watched me with their stony eyes, the dungeon-like locker rooms where tarantula-sized spiders lurked in the corners, the sudden floods that devoured homework and caused mass hysteria.

I didn't expect the ghost of a drowned girl to wander the hallways.

I certainly didn't expect to make the most chilling discovery of all: the secret of the Ladies of the Lake.

1

The Drowning

In the moonlit landscape surrounding Our Lady of Sorrows, a blindfolded girl stumbled through the snow. It was the night before Thanksgiving, and only hours before, she had looked forward to several days of Thanksgiving vacation away from school. Now the idea of turkey and sweet potatoes seemed a remote, unlikely image – something that part of her mind realized she might never experience again.

Where was it that she had been trying to go? Was she truly alone, or were they still watching her?

She touched the smooth fabric of the blindfold that was tied so tightly across her eyes, it almost cut into her cheeks. Her nose and lips were numb, and as she struggled to remove the blindfold with clumsy fingers, it seemed that she might as well be touching someone else's face. She gave up and left the blindfold on. They would only make her pay some price if she disobeyed the rules.

Waving her arms in front of her, she discovered that there were no longer tree branches to push out of the way. *Maybe I finally found my way back onto the main path,* she thought.

But now a new emptiness surrounded her – a fresh, frozen silence, as if the world was waiting for something to happen. She walked a few steps and found that the earth had suddenly become perfectly, absurdly flat. As she took another step, her tennis shoes shot out from under her and her tailbone hit the ground with a thump.

Ice. For a moment, she lay on the comforting ice, the snow as soft as a powdery blanket. She had an overwhelming urge to give up – to allow herself to fall asleep. *But falling asleep could mean freezing to death,* she told herself. *You have to keep moving.*

She rolled onto her side, forced herself to move onto her hands and knees, and stood up shakily.

I don't care anymore, she thought, struggling once more to pull the freezing blindfold from her face. This time, she lifted the fabric enough to peek out at her surroundings with part of an eye.

The world was surprisingly bright in the moonlight: blank, white snow edged with a row of naked trees that seemed to observe her from a distance – a row of quiet, cold skeletons.

I'm standing on the lake. The girl forced the blindfold over her temples and finally freed herself from it completely.

Disoriented because the snowfall blurred all boundaries between the lake and the shore, she

4

decided to make her way towards the trees that beckoned with thin, leafless arms.

A soft crunching sound broke the silence – a sound that did not bode well.

Weren't there people across the ice, waiting for her? A group of slender girls? If only she could hurry across before it was too late!

She took another step, and again heard the sickening crunch of ice beneath her feet grow louder. A series of cracking sounds followed like gunshot – multiple fissures hacking apart the flat surface of the ground.

Cold shot through her body, as if ice water had suddenly been injected into her veins and poured into her skull. The shock of plummeting down, down, down into a world without air; the lead weight of the chains on her limbs that only a split second before had been mere clothes. She gasped for oxygen and inhaled icy water; her lungs were dunked and crushed in a liquid black hole.

As her pain receded, she glimpsed the water nymphs who reached towards her with slender hands and flowing hair, pulling her down, deeper into the water to join them where they lived at the bottom of the lake.

2

Our Lady Of Sorrows

Dear Dad,

Sometimes I don't understand Mom at all. I know she hates miniskirts, so why is she so excited about the prospect of her daughter donning a Britney Spears outfit and going to private school for girls?

I know I'm the one who wrote the application essay and everything, but that was when I thought there was no way they would give me a scholarship! The last thing I want is to hang around a bunch of debutantes who will probably give me the stink eye because I live on the 'wrong' side of town.

There is NO WAY I'm going to Our Lady of Sorrows.

'Gilda, you should at least give this school a *chance.*'

Gilda slumped in the front seat of her mother's Oldsmobile and fanned herself with the glossy brochure from Our Lady of Sorrows School for Girls.

The air conditioner in the car was broken, and in the August humidity, the tights her mother had forced her to wear with her skirt and blouse made her feel as if she were sweltering in a tropical swamp. Everything about the outfit she was wearing – the high-heeled, secretarial pumps purchased at Payless Shoes, the polyester blend of her navy blue skirt (not to mention her fear that there *might* be sweat stains on the armpits of her blouse following the ride in an overheated car) felt just plain *wrong*. At the moment, Gilda felt intense irritation with her mother, the whole notion of a private school for girls, and the entire world in general.

'Gilda you're being way too judgmental. Don't forget, I went to a private school myself, and I am obviously no debutante.'

Gilda knew that this was true; her mother was a hardworking nurse who wasn't afraid of things like needles, blood, and drains clogged with hair. On the other hand, Gilda knew that the Catholic school her mother had attended in Southfield had little in common with the rarified, exclusive atmosphere of Our Lady of Sorrows in the Detroit suburb of West Bloomfield, commonly known as 'one of the wealthiest communities in the entire United States.'

They passed a sign announcing the West Bloomfield City Limit, and the neighbourhood of well groomed lawns through which Mrs Joyce had just driven suddenly became a landscape of progressively larger, more elaborate houses.

'Who *lives* in these places?' Gilda's mother wondered, slowing down and gaping at an enormous white house with pillars. The house seemed to peer down at Mrs Joyce's aged, unwashed car with disapproval.

'The girls who go to Our Lady of Sorrows live in these places.' *If the houses in this neighbourhood seem to look down their noses*, Gilda thought, *what will the girls at Our Lady of Sorrows be like?*

'Gilda, they don't give out many scholarships, so keep in mind that this is a rare opportunity. Especially considering the fact that your grades from junior high were all over the place, I think it was very nice of Brad to pull some strings and convince the headmistress to consider your application so late in the summer.'

'Nobody *asked* Brad to pull any strings.' Brad Squib was Mrs Joyce's new boyfriend, and since Gilda found him annoying, she resented the fact that he had done something to help her. Now she would have to express gratitude and appreciation rather than sullen grimaces when he was around. 'Besides,' she added, 'plenty of total geniuses have got bad grades.'

Gilda stopped fanning herself with the school brochure and paused to examine the image on its cover: a pretty girl sitting by the side of a lake and gazing dreamily into the distance.

Our Lady of Sorrows

Our Lady of Sorrows provides a beautiful, stimulating environment for girls who truly want to learn. The school also provides structured discipline to protect girls from potentially unhealthy influences.

Originally built as a country estate by automotobile tycoon Stanton Jackson and his wife Martha in the year 1900, the Castle House that is now Our Lady of Sorrows reflects the Jacksons' passion for medieval and Renaissance architecture and the couple's love of the arts. Surprise, beauty and mystery are found at every turn.

The Jacksons willed part of their entire estate to an order of nuns who opened Our Lady of Sorrows in 1951. Throughout the 1950s and 1960s, Our Lady of Sorrows was an elite finishing school for young women who wished to improve their skills as future wives, mothers, and elegant hostesses.

Our Lady of Sorrows has evolved into a school with an outstanding academic programme that emphasizes both creativity and the scientific method. Many of our graduates have continued their education at Ivy League colleges

What do students say about Our Lady of Sorrows?

'I feel so at home here! Everyone is so nice all the time!' – Marcie

'At my old school, I used to spend hours putting on make-up and picking out clothes to wear every morning. Now I can roll out of bed and get dressed in ten minutes! Who knew I would love wearing a uniform!' – Eloise

'I've been able to concentrate better on my studies without having boys around all the time.' – Nichole

'You know,' said Gilda, tossing the brochure aside, 'since I've never actually *had* a boyfriend, I find it a little strange that I'm being locked away in a convent where I'll never *get* one.'

'I always found plenty of chances to meet boys when I was a teenager at a girls' school,' said Mrs Joyce. 'Probably too many.'

'That was because you were a tart.' The words seem to come out before Gilda could stop them.

Her mother abruptly stepped on the brake and pulled her car to the side of the road. 'What did you say to me, young lady?'

Gilda stared at her lap. 'I didn't mean it.' She *had* heard stories about how her mother had smoked in the girl's bathroom and snuck out at night while her parents were asleep, but Gilda guessed that now was not the time to remind her mother of these facts.

Mrs Joyce sighed with exasperation as she manoeuvered back onto the street, following a series of winding roads with whimsical names like Butter Creek Road and Cherrybrook Lane. Gilda scowled out of the window at enormous houses that sprawled on perfectly landscaped lawns. The surroundings seemed more like a series of little kingdoms than a single neighbourhood.

Cherrybrook Lane ended abruptly, and Gilda found

herself peering through the windshield at a landscape of soaring pine trees; it seemed that they had arrived at the edge of a forest. She and her mother faced an iron gate that had been left open. A small sign announced: *Our Lady of Sorrows Upper School for Girls*. An arrow pointed to a long driveway that disappeared into the trees.

'I guess this is it.' Mrs Joyce drove slowly through the gate and followed a curving drive where tall trees provided a moment of relief from the scalding sun.

As the car entered a sunny clearing, both Gilda and her mother gasped.

'Well, will you look at *that*?' said Mrs Joyce. 'Brad said it was interesting, but I had no idea it was like *this*. No wonder they call it the Castle House.'

Gilda felt a rush of adrenaline and a ticklish sensation in her left ear that usually meant that she was on the verge of having an encounter with something beyond the realm of the ordinary. She knew that there was something very interesting indeed about this school.

Our Lady of Sorrows appeared amidst the trees like an image from a dream. The school looked nothing like the institutional brick building where Gilda had attended junior high school. It also looked nothing like the self-consciously perfect houses in the surrounding West Bloomfield neighbourhood. Gilda actually had to blink several times to make sure that her eyes weren't deceiving her. It was as if Mrs Joyce's car had slipped through a time portal into a mediaeval world.

'It looks just like a castle,' Gilda breathed.

Instead of an ordinary roof, the enormous building had battlements and turrets that soared against the blue sky. Gilda half-expected to see a soldier wearing an iron helmet and carrying a spear peering down at her from above. The stone walls were laced with creeping vines that partially concealed arched, stained-glass windows. Gilda sensed a brooding sadness about the building: there was something ominous about the weighty silence in the air.

Mrs Joyce parked in a small car park behind the school where a handful of expensive cars huddled together in a corner of shade, then checked her reflection in the rear-view mirror, fluffing her hair. Gilda was already making her way towards the school as if pulled toward it by an overwhelming magnetic attraction.

'Wait!' Mrs Joyce called after Gilda. 'Don't you need to comb your hair first?'

'Nope.'

'Don't you want to make a good impression on the headmistress?'

Gilda had already disappeared around the corner. Her mother followed behind, wobbling a bit in the high heels she rarely wore.

3

The Ghost In The Lake

Because she was used to schools where institutional lockers lined drab corridors and ancient drinking fountains spewed trickles of rusty water, Gilda was particularly thrilled to discover that the interior of Our Lady of Sorrows was just as imaginative as its castle-like exterior promised. She wandered past a vacant receptionist's desk into a room filled with ornate furniture drenched in jewel-like shades of maroon, green, and gold. Whimsical images of animals and magical creatures were everywhere: pheasants and peacocks covered the silk wallpaper; a trio of mermaids supported a marble coffee table; gilded cherubs perched at the edges of mirrors; plaster dragons and ogres with scowling faces hovered at the tops of walls, as if holding up the complicated moulding of the ceiling. Gilda walked slowly through the room, touching objects here and there. She paused at a bookshelf to pick up a book with the intriguing title *Tales of Woe*.

'Oh, there you are, Gilda. Can you believe this

place?' Mrs Joyce appeared, wiping perspiration from her forehead with a tissue.

At the same moment, a strikingly thin young woman with long, black hair emerged from an adjacent office. 'Are you Gilda Joyce?'

Gilda shoved *Tales of Woe* back into the bookshelf and struggled to control her surprise as she turned to meet the gaze of the thin woman, whose obviously dyed black hair hung past her waist in long, uneven locks. Gilda couldn't help noticing her striking resemblance to a vampire.

'My name is Velma Underhill.' The woman spoke with a nasal voice, extending a limp, pale hand and revealing small, pointy teeth that resembled little fangs. 'I'm the headmistress's assistant.'

Gilda shook Velma's hand. 'I've never met anyone named Velma before,' she blurted, noting that Velma's hand felt unpleasantly damp and slippery. Her mother shot her a familiar look that meant '*Please censor yourself.*'

'You may call me Miss Underhill.' Velma turned to Mrs Joyce and extended her clammy hand. 'Nice to meet you, Mrs Joyce. Mrs McCracken will see both of you in her luncheon room.'

'Is this a lunch meeting?' Gilda asked.

'No, but Mrs McCracken always wants guests to see her luncheon room.' Velma turned to give Gilda a wry look. 'Maybe she'll give you a muffin or something.'

Gilda was about to explain that she wasn't hungry,

14

but she was silenced by the sight of Mrs McCracken's luncheon room as she followed Velma through the next doorway.

If an enormous, pink wedding cake could turn itself into a room, Mrs McCracken's luncheon room would be the likely result. Everything in the room — furniture, walls, draperies — radiated a soft shade of pink. Gilda's eyes were drawn up to the creamy plaster decorations on the ceiling — a pattern of pink feathers, leaves, birds, mermaids, cherubs, and fish.

'It's breathtaking,' said Mrs Joyce. 'Isn't this just amazing, Gilda?'

Gilda nodded, but couldn't help thinking that it also looked as if a bunch of the mermaids and cherubs on the ceiling had puked after eating too much cotton candy for lunch.

'Absolutely stunning, isn't it?' A stout, energetic woman appeared from behind and shook Mrs Joyce's hand with a firm, business-like grip. 'I'm Shirley McCracken, the headmistress.' She spoke with a bright, twangy voice that hinted of a southern drawl.

Mrs McCracken was the exact opposite of her assistant, Miss Underhill. Whereas Miss Underhill was tall and rail-thin with long, stringy hair and not so much as a dab of make-up, Mrs McCracken was short, broad, and plump with yellow hair that towered above her head in an outdated beehive. Her skin was caked with bronzing powder and bold, coral pink lipstick that looked as if it might glow in the dark.

15

'You must be Gilda.' Mrs McCracken grabbed Gilda's hand and mashed it between two chubby palms. 'I'm so very glad to meet you, sweetie. Such a pleasure. Shall we have a seat? Help yourself to some tea and muffins, darlin'.'

Gilda noticed that Mrs McCracken wore a bejewelled cross around her neck and a chunky diamond on her finger. Her nails were long, pink claws, painted to match her lips.

Gilda and her mother followed Mrs McCracken to a sideboard where they assembled cups of tea in china tea cups, then sat across from the headmistress at a small table decorated with a fluffy pink tablecloth.

Mrs McCracken gazed at Gilda with a fierce expression that seemed simultaneously admiring and sceptical. 'Gilda, our English department was very interested in your application essay.'

Gilda had completed the personal essay section of her application hastily and in a decidedly begrudging frame of mind, but she remembered that she had said something about 'remaining steadfastly brave' despite the trauma of her father's death from cancer a few years ago. She also remembered the bold and possibly overblown statement that she constituted a 'triple threat' as a 'novelist, psychic, and crime-fighter.'

'My colleagues said to me, "Shirley, this girl has a flare for writing and a gift for satire. Bring her onboard!" '

'Gilda is always writing something,' Mrs Joyce interjected. 'She's written whole novels already!'

'You must be darn proud.' The headmistress beamed at Gilda.

'Gilda's only problem is that she works on just about every project under the sun except her homework!' The headmistress raised her eyebrows, and Mrs Joyce grimaced, immediately realizing that her last statement had cast her daughter in an unfavourable light. 'I mean, she does her homework, mostly, but she always has her own projects to work on too.'

'We like self-motivated students here at Our Lady of Sorrows. Lots of the girls tell me they feel really inspired here.'

'That sounds good,' said Mrs Joyce, glancing at Gilda hopefully.

Gilda looked away, irritated with her mother's eagerness. Did she *want* to attend this school? True, the surroundings were spectacular, and both Miss Underhill and Mrs McCracken struck her as intriguingly odd characters. On the other hand, something about the ornate formality of Mrs McCracken's luncheon room made her feel claustrophobic. Gilda remembered reading that prisons sometimes use the colour pink to calm the inmates. What if Our Lady of Sorrows was simply a gilded prison?

'Gilda, honey, you must have a whole heap of questions you want to ask me.' The headmistress fixed Gilda with another intense stare.

Gilda really wanted to ask Mrs McCracken how she managed to get her hair piled up so high on her head.

She also wondered about the headmistress's personal life. Did she eat lunch in her luncheon room every day by herself? And what about Miss Underhill? Did her resemblance to a vampire have any basis in fact? Gilda knew that her mother would disapprove of these questions. She thought for a moment and came up with a more educationally relevant query. 'How severe is the corporal punishment here?'

Mrs McCracken guffawed. 'Honey, nobody's going to spank you here. No corporal punishment whatsoever.'

'I just figured that the nuns probably can't resist a little knuckle rapping here and there, at the very least. Maybe a good sound thrashing for bad behaviour.'

The headmistress let out another cackle. 'My gosh, you are a live wire! Are you pulling my leg?'

'That was just Gilda's idea of a joke,' said Mrs Joyce, nervously.

'I've heard that some of these schools are going back to the old ways,' said Gilda, ignoring her mother's discomfort.

Mrs McCracken regarded Gilda steadily, as if she were trying to determine how much trouble this girl would actually be, and whether the advice of her English department had led her astray. 'Well, Gilda, you might be interested in the fact that only three of our teachers are actually nuns. I myself grew up Methodist, so as much as I'd like to, I can hardly expect every member of our faculty to be a nun! Same thing goes for the girls. Nobody's perfect, right?'

'Right.'

'Well, if you have no further questions, I'll ask Miss Underhill to give you a little tour of the grounds, and then you can think about whether or not you want to accept our invitation. Normally girls from our sophomore or junior class are the tour guides, but you'll be stuck with Miss Underhill today, if that's OK.'

'Thanks so much, Mrs McCracken,' said Mrs Joyce. 'Gilda is so honoured to have this opportunity.'

'You're very welcome. And Gilda, I'm sure you'll absolutely love it here.'

Miss Underhill led Gilda and her mother through a dining hall covered with oil paintings of church officials, a gilded ballroom that was now used as the school's theater, a second parlour, and a chapel where the stained glass and soaring ceilings resembled a scene from a European postcard.

Throughout the tour, Miss Underhill couldn't have been a more sullen guide. She made no attempt at conversation and provided only the most cursory introduction to each room. As Gilda and her mother looked around, she sulked and picked her cuticles or stared at her watch.

'*What's eating Morticia?*' Gilda whispered to her mother.

Mrs Joyce suppressed a giggle.

'That's about it,' said Miss Underhill, sounding bored. 'I can show you some of the grounds outside, if you want.'

'But what about the classrooms and teachers' offices?' Mrs Joyce asked.

'That's not part of the tour,' Miss Underhill replied, unapologetically. 'I'm supposed to focus on the selling points.'

Mrs Joyce looked taken aback by this response, but Gilda was intrigued. 'What's wrong with the rest of the school?' she asked.

'Nothing's *wrong* with it, exactly, but it takes a ton of money to maintain all the historical detail, and after a while, things start going downhill.'

Gilda wondered what Mrs McCracken would say if she had been around to hear this last comment.

'Plus, there were a few infestations this summer.'

'*Infestations?*' Mrs Joyce's mouth fell open in disbelief.

'Just some baby raccoons and a few bats.'

Gilda imagined herself taking a geometry test only to be interrupted by a litter of infant raccoons rolling around on the floor like furry kittens. 'I caught one!' she would yell as the teacher threw up her hands and declared the test pointless. She would take the baby raccoon home and keep it as a pet.

'Raccoons and bats?' Mrs Joyce still seemed shaken.

'Don't worry about it, Mom,' said Gilda, who viewed this bit information as a selling point in favour of the school.

Miss Underhill led Gilda and her mother outside. 'Will you both be OK in those shoes?' She peered down at their high heels. Gilda noticed that

Miss Underhill herself wore flat loafers with her black pantsuit.

'I guess,' said Mrs Joyce, reluctantly.

'We'll be fine.' Gilda was used to wearing costumes that included uncomfortable shoes of all types. She couldn't help feeling a moment of sadistic satisfaction; her mother obviously regretted insisting on high heels.

Outside, Miss Underhill led Gilda and her mother down a shady path where pine needles carpeted the forest floor. They reached a garden with a stream that flowed into several tiny waterfalls, filling the air with the happy sound of rushing water. Next to the stream, neatly trimmed hedges grew in a maze-like design around a small sculpture of the Virgin Mary.

'This is our Garden of Contemplation,' said Miss Underhill, leading Gilda and Mrs Joyce over a miniature wooden bridge that arched across the stream.

'Oh!' The heel of Mrs Joyce's shoe stuck in a crack in the wood, and she waved her arms, struggling to avoid a spill into the shallow water below. 'That's it; I'm taking these things off!'

'Mine aren't bothering me at all.' Gilda skipped past her mother and followed Miss Underhill up a small hill where she suddenly found herself gazing across a sizeable body of water. *There really is a surprise at every turn in this place*, Gilda thought.

'This is Mermaid Lake,' said Miss Underhill. 'You probably can't see it from this angle, but it's actually shaped like a mermaid.'

Gilda felt a drop of sweat trickling down her back, and wished she could hurl herself into the water, clothes and all.

'Do people ever go swimming here?'

'No swimming allowed.'

'Why not?'

Instead of replying, Miss Underhill continued to trudge along the edge of the lake.

'Wait!' Carrying her pumps in one hand, Mrs Joyce struggled up the path, trying to catch up with Gilda and Miss Underhill. 'Listen, you two go on with the rest of the tour; I think I'm going to sit down in that Garden of Contemplation for a moment.'

'We can turn back if you want.'

'No, you two go on and I'll meet you in a minute. My blisters have blisters!'

Miss Underhill shrugged and turned to continue with the tour.

'We'll hurry,' said Gilda, feeling that Miss Underhill should have offered at least a polite word of sympathy for her mother's blisters even though she herself had been unsympathetic. As she walked next to her glum tour guide, Gilda tried to think of something to say. 'Have you worked here long?' she asked.

'Long enough.'

Miss Underhill was obviously in no mood for small talk. As Gilda left her mother further behind, she imagined that the secluded setting might provide a perfect opportunity for the vampire-like tour guide to bare her little fangs and steal a swift, deadly chomp on the neck.

Just then, Gilda noticed something strange. Across the lake, she saw a miniature castle – or rather, the crumbling remains of a castle. A solitary window peered from the only intact portion – a cylindrical structure large enough to contain a single room. All that remained of the rest of the little castle was a broken wall and the skeleton of an arched ceiling. It looked as if someone had built a small replica of the Castle House next to the lake, and then thrown a grenade at it.

'What's that?' Gilda asked, pointing.

'The ruins.'

'What happened to it? Did someone live there?'

'It was built to look like a ruined building on purpose. It's supposed to be picturesque or something. They have lots of fake ruins in England, so naturally the Jacksons had to have one for themselves when they built their estate.'

Gilda stared for a moment, as if hypnotized. The ruins suggested a sense of tragic decay, but it was strange that they were created as a kind of trick – to look much older than they really were. *This is a place of illusions*, Gilda thought.

Gilda and Miss Underhill passed a sculpture of four slender water nymphs dancing at the edge of the lake. Walking in a prickly silence, they reached a stone bridge that arched over a narrower portion of the lake.

Gilda noticed a memorial plaque cemented into the side of the bridge:

```
  Dedicated  to  the  memory  of
Dolores  P.  Lambert  whose  time
     with  us  was  too  short
```

Gilda approached the bridge, hoping to get a better view of the ruins. 'Who was Dolores Lambert?'

Gilda let out a little yelp of shock as Miss Underhill seized her arm with a violent, pinching grasp.

'Keep your voice down around the dead,' Miss Underhill hissed.

Gilda was speechless with surprise and confusion. Who was dead? She hadn't seen any tombstones around, so what was Miss Underhill talking about?

'A girl died here,' Miss Underhill whispered, dropping Gilda's arm. 'Dolores Lambert was a freshman when she drowned in the lake. You'll hear it from the other girls, so I may as well tell you now. If you make any noise as you walk over the bridge, her ghost rises out of the water, screaming.'

Gilda stared into the dark, bruise-coloured circles under Miss Underhill's eyes and cringed from the sour-coffee smell of her breath. In the heat of the afternoon sun, she felt a delightful shiver of horror. 'And then what happens?' Gilda whispered.

Miss Underhill frowned at Gilda as if she were suddenly speaking a foreign language. 'What?'

'You said her ghost rises out of the water screaming. Then what happens?'

'I don't think I want to find out.'

Gilda's mind raced with questions. *Was Our Lady of Sorrows truly haunted, or was Miss Underhill simply trying to scare her? How had Dolores Lambert drowned? Was the headmistress's assistant completely mad?*

Gilda had just made up her mind; she wanted to attend Our Lady of Sorrows.

4

No Escape

'You've got to be kidding me. You're actually going to attend Our Lady of Wallet?!'

'It's called Our Lady of Sorrows, Wendy.'

Gilda lay on the purple carpeting of her bedroom floor. With her legs propped up on her unmade bed, she rested her head on a makeshift pillow of dirty laundry. She was attempting to carry on a telephone conversation with her best friend Wendy Choy while also eating crisps and salsa. Every now and then, a drop of salsa fell onto her polyester blouse, permanently staining it.

'Everyone knows that all the girls who go there are like millionaires or something,' said Wendy. 'What are you munching?'

'Crisps. Aren't you curious about *why* I decided to go to Our Lady of Sorrows?'

'Clearly you hate me and feel the need to get as far away as possible.'

'True,' Gilda joked, 'but there's also another reason. I've got a psychic investigation on my hands.'

'Would you please stop it?'

'Stop what?'

'I said stop that right now! Sorry, Gilda – my brother was just stuffing the cat into the cupboard again, even though I told him a thousand times HEY! STOP IT RIGHT NOW!'

Wendy's little brother, Terrence, was always doing things like sticking gum in his hair or trying to give the cat a bath with laundry detergent. Wendy often had to baby-sit Terrence after school while also attempting to finish her homework, and as a result, she was very impatient with him. Gilda felt a little sorry for Terrence, since she knew what it felt like to be the younger sibling. She couldn't understand why Wendy was so stingy about letting him tag along when she and Gilda got together to watch television or to spy on neighbours. What was so bad about having a small, clueless fan who found everything you did fascinating?

'Go watch television and leave me alone for half a minute!' Wendy yelled. 'Sorry, Gilda. So what were you saying about a psychic investigation?'

Gilda explained the bizarre exchange with Miss Underhill and the story she had heard about Dolores Lambert's ghost.

'Weird.'

'I know. I may need your help with this one.'

'OK, but I'm going to be really busy this year,' said Wendy. 'I'm signed up for a college-level maths class and I also have a big piano competition coming up.'

In the old days, Wendy had had plenty of time to do things like perform séances, spy on neighbours, or try on purple toenail polish, but then her parents decided that it was time for her to get serious about her studies, become a concert pianist, and look after her little brother several afternoons a week besides. At any rate, Wendy *claimed* that it was her parents who put the pressure on her to become a high achiever. Gilda suspected that Wendy herself was the force behind most of the pursuits, despite her repeated claim: 'All I want to do with my life is sleep!'

Gilda heard Terrence crying in the background.

'See?' said Wendy in a high-pitched whine. 'I *told* you she would scratch you. Now your arm is going to be infected, and we might have to amputate it. Look, Gilda, I've got a cat trauma to take care of, so I'd better go.'

Gilda sat down at her manual typewriter to write a letter to her father. It was something she did almost every day – much like keeping a diary. Gilda liked to think that her father could somehow read her letters, especially when they were typed on the antique typewriter that had once belonged to him.

Dear Dad:
Mom has no idea that I want to go to Our
Lady of Sorrows just to investigate a
haunting.

I have a gut feeling I'm going to feel like
an outsider at this school, but that's the price
I pay for being a psychic investigator. Like
my *Master Psychic's Handbook* says, 'Being a
psychic isn't a normal career, like being a
doctor or a lawyer. At some point, there may
be a price to pay for such an unusual,
misunderstood lifestyle.'

I don't mean to put you in a bad mood, but
I think Mom is going on a date with Brad
Squib tonight.

Don't worry – *I* still can't stand him!

Character Flaws of Brad Squib – official documentation:

1. Too much nose and ear hair.
2. Takes up too much space when he sits on the couch.
3. Tries too hard to be likeable, and this makes him doubly revolting.
4. Jingles car keys in his pocket while talking. Always a sign of perversity.
5. Grins in a sinister, cheesy way when he finds something funny, but doesn't actually laugh.
6. Wears aftershave that smells like motor oil.
7. Always has to say *something* even if he knows nothing about the topic being discussed.

As she documented Brad Squib's flaws, Gilda felt a surge of creative inspiration. She was tired of thinking about Brad Squib, so she decided to begin a sordid tale about Miss Underhill and Mrs McCracken instead:

As the door closed behind their new victim (a sparkling, witty student on scholarship), Velma Underhill and Shirley McCracken shared a fit of irksome giggles that ricocheted across the forest. The hags cracked their knuckles and grinned like two arthritic hyenas ready to tear apart a carcass.

'She doesn't suspect a thing,' cackled Velma.

'Of course she doesn't!' her plump cohort replied. 'They never do!'

'You don't think she noticed my fangs?'

'No. But she *might* have noticed my tail.' Mrs McCracken lifted her long skirt daintily to reveal a scaly, reptilian tail that swished back and forth.

'It's a magnificent tail.'

'Don't patronise me, Velma. I'm hungry. Get me a snack!'

Velma slithered into the hallway, where a herd of plump, jolly schoolgirls skipped blithely to their next class. Velma grabbed a girl who was moving more slowly than the others by her long ponytail and dragged her whimpering back to the headmistress's office.

Behind a locked door, both fiends sunk their little fangs into the slow-witted girl's neck until there was not a single drop of blood left in her body. Then they tossed her into the lake.

The evil school marms panicked for a moment, realizing that they had forgotten to find out their victim's name.

'What will we do?' Velma fretted. 'We don't know which school records to delete.'

'Don't worry,' said Mrs McCracken, picking a bit of flesh from her teeth with a toothpick. 'Nobody will notice she's missing—'

'Gilda?' Mrs Joyce poked her head into Gilda's bedroom. She had tied her wet hair in a towel turban and applied only part of her make-up. With one eye darkened with charcoal eyeliner and mascara and the other bare, she appeared to have a black eye. 'Oh. I thought you said you were going to clean your room today.'

'I'm in the middle of something.'

'Gilda, Brad is at the front door, and I'm not quite ready.'

Gilda turned to scrutinise her mother's half-assembled appearance. 'You look fine,' she lied. 'Dad's pretty casual himself, so I'm sure he won't mind if you go out like that.'

'Would you mind going downstairs to chat with

Brad for two minutes? You can tell him that you liked Our Lady of Sorrows.'

'You want me to "chat with Brad"?' Gilda looked at the ceiling dramatically as if begging for some divine assistance.

'Gilda, please.'

'Oh, all right.' Gilda reluctantly trudged downstairs to face Brad Squib.

'So you liked Our Lady, huh?' Brad Squib sprawled on the couch, legs and arms spread wide apart, as if he were competing with the very furniture to see who could take up more space in the room.

Gilda stood across from him, her arms folded defensively. She didn't want to sit down, because then she'd be stuck in a lengthy, one-sided conversation from which there might be no escape. Whenever her mother said 'I'll be ready in two minutes' it usually meant that she would be ready in something closer to thirty minutes.

'It was interesting,' Gilda said primly. 'Thanks so much for, you know – passing along my application and everything.' As she spoke, Gilda noticed that Brad chewed a piece of gum with a little too much gusto. The sight of his moving jaws filled her with inexplicable rage.

'That place just blew me away first time I saw it.'

'So how do you know the headmistress?'

'Sold her a car back in the days when I worked at a

dealership, and she came back for two more, that's how. Got her amazing deals on all three of them too, so she owed me one.' Brad grinned. 'Owed me three, actually.'

'She's letting me into the school because she bought *cars* from you?'

'Well, my company also donated a car to the school, and she raffled it off at a fundraiser a few years ago. Not that you didn't get into the school completely on your own merits, of course. Shirley just did me the favour of taking a look at your application after the deadline.'

'Thanks.'

'I made quite a few friends back at the dealership. I had a way with people, and that's why they pay me the big bucks to direct regional sales now. Did I ever tell you how I—'

'Oh, I almost forgot to ask,' said Gilda, interrupting Brad. She had learned that if she didn't cut him off in mid sentence, he would go on for hours, telling her one success story after another. She didn't know how her mother could stand it. 'Did you ever notice anything strange about Mrs McCracken – or hear anything unusual about Our Lady of Sorrows?'

'Strange?' Brad squinted at the ceiling and worked his chewing gum. He pointed at Gilda. 'The hair. Am I right?'

Gilda couldn't help but crack a smile, and Brad grinned broadly. 'Does Shirley still have that crazy Queen of England hairdo?'

'You mean her beehive hairdo?'

'Is that what you call it? It's like those furry hats the English soldiers wear when they guard the palace.' Brad raised a finger to emphasize his point. 'Her hair is nuts.'

'But did she ever mention anything about a girl who drowned at the school?'

Brad frowned. 'Oh, I think I know what you're talking about. The little girl who fell through the ice, right?'

'All I know is that there's a bridge dedicated to a girl who drowned in the lake.'

Brad nodded vigorously. 'I remember because it was colder than a witch's behind that year on Thanksgiving, and we were all glued to the local news.' Brad got a wistful, faraway look, as if he had just pictured something that made him sad.

'I wonder what she was doing trying to walk across the lake on Thanksgiving weekend?'

Brad gave Gilda a wry look and tapped the side of his head with his index finger. 'Maybe this kid wasn't the sharpest knife in the drawer, if you know what I mean. Anyway, Shirley McCracken was one "chatty Cathy," believe me, but a drowned girl was not the type of subject she wanted to discuss at the car dealership. She *did* go on and on about her dead husband and how he always drove a beat-up, used car. I said, "Shirley, when is it going to be about *you*? When is it time for the car of *your* dreams? *Now* — that's when". And damned if she didn't get herself one helluva new car. At a bargain too.'

Gilda felt irritated that Brad had managed to turn the conversation back to the subject of selling cars. 'Mrs McCracken is widowed?'

'That's right.'

There was an uncomfortable silence. Rather, it was uncomfortable for Gilda, but Brad seemed to feel right at home as he stretched his legs in front of him. *A little too at home*, Gilda thought. Why wouldn't her mother hurry up? In the old days she would have run out the front door wearing sweats and not so much as a swipe of lip gloss. But over the summer Mrs Joyce had started dating for the first time since her husband's death, and had rediscovered things like blusher, lipstick and a hairspray. Gilda suddenly felt puritanical and resentful. *Why am I the one sitting here, talking to my mom's boyfriend? She should be sitting here talking to MY boyfriend — if only I had one.*

On the other hand, Gilda had to admit that talking to Brad had yielded a bit of information. She now knew a bit more about Mrs McCracken and the girl who drowned in Mermaid Lake — Dolores Lambert.

5

Going Undercover

As she studied her reflection, Gilda felt that the Catholic schoolgirl she saw in the mirror – this girl who wore a school uniform and had no fashion sense – must simply be a character she was impersonating. She herself would never dress in such an uninspired outfit.

The uniform for sophomores, juniors, and seniors at Our Lady of Sorrows was 'a light-blue skirt and white polo top in fall and spring, and a plaid skirt in shades of burgundy and grey during the winter. IMPORTANT: THE SKIRT MUST BE NO SHORTER THAN THREE INCHES ABOVE THE KNEE!'

The freshman uniform was slightly different and distinctly horrible: a pink, pleated skirt with a matching pink, short-sleeved shirt. The colour scheme was Mrs McCracken's idea: she wanted to give the freshmen a more 'fun and feminine' outfit. As a result, the new girls looked more vulnerable and unsophisticated than ever.

At public school, Gilda had often dressed in

expressive combinations of vintage clothing and costume jewellery. She created outfits to reflect every mood (her burgundy velvet 'Bloody Mary' dress, worn with leather boots on test days, was among her favourites). Now the full realisation that she would have to wear the same clothes to school for an entire year made her feel itchy, as if she might break out in a full-body rash. As she practised walking around the room in her school uniform, she felt exposed and drafty in the short skirt.

There must be something I can add to this uniform to make it look more like something I would actually wear, Gilda thought. She considered adding a denim jacket and black tights, but realised that this would be completely against the rules. *Mom will kill me if I get sent home from school on the first day.*

After digging through her wardrobe for several minutes, Gilda settled on an ironic heightening of her extremely girlie look with pink lipstick, a glittery rhinestone hairclip, and a 'Little Mermaid' Disney bandaid, which she stuck on her bare knee.

She peered into the mirror one last time. *I look like the kid who's going to get beaten up in the playground,* she thought. She removed the Disney bandaid and the hairclip.

'Oh, don't you look adorable!' Mrs. Joyce clutched her cup of coffee and beamed at Gilda. 'I should get the camera. Doesn't your sister look cute, Stephen?'

Seized by a fit of laughter, Gilda's older brother spat some Cheerios back into his bowl.

'Don't say anything,' Gilda warned him. 'Not one thing.'

'I hope I have some film,' said Mrs Joyce, rummaging through a kitchen drawer where things like scissors and tape were mixed together with old telephone bills and bank statements.

'Mom, there shall be no record of this moment.'

'But you look so nice. Stephen, tell your sister she looks nice.'

'You look nice.' Stephen's mouth contorted in a smirk. 'I didn't realise you were a figure skater.'

'I didn't realize you were a doofus.'

'Well, maybe you should pay better attention.'

'You just burned yourself, you know.'

'I *meant* to.'

'Gilda you'd better hurry and grab some breakfast or you're going to be late on your first day. It takes almost half an hour to get all the way over to West Bloomfield from here during rush hour.'

'But you're driving me, right?'

'I will this morning, but you'll have to catch the city bus home after school. I'll be at work.'

Gilda grabbed a bagel from the cupboard and slapped some cream cheese on it. She located her faded pink backpack in the closet and tossed it over her shoulder. Because the backpack was covered in graffiti, Gilda's mother had urged her to purchase a new one for the school year, but Gilda had refused. The old backpack was simply too covered in history – an intricate pattern of phrases and doodles that she and Wendy had scribbled during dull moments in school. Gilda smiled as she skimmed one of their exchanges:

Psychic investigators rule.
Are you going to watch 'Buffy' tonight?
Of course; I never miss it
Call me later
OK
Do you still like Craig Overcash?
Don't write stuff like that on my backpack, please
Do you still LOVE Craig Overcash?
Why, do you think he likes me?
He's going out with Charlene.
Her nostrils are too big. They're like this (oo).

'OK, Mom,' said Gilda. 'I'm ready to go.' She sighed and headed outside to make the journey to her new school.

A tangle of balloons, streamers, and toilet paper draped from tree branches greeted Gilda and her mother as they approached Our Lady of Sorrows. Suspended across the Castle House was an ominous banner:

BEWARE, UNDERLINGS! SENIORS RULE
AT OUR LADY OF SORROWS

Mrs Joyce gaped at the sign. 'And I thought you were going to be hanging around some refined people for a change.'

'Everyone knows there's nothing wilder than a Catholic schoolgirl.'

'Gilda, please don't align yourself with the bad crowd, OK?'

'When have I ever aligned myself with the "bad crowd"? I realise Wendy Choy and I are wanted by the police and the FBI, but—'

'You know what I mean, Gilda.'

'Fine. I'll only make friends with the nuns.'

'That would be perfect. Have a wonderful day, Gilda. Just smile and be yourself, OK?'

Gilda bared her teeth and waved at her mother in a hysterical parody of good cheer as she exited the car. She trudged through a parking lot teeming with new SUVs, many of which were adorned with heart-shaped bumper stickers that announced, 'I love Our Lady of Sorrows!'

Inside the school, Gilda found pandemonium. Everywhere she looked, girls screamed with delight and hugged each other as if shocked to find their friends alive after a long summer of beach vacations. Gilda noticed a couple of prevalent characteristics: deep tans from outdoor recreation (Gilda herself remained pale with only a smattering of darkened freckles across her nose), and long, sleek hair worn straightened with a flat iron, pulled back in a ponytail, and tied with a silk ribbon.

Among the giggling clusters of girls were a few young women who exuded superiority – girls who literally shimmered. Their suntanned skin glowed. Their hair, whether blonde or brunette, glistened with subtle, gold highlights. Instead of the regular uniform, they wore polo shirts with khaki pants and high-heeled sandals. Their accessories were small, whimsical purses, delicate necklaces from Tiffany's, and lattes and frappucinos from Starbucks. Gilda gradually realised that these girls were the seniors.

On the other end of the spectrum were the hapless freshmen who stood watching silently in their pink skirts. The few who knew each other from junior high gravitated towards each other for safety. The others glanced around, shooting nervous smiles to anyone who looked in their direction – smiles that were calculated to appear delighted but instead looked like glassy-eyed stares of panic. Gilda hoped that she herself didn't look quite so overwhelmed. *I'm just here to investigate a paranormal phenomenon*, she told herself. *I'm undercover, so I don't have to fit in.*

She reminded herself of something she had recently read in a book called *The Spy Next Door*:

The undercover agent must become more than a person in disguise; he must become a true part of his surroundings, living the whole life of the scene he's investigating – all the while keeping a portion of his mind separate and entirely secret. Few people have the mental stamina to go this deeply undercover.

Gilda resolved that she would be one of the few who *could* go deeply undercover – a secret psychic detective in a Catholic girls' school.

Without warning, someone clobbered Gilda. It took her a second to realise that she was actually being *hugged* by a short, stocky girl who had most likely mistaken her for someone else. Should she hug the girl back just to be polite? 'I don't think we've met,' said Gilda, fighting an urge to duck under the girl's meaty arm to free herself.

'You *are* Gilda, aren't you?' said the girl, abruptly releasing Gilda and peering at her through glasses that were too large for her round face. 'Please tell me you are! Miss Underhill pointed you out to me.' The girl wore her hair in a puffy, hairsprayed bob that made Gilda think of a middle-aged librarian or a politician's wife.

'You're right; I'm Gilda.'

'Whew! My name's Marcie Dinklemeyer. I'm a sophomore, and – lucky you – I'm your big sister!' Marcie smiled at Gilda with rosy anticipation, as if she expected Gilda to jump up and down with excitement. 'My job is to help you find your way around. I'll also point out the rules so you don't get too many detentions and stuff like that.'

'Thanks.' Gilda already missed the freedom of being a completely anonymous stranger.

'Can I be honest?' Marcie looked at Gilda imploringly. 'The truth is that most of the big sisters *ditch* their freshman little sisters after the first day of school. It happened to me, and it's so *wrong*. But I'm not going to do that to you, Gilda. I *promise* I won't!'

'Oh, you don't have to worry about me.' Gilda instinctively recoiled from Marcie's motherly attitude. For one thing, she hated being regarded as someone who needed help. For another thing, she had a gut feeling that Marcie was the type of person who would get in the way of a psychic investigation.

'It's almost 8:30, so we should head to the chapel,' said Marcie. 'We meet there each morning for prayer and announcements.'

'Uniform check!'

A few feet ahead, Miss Underhill grabbed a girl by the arm and pressed a ruler against her leg. 'An inch too short!' she declared. 'See you in detention.' She pulled a little pad of paper from her pocket, tore off a piece, and thrust it at the girl like a police officer giving a speeding ticket.

'But it's the first day of school,' the girl protested.

'Exactly.'

'Watch out for Miss Underhill,' Marcie whispered, glancing down at Gilda's skirt. 'She hides behind corners, and then jumps out with her ruler to measure your skirt. She gives about twenty detentions every day. Your skirt length looks right, though, just like mine. Good for you!'

43

Gilda made a mental note to shorten her skirt as soon as possible. She glanced up and caught Miss Underhill staring at her with a sharp little smile on her face. Gilda felt a wave of creepiness, remembering the bizarre exchange next to Mermaid Lake – Miss Underhill's warning to 'Keep your voice down around the dead.'

'Marcie,' Gilda ventured, 'do you know anything about the ghost in Mermaid Lake?'

Marcie stopped in her tracks. 'Who told you that?'

'Miss Underhill.'

'Now *she's* scaring the freshmen too? I have half a mind to say something to the headmistress about that. Listen, Gilda, you don't have to be frightened, because I think that story is just something the sophomores made up to scare the freshmen. Some girls actually decide not to go to school here because they think it's haunted! Can you believe that?' Marcie shook her head as if this ghost story was one of the greatest travesties she could imagine.

Gilda decided not to mention that she had actually decided to attend the school because she *hoped* to investigate a ghost. She had a sense of vast disappointment, as if she had pinned all the money she owned on a racehorse that had just broken its leg. Had Miss Underhill merely been teasing her?

'But there *was* a girl who drowned in the lake, right?'

Marcie nodded. 'Dolores Lambert. She was a

freshman. That's why Mrs McCracken had that bridge built, because people used to take shortcuts across the ice during the winter, and I guess Dolores tried to do that before the lake was completely frozen. They used to allow ice-skating on the lake in January, but we can't do that any more.'

Marcie's matter-of-fact explanation for Dolores Lambert's death was a calm, logical contrast with Miss Underhill's warning, '*Keep your voice down around the dead.*' The whole experience now seemed like an intriguing nightmare that didn't quite match reality.

And now I'm stuck going to school here, Gilda thought, as she and Marcie made their way to the chapel.

With a microphone in hand, Mrs McCracken stood in front of an ornately carved pulpit, facing the entire student body. The girls sat in pews in the order of their grade level: seniors at the front; freshman clumped together at the back of the room with their sophomore big sisters – many of whom were already in the early stages of ditching their bewildered 'siblings.'

Gilda was surprised to realise just how small the school was: there were only about twenty or thirty girls in each class of students. It was clearly a place where *everyone* knew each other.

'Good morning ladies!' Mrs McCracken's twangy voice echoed through the room. 'Looks like you're all well-rested, suntanned, and ready to dig right in to your studies, right?'

A few morose titters were her only response.

'You're ready to hit the books, RIGHT?'

'RIGHT.'

'That's more like it. Now, before we get down to business, let's sing the Our Lady of Sorrows school song together':

Our lady, our lady
I know you'll walk with me
Our lady, our lady
Upon the shining sea,
Along the highways of my life
A true sorority!
Our lady, our lady
Your sorrows set me free!

Sitting in a wooden pew surrounded by shy girls in pink skirts, Gilda felt as if she had been sent to another planet to attend school. She wondered what Wendy Choy was doing and wished she could pass her a note.

'Now we'll introduce this year's clubs and activities,' said Mrs McCracken, when the song ended. 'Whatever you're interested in, there's a club here for you to join!'

Gilda doubted that they had a club for psychic investigators.

A tall, willowy girl who wore her dark hair in a chic, short haircut approached the microphone.

'That's Danielle Menory,' Marcie whispered. 'She's a senior. She's a member of about twenty clubs, and she does a *ton* of community service.' Marcie gazed at Danielle with sparkling eyes, as if she were staring at a celebrity.

Danielle adjusted the microphone and began to speak in a soft voice. 'Hi. I'm Danielle Menory, and I want to invite anyone who's interested to join the Eating Disorders Awareness Club. Many of you know that when I was a sophomore, I had a pretty severe eating disorder, and even had to be hospitalized. After I recovered, I realized that lots of other girls have this problem too.'

Gilda reflected that at her old school, nobody would have been willing to stand in front of the whole school and share something so personal.

Danielle's introduction to the Eating Disorder Awareness Club was followed by a long series of clubs – everything from the 'Young Democrats' and 'Young Republicans' to clubs with unusual names like 'Kite-Flyer's Club,' 'Psoriasis Awareness Club,' and 'Future Podiatrists and Gastroenterologists of America.' There were also some religious groups with names like 'Mary's Way.'

Marcie peered at Gilda. 'See anything you like?'

'It's a toss-up between the Future Podiatrists club and the school newspaper.'

'Do you have any hobbies?'

'I like writing.' Gilda sensed that Marcie would be completely baffled if she mentioned her work as a psychic investigator.

'We'll find something you like, Gilda. I promise!'

Mrs McCracken approached the microphone again. 'Let's have a moment of prayer.'

The girls bowed their heads and squeezed their eyes shut.

'Lord, we pray for a happy school year – a year filled with learning and growing. A year of friendship with each other. We pray also for those we have lost.' Mrs McCracken paused for a moment. 'We pray for the spirit of Dolores Lambert, who would have been a senior this very day.'

Gilda's ears perked up at the mention of Dolores's name.

'We pause in silence to consider others who are in need of our prayers.'

A loud dripping sound broke the silence: *plop, plop, plop, plop* . . .

While Mrs McCracken and most of the other girls did their best to ignore the sound, Gilda cautiously peeked up and noticed Miss Underhill staring straight ahead, gazing with horrified fascination at a small, metal drinking fountain attached to one of the walls – the apparent source of the dripping. *It's odd that we only heard the dripping echoing through the room after Mrs McCracken mentioned Dolores Lambert's name*, Gilda thought. *Maybe Marcie is wrong. Maybe there really is a ghost.*

6

The First Week Of Suffering

Dear Dad:

Miss Underhill was right about one thing:
most of the classrooms are pretty crummy
compared to the stuff you see when you go
on the tour of the school. They all have
peeling wallpaper and stained carpeting that
smells of mould. The hallways in the school
are a little creepy because they're lined with
marble busts of historical people like
Shakespeare and George Washington who just
sit there like disembodied heads, watching us
as we walk to our classes. Most of the rooms
have fireplaces, but I guess they don't work
any more, and now they make good places
for critters to nest. I think I saw a rat in the
freshman locker room, and there was some
kind of toxic crud in my locker, which,
incidentally, is too small for my backpack.

Interestingly, the seniors have a Common Room all to themselves that is rumoured to have velvet couches for mid-day naps, an entertainment centre with a flat-screen television, and a small kitchen for making snacks. Of course, no freshman has ever set foot in this room, so it's hard to say whether this is truth or rumour.

GOAL: find a way to sneak into the Senior Common Room without getting killed.

Excuse me; I hear the dulcet tones of Stephen bellowing, 'GILDA! PHONE!!' from downstairs. Probably Wendy Choy calling with all the gossip back at ye olde public school!

Big disappointment. The phone call was from Marcie Dinklemeyer, who asked whether I got home safely on the city bus. I told her, 'I got mugged a few times, but it's no big deal; I'm used to it!' (I actually _did_ get a couple of slack-jawed looks because of the pink school uniform.)

I have a tonne of homework tonight, by the way. Anyone who goes to a girls' school hoping to do assignments about lip gloss and how to make extra moist fudge brownies (like me) is in for a rude awakening.

Loud dripping of a water fountain followed
the mention of Dolores Lambert's name
during Mrs McCracken's prayer. Could this be
significant?

Pausing to see if her *Master Psychic's Handbook* could
offer any insight, Gilda turned to a chapter entitled
'Modes of Spirit Communication.'

A spirit who died under traumatic circumstances may occasionally communicate
using the material that caused his or her death. In other words, an individual who
was electrocuted may 'speak' through the use of electricity (turning televisions and
under appliances on and off, etc.), a person whose death resulted from drowning
may use water as a kind of 'medium.'

Gilda thought for a moment, then turned back to
her typewriter:

Was Dolores's ghost trying to make her
presence known through the dripping of a
water fountain? Marcie says the school isn't
haunted, but I think I picked up some kind of
psychic vibration today.

THE SECOND DAY – A DAY OF
SOUL-SEARCHING AND INNER ANGST:
Dear Dad:
Remember the stories Mom used to tell

51

about her religion teacher in high school –
the nun who used to bang her wooden leg on
the desktop to get her students' attention?
Well, I was hoping my religion teacher would
be just as bizarre and entertaining, but it
turns out that Miss Appleton is
disappointingly young and normal. She kept
saying how she wanted us to enjoy her class.

'You don't have to win a Nobel Peace Prize
or save someone's life to be "good",' she said.
'It's the little things – the smile someone gave
us when we needed it most, the helping hand,
the homemade chocolate chip cookies baked
on a rainy fall day that matter most. Good
behaviour doesn't always get directly
rewarded.'

Then Miss Appleton made us write two
lists: 'Bad things I've done recently' and
'Good things I've done recently.'

<u>Bad things I've done recently:</u>
1. 'Forgot' to give Mom the message when
   Brad Squib called.
2. Congratulated Stephen on the birth of his
   new zit.
3. Stuck gum under desk at school.
4. Whispered 'under Canada' instead of
   'under God' during Pledge of Allegiance.
5. Wished that Marcie Dinklemeyer would

wake up with a sudden case of
Alzheimer's, causing her to forget all about
her big sister duties.

6. Shortened my uniform skirt one inch below
the uniform regulation length to avoid
looking like Marcie Dinklemeyer.

<u>Good things I've done recently:</u>
1. Initiated psychic investigation.
2. Flossed teeth regularly.
3. Abstained from gossip due to lack of
opportunities at new school.

THE THIRD DAY – A DAY OF UNDERWEAR JOKES:

Dear Dad:
Have I told you how everyone supposedly
gets a crush on my English teacher, Mr
Panté? I've decided that won't happen to me,
though, because he isn't my type. He has
dark, curly hair that hangs down almost to
his shoulders, and a kind of puffy,
bedraggled, razor-stubbly look. He *could* be
good looking, but he looks like he needs a
shower. (Considering the dress code here, I'm
surprised Mrs McCracken hasn't mentioned
something to him about that. Maybe she did
and he refused.) If he would just shave and

put on some clothes that don't look as if he spent the night camping out in a lawn chair, he might actually be cute. But like I said, he isn't my type.

Mr Panté told us that he's a poet as well as a teacher. This made us all pretty curious, so we started asking him lots of questions. We learned how he dropped out of law school and got married to a banker who pays most of the bills so he can spend his spare time writing.

'My wife's friends like to call me her "trophy husband",' he said.

I get the feeling Mr Panté can't stand his wife's friends. I don't see why anyone would call him a 'trophy husband' in the first place, though.

Then a girl named Sheila who seems kind of daft called him 'Mr Panty' by mistake, and he got really mad.

'My last name is pronounced PANTAY,' he said. 'I've already heard all the jokes, so don't even bother.' He wrote his name – 'PANTÉ' on the blackboard in big letters.

'But I wasn't *joking*, Mr Panty,' Sheila said. And she wasn't either – I could tell – but he gave her a detention anyway.

GOAL: Come up with a panty joke Mr Panté hasn't heard yet.

THE FOURTH DAY – A DAY OF CRINGING
AND DASHED HOPES:

Dear Dad:

Because this school is so small, a bunch of
the same girls are in almost all of my
classes. I have to admit that a few of them
are already becoming irksome.

AMELIA

Always notices when the teacher spells
something wrong on the blackboard. Drives
everyone crazy because her hand shoots up
to answer *every* question the teacher asks.
Then, after she's just finished giving a five-
minute lecture, she raises her hand AGAIN!

SHEILA

Amelia's best friend from junior high, and
the one who keeps calling Mr Panté 'Mr
Panty' by mistake. Her mobile phone goes off
almost every day in class, and then the
teacher gives her a detention. She must have
about fifty detentions already, and it's only
the first week of school.

"THE TRIPLETS"

Britney, Lauren, and Ashley all went to
junior high together. I think of them as 'the
Triplets' because they all wear ribbons in

their long hair and have faces with features
that look weirdly similar, as if they're
actually related. They're always passing
notes and looking as if they're all in on some
big joke that's just killing them because it's
so hilarious. Then, when the teacher
reprimands them, they do a really bad job of
acting as if they were just asking each other
'a question about the material.' That's the
oldest trick in the book, and it *never* works.
Just ask me and Wendy!

TIARA

Stands out because her hair is dyed blue and
really spiky. She also wears leather cuff
bracelets and a necklace covered in pointy
metal studs. There were a bunch of kids
who looked like her at my old school, but at
Our Lady of Sorrows she looks freakish
because her spiky hair and jewellery are
definitely against the uniform policy. How
can she get away with that stuff? Maybe her
parents donated money to the school or
something.

CONCLUSION

The potential for *real* friends at Our Lady of
Sorrows looks dubious. On the positive side, a
dearth of close friends will make it easier for

me to stay undercover and on-task with my psychic investigation.

I just overheard Mom gabbing on the phone about Brad:

'I don't want to speak too soon, Lucy,' she said, 'but I think he's pretty wonderful. He took me to the most fabulous dinner the other night, and he brought me flowers for no reason at all! He's just so generous, and he's fantastic with the kids, too! I told you how he helped Gilda get into this wonderful private school? And now he's even looking for a car for Stephen. Can you believe *that*?'

Dad, I'm trying not to barf.

7

Ghost Stories

'I swear he's wearing eyeliner today,' Britney whispered.

'He is not,' said Ashley.

'I'm serious. Just look.'

Mr Panté paused to glance behind him, causing 'the Triplets' to fall apart with laughter.

'What's so funny?' Mr Panté asked. 'Actually, don't tell me. I don't want to know.'

'We find you amusing,' said Britney, coyly.

'I'm glad someone finds me entertaining.'

Mr Panté stood aside to let the three girls walk in front of him, then fell back into step on the path next to Gilda.

He must be sick of listening to their cackling, Gilda thought. As she walked next to her teacher, Gilda felt nervous. She tried to think of something interesting to say, but it seemed that her brain had turned to potatoes.

Listening to the rushing of wind in the trees combined with the shouts and yelps of girls playing lacrosse on fields behind the school, Gilda had to admit that she felt happy to be at Our Lady of Sorrows, heading toward Mermaid Lake for a poetry discussion, instead of inside a stuffy classroom. Besides, she was hoping for an opportunity to snoop around the bridge dedicated to Dolores Lambert.

'So, Gilda; what are you reading these days?' Mr Panté asked.

Gilda's 'get-to-know-you' questionnaire highlighted the numerous titles she had read in addition to her regular schoolwork. She knew Mr Panté hoped she would say something like 'Chekhov's *Collected Plays*' but the truth was that she had recently reread *The Master Psychic's Handbook* for the fourth time in a row and then started another book by psychic Balthazar Frobenius entitled *Ghost Encounters*. There was also the disappointing thriller entitled *Nun's Dungeon* that she had read to help get her into the mood to attend a Catholic girls' school.

'I was just about to start *War and Peace*,' said Gilda, embellishing the truth, 'but then this book called *Nun's Dungeon* caught my eye.'

Mr Panté nodded and frowned. 'Not familiar with that one.'

'It wasn't as good as I thought it would be,' Gilda admitted.

'So you're a fan of the Gothic.'

'I guess.'

'The uncanny.'

'You mean, ghost stories?'

'All that wonderful spooky stuff with treacherous staircases and mysterious strangers,' said Mr Panté, waving his hand as if drawing an exuberant picture in the air. 'Ghosts, moody atmospheres, that sort of thing.'

'Like Our Lady of Sorrows.'

Mr Panté chuckled. 'You have a quick wit.'

Somehow, the backs of the Triplets' heads seemed to smirk.

'You should read the works of writers like Edgar Allen Poe.'

'OK.' Gilda felt paranoid as she noticed Ashley glancing behind slyly, then immediately whispering something to Britney. *They hate the fact that Mr Panté is talking to me.*

Mr Panté led the class to a grassy spot by the edge of the lake. Across the sparkling water, the ruins looked melancholy in the sunlight, and Gilda felt a familiar light-headed sensation combined with a tickling in her left ear. *I can't put my finger on it, but something isn't right about this place.*

'Let's talk about poetry,' said Mr Panté, 'Any favourite poems? Things you like or dislike?'

'I like rhyming poetry the best,' said Sheila.

Something about this response seemed to irk Mr Panté because he sighed deeply. 'Can you say more about that?'

'I just like rhymes. But one thing I hate is

Shakespeare, because we did that in my other school, and maybe it's too wordy or something, but I don't like it!'

'You'll be pleased to know that we'll be starting an extensive unit on Shakespeare shortly, beginning with the rather wordy play *Hamlet.*'

The girls groaned, but Gilda was secretly delighted. She had read Shakespeare's *Macbeth* in eighth grade and remembered being very intrigued with the witches.

'I've already read four of Shakespeare's plays,' said Amelia, peering through her small, round glasses. 'Shakespeare writes in iambic pentameter.'

'Very true, Amelia,' said Mr Panté. 'Hold that thought for our Shakespeare unit.'

Mr Panté asked them to open their poetry books to a poem by Emily Dickinson. 'You'll be happy to know it's a rhyming poem, Sheila.'

> *My friend must be a Bird—*
> *Because it flies!*
> *Mortal, my friend must be,*
> *Because it dies!*
> *Barbs has it, like a Bee!*
> *Ah, curious friend*
> *Thou puzzlest me!*

'It seems to be about a bird,' said Amelia, after Mr Panté read the poem aloud. 'But maybe it was a poisoned bird, or something?'

'An interesting interpretation,' said Mr Panté. 'Anyone else have any thoughts?'

Something about the poem reminded Gilda of a friend she'd had in fourth grade – a girl named Charlene who, without warning or explanation, stopped speaking to Gilda when her other friends were around. Gilda remembered the confused, surprised feeling she had one morning when she approached Charlene and two other girls who were walking to school, and sensed that there was some secret she had missed – some mean joke at her expense. She remembered gazing down at her new, red tennis shoes – shoes that had seemed whimsical and fun only a minute before – and wondering if they were the *wrong* shoes. Maybe they were *dumb* shoes. Why else would Charlene suddenly become best friends with girls she had made fun of only days before?

Her father told her: 'If you have to keep wondering whether this girl is your friend, maybe she isn't.' Finally, Gilda had stopped wondering, and had become best friends with Wendy Choy instead.

'It's about friendship,' said Gilda. 'A really confusing, disappointing friendship.'

After class, as Mr Panté and the other girls headed back towards the Castle House, Gilda made a bold move and slipped away in the opposite direction, towards the bridge over Mermaid Lake.

When she reached the centre of the bridge, she

looked down at the sparkling water beneath her. Surrounded by red–winged black birds perched on cattails and the soft rustling of trees under a cerulean blue sky, it was hard to imagine someone plunging through ice to her death. Still, there was something eerie about the sight of the ruins just across the water — something that made Gilda feel anxious despite the serenity of the scene. *There's a powerful vibration here*, she thought.

Beneath the water, shadowy plants weaved back and forth like the flowing hair of water nymphs. Gilda glimpsed something gold beneath the water — something that moved. Was it a fish?

If you make any sound, she rises out of the water, screaming.

Summoning all her courage, Gilda decided to take a huge risk and find out whether Miss Underhill's warning had any basis in reality. 'Hey!' she yelled. Her voice sounded small and lonely in the outdoor space.

Gilda watched the water, but nothing happened. She walked to the opposite side of the bridge, leaned over the railing, and yelled louder: 'HEY, DOLORES!'

She heard a small splash — a sound that filled her with trepidation.

'You shouldn't have done that,' said a hoarse voice behind her.

8

Tiara

Tiara leaned against the railing of the bridge. Her studded cuff bracelets made her thin, white wrists look fragile rather than tough. *She looks like she's wearing little bits of armour*, Gilda thought.

How long had she been watching? How had Gilda not seen her approaching?

'Mr Panté told me to come get you,' Tiara said. 'You were supposed to go back to the school after class.'

'I was just looking for something I lost on the bridge,' said Gilda, realizing this excuse sounded unlikely.

'She *will* come out, you know. But it won't happen until you're least expecting it.' As Tiara spoke, something glinted in her mouth; her tongue was pierced.

Gilda had the eerie sense that some magical creature from a fairy tale had appeared from beneath the bridge to scare her.

'She doesn't exactly jump out of the lake the way they tell you. What happens is that she haunts you *personally*. I did the same thing you just did, and now Dolores's ghost is after me.'

'Her ghost is "*after you*"? What do you mean by that?'

There was something sly and crafty about Tiara that put Gilda on guard. In class, she sometimes made dramatic statements just for their shock appeal. 'I nearly died once,' Tiara had commented during a discussion of the poem 'Death Be Not Proud.' 'My fever was so high that all my hair fell out in the shower.'

Tiara looked Gilda directly in the eye. 'This morning, when I looked in the mirror, my face was all puffy and greenish-white, like the face of a drowned girl. It was like I was *possessed* or something.'

Does she really mean what she says, or is she just trying to scare me? Gilda also had a penchant for embellishing the truth, but she found this tendency annoying when she encountered it in other people. It bugged her that she couldn't tell whether or not Tiara was lying.

Gilda observed Tiara closely. She didn't *appear* to be lying. 'So what did you do?'

'I totally freaked out. I was crying, and I think I might have passed out or something. Anyway, the next time I looked in the mirror, my face was back to normal.'

Gilda wondered how she would react if she ever had a similar experience. Would she be able to keep her wits about her and remember that she was a psychic investigator, or would she start crying? 'Tiara,' she said, 'if that happens again, you should try to ask Dolores's ghost some questions.'

'I was in no state to ask questions.'

'Just tell her she's scaring you, and then ask her what she wants.' Gilda hadn't yet had an opportunity to use this technique, but she had read about it in her *Master Psychic's Handbook*.

Tiara turned to head back to the school. 'You seem pretty calm about all this stuff.' She sounded vaguely disappointed.

'It's my business.' Gilda caught herself, remembering that she had intended to remain completely undercover. Here she was, already about to tell someone she was a psychic investigator.

'It's your *business*?'

'I mean, I have an interest in ghosts and things like that, that's all.'

'In that case, you should come over to my house sometime.'

'Your house is haunted?'

'Weird things are happening to me lately, Gilda. If you're interested in this stuff, you should come over to my house after school. You'll see what I mean.'

At Tiara's house, Gilda perched on a stool next to the gleaming counter of an enormous, immaculate kitchen. She watched as Tiara poured Diet Coke into two wine glasses, then tore open a box of Oreo cookies.

Gilda felt smaller than usual inside the vast house – a house with a huge garage by the drive and neutral-coloured rooms as shiny and spotless as elegant hotel suites. As she nibbled a cookie, Gilda concentrated on picking up a psychic vibration – some sense of a phantom presence in the house – but she only sensed a cool emptiness and loneliness in her surroundings, as if all traces of warmth had been scrubbed away. The loud drone of a vacuum cleaner abruptly filled the silence, and Gilda glimpsed a grim-looking housekeeper sullenly pushing the machine across white carpeting in the next room.

Tiara's face looked smudged and bruised with remnants of black lipstick and eyeliner. During the school day, she had torn out the hem on one side of her pink skirt while cutting the material on the other side short enough to reveal the plaid boxer shorts she wore underneath. She had pinned several detention slips to the ragged, asymmetrical edge of her skirt: 'Skirt length is WRONG!' and 'This is UNACCEPTABLE!' Constantly in motion, Tiara bounced a knee nervously and tapped her chipped fingernails on the counter.

She looks out of place in her own house, Gilda thought.

Tiara stuffed an entire cookie into her mouth and stood up very suddenly, as if she had just remembered something urgent. 'Gotta pee,' she declared.

'Thanks for letting me know,' said Gilda.

'We don't have a bathroom here, by the way – just an out house.'

'That's what I figured,' said Gilda. 'Watch out for butt splinters.'

Tiara stared at Gilda for a moment, as if trying to decide whether continued attempts to pull Gilda's leg were worth the effort. Finally she turned on her heel and left the room.

A moment later, Tiara reappeared in the kitchen looking stricken, as if she had just realized that she was coming down with a bad case of stomach flu.

'What's the matter?'

'I need to show you something.' Tiara picked up her glass of Diet Coke and left the room without another word.

With some trepidation, Gilda followed Tiara into a very beige living-room with soaring ceilings. As she surveyed her surroundings, she caught her breath. Something ghastly loomed over the fireplace.

'This is the kind of thing that keeps happening,' Tiara whispered.

Gilda gazed up at a larger-than-life oil painting of a haughty-looking woman who shared Tiara's pale complexion and elfin features. It was difficult to see the portrait clearly because it was splattered with what appeared to be streams and clots of blood.

Gilda's stomach turned. *I've never seen anything like this before*, she thought. Was it possible that the ghost in Tiara's house was the kind of violent, murderous spirit people encountered in horror movies? For some reason the spotlessness of the room made the angry mess covering the painting particularly disturbing.

'This is the worst thing I've seen yet,' said Tiara, whose face looked ashen. 'A couple of weeks ago, there were broken eggs all over every mirror in the house. And then a few days ago, we found all my mom's antique china shattered. But this is definitely the *worst*.'

Gilda reminded herself that feeling grossed out was no excuse for shirking her psychic investigator duties. She forced herself to move closer to the painting to get a closer look. 'I should take a sample of this stuff for testing,' said Gilda, not knowing exactly what sort of testing she had in mind.

With shaking fingers, Gilda reached up to touch the edge of the painting and managed to remove a clump of something dried and red. She squinted closely at the substance in her hand and noticed something odd: the blood contained tiny seeds. She sniffed the substance and suddenly felt suspicious of Tiara. Was this simply an attention-seeking prank? 'Tiara, I'm pretty sure this is tinned tomatoes,' she said, accusingly.

'You mean it isn't blood?'

'Don't play dumb.'

'I'm not! All I know is, I walked into the room, looked up, and saw what looks like blood all over this painting.' said Tiara. 'Even if it is tomatoes, the ghost must have put them there!'

'You swear you didn't do this yourself?'

Clutching her wine glass between her ring finger and pinky, Tiara traced an 'X' over her pink shirt with her index finger. 'I *didn't*. Cross my heart and hope to die.'

Gilda reflected that there was something eerie about the phrase 'Cross my heart and hope to die' – a vow she and Wendy had used when they were much younger. Strangely, the words still seemed to have a magical persuasive power, and Gilda found herself wanting to believe Tiara. 'Then it looks like you have a poltergeist.'

'It has to be the ghost from Mermaid Lake.'

'It *could* be the ghost from the lake, but did you or your parents have any special connection with Dolores Lambert – any reason she would be haunting your house?'

The sound of the vacuum stopped, and the girls were suddenly aware of a thick silence.

'All I know is that ever since I broke the rule and shouted into the lake, weird things have been happening.' Tiara fixed Gilda with a portentous stare. '*You* did the same thing, so you'll see what I mean soon enough.'

Gilda did her best to ignore a twinge of anxiety caused by Tiara's ominous tone. 'We'll need to do more research before we can be sure of the ghost's identity.'

'What kind of research?'

Gilda thought for a moment. 'Why don't you show me where you first saw Dolores's ghost in the mirror?'

Tiara's room reminded Gilda of a cave. Dark curtains covered the windows, and the air was still and heavy. Gilda wondered what it would be like to wake up in the morning and find herself surrounded by such complete darkness.

'What's the matter?' Tiara asked, turning on a series of lights with bulbs the size of small candle flames. 'Never seen a room with black walls before?'

'Only in the homes of vampires,' Gilda joked.

Tiara stared a Gilda with a spooky intensity, as if trying to hypnotize her. 'How do you know this *isn't* the home of a vampire?'

'Because, for one thing, you'd have an unusually high tolerance for sunshine and crucifixes if you're a vampire attending a Catholic girls' school.'

Tiara's mouth twitched; she suppressed an urge to giggle. 'Well – don't you wonder why my room is so *dark*?'

Gilda shrugged, feigning nonchalance. 'Some people like it dark.' Secretly, she was very curious indeed, but for some reason, she didn't want to give Tiara the satisfaction of knowing that.

Tiara sat down on her bed and gulped down the last bit of her soda. 'My mom told me I could decorate my room any colour I wanted, so I picked black because I thought it would be cool. I'll never admit this to her, but sometimes it's kind of depressing in here.'

'You should put some glow-in-the-dark stars on the ceiling,' Gilda suggested. 'And maybe add a Disco ball.'

'But that sounds cheesy.'

Gilda breezed past Tiara toward an oblong, full-length mirror that perched on a pedestal. 'Is this the mirror where you first saw the ghost?'

Tiara nodded.

In the dim light, the two girls peered into the mirror, gazing at the yellowed, shadowy features of their faces and the spiky silhouette of Tiara's hair. Gilda couldn't help but think that in the tomb-like atmosphere of Tiara's room, it seemed entirely plausible that if she stared into the mirror, she might see someone else's face instead of her own reflection.

'Have you ever considered bleaching your hair?' Tiara whispered, instantly breaking the sombre mood.

'Excuse me?' Gilda noted that Tiara's habit of constantly switching from one topic or activity to another was not at all helpful for a psychic investigation.

'I just think it would look cool if we bleached a couple streaks in your hair.'

'I prefer wigs,' said Gilda, thinking that her mother would ground her for several weeks if she came home with bleached hair. 'That way, I'm not stuck with a single look.'

'Nobody wears wigs.'

'By senior year, we'll all be wearing wigs. They're due for a comeback.' Gilda couldn't understand why people who could afford high-quality wigs didn't seize the opportunity to wear them more often. She herself owned several costume wigs that she sometimes used for disguises.

Tiara covered her short hair with her hands and scrutinized her face in the mirror. 'How do you think I'd look with long, platinum blonde hair?'

'Fantastic, of course. Who *wouldn't* look fantastic with long, platinum hair?'

Tiara grinned. 'Wouldn't it be awesome if we could go to school with different hair every day of the week?'

'There would be no such thing as a bad hair day.'

'Gilda,' said Tiara, shaking Gilda's shoulders, 'we have to start this wig trend right away!'

'OK. But what about the school uniform?'

Tiara swatted the air dismissively. 'McCracken's big secret is that she needs every bit of our money to keep her in pink fingernail polish. So as long as your parents are paying your sky-high tuition, believe me, there's no way she'll kick you out of school for wearing a wig. You might get a few detentions, of course.'

'Well, I'm on scholarship, so I'm not adding much to McCracken's fingernail polish budget.'

'Oh.'

Gilda noticed that something in Tiara's face changed. It was a momentary flinch, a very slight raising of the eyebrows as if, in spite of herself, she was seeing Gilda in a different light and placing her in a new mental category – a category labeled 'Girls on Scholarship.'

Gilda felt irritated to discover that a secret snobbery might lurk beneath Tiara's rebellious exterior. She also realized Tiara was steering her psychic investigation off-track. 'Listen, Tiara, I have to be home soon, so do you want to try a séance or not?'

'How do we do it?'

Gilda thought for a moment. 'It helps to have an object that has some personal connection with the spirit, and I usually use a Ouija board too. We can try using this mirror, since this is where you saw the image of the spirit's face.'

Gilda sat on the floor next to the mirror. 'Now you sit across from me here and place your fingers on the mirror like this. The most important thing is to take the séance seriously, and to concentrate.'

Tiara sat down, carefully placing her empty wine glass on the floor.

'Now we both close our eyes and focus.'

The girls waited for a moment, listening to the silence of the house.

'We sense a troubled spirit here in this house,' said Gilda. 'Oh spirit, if you are here with us, please make your presence known.'

Gilda's heart beat faster as she sensed the surface of the mirror vibrating beneath her fingers. Then, without warning, a shrill shriek seemed to explode into a brittle cascade of shattering of glass.

Gilda opened her eyes to find Tiara staring with a strangely enthralled expression at blood dripping from a deep gash on her finger. Both the mirror and Tiara's wine glass were broken.

TO: Gilda Joyce
FROM: Gilda Joyce
RE: Progress Report – The Ghost in the Lake

STATUS: Clear evidence of a violent poltergeist in Tiara's house. Tiara believes that she's haunted by Dolores Lambert because she shouted Dolores's name on the bridge over Mermaid Lake. (By this logic, I should also be expecting a visit from Dolores's ghost!)

There's just one problem with the evidence: when we were conducting our séance, I didn't actually *see* Tiara's glass pick itself off the floor and hurl itself at the mirror, so I suppose it's *possible* that she threw it herself, then just acted surprised. But what about the tomatoes splattered all over the painting of her mom? Tiara wouldn't have had time to do that herself unless she did it in the morning, before she went to school. And wouldn't someone in the house have noticed by the time she got home?

Wearing her pyjamas, Gilda turned from her typewriter to her *Master Psychic's Handbook*. She flipped through the dog-eared pages until she found a chapter on 'Poltergeists':

One of the defining characteristics of a poltergeist is psychokinesis – the spontaneous movement of objects. The interesting thing about poltergeists is that their mischievous, annoying, loud, and sometimes even dangerous activities so often occur around a particular individual in a household. For some reason, girls around the age of thirteen or fourteen are particularly vulnerable to such occurrences. It is unclear whether this is because the 'immature' ghost gravitates to a similarly volatile or immature subject, or because something in the young person's psyche – possibly some repressed rage or unstable emotion – is triggering explosive and unpredictable energy disturbances that causes objects to spontaneously move.

QUESTIONS TO SLEEP ON:
Is there something 'volatile' about Tiara that's attracting Dolores Lambert's ghost?

TO DO:
1. Keep an eye on Tiara.
2. More research needed to understand ghost motives: must learn more about Dolores Lambert.

PANTY JOKE PROGRESS:
Mr Panté gave me two detentions today. The first one was for my 'failure to return to the school building at the end of class.'

'It won't happen again, Mr Panty,' I said, pretending to accidentally mispronounce his

name. Tiara was standing right there, and I
thought I might as well try to get a laugh out
of the situation.

I guess he had heard that joke before (the
'slip-of-the-tongue' panty joke), because he
wrote another detention slip without a
moment of hesitation. I had an urge to see
how many detentions he would give me if I
kept saying 'panty,' but luckily I came to my
senses and dropped it.

Good thing the weekend is here, because I
have a lot to think about and research.
T.G.I.F!

9

The Ghost In The Rain

Dear Dad,

I had *planned* to spend my Saturday reading
Shakespeare's *Hamlet* and researching
poltergeists, but along comes Brad Squib with
this 'big surprise for the whole family.'

Gather 'round everyone! Slaughter the
cattle and break open the champagne,
because Brad Squib has saved the day with
FOOTBALL TICKETS!!!

Sure, it was NICE of him to take us to a
University of Michigan football game, but he
acted as if he was this outrageous hero. He
seemed to think that all our problems would
be fixed if we would just sit down and watch
some butt-slapping men wearing helmets.

ME: To be honest, Brad, I've never been
that interested in football. I find it to be a
slow, boring sport.

BRAD: Come on, Gilders. Lighten up
a little!

MOM: Yes, Gilda. Try to enjoy life a little.

ME: YOU were never interested in football before.

STEPHEN: The problem is, Gilda just doesn't *understand* football.

After that, Brad felt the need to educate me. He kept leaning over to shout things like, 'NOW THEY'RE GOING INTO THE HUDDLE, GILDA!'

I made an effort to ask the dumbest questions I could think of ('Now that guy in the black and white; is he someone's dad?' and stuff like that).

PEOPLE-WATCHING REPORT!:

I saw a girl from Our Lady of Sorrows at the game – one of the seniors. She stands out because she has wild curls and a really loud voice. I think her name is Nikki. She and her boyfriend kept standing up and screaming their heads off. They seemed like they were kind of . . . drunk, too, which is odd since I'm almost positive Nikki introduced the 'Alcohol Awareness Club' on the first day of school.

AN EMBARRASSING MOMENT!:

I don't mean to upset you, but when Mom and Brad were walking along together towards the stadium, I saw Brad stick his

hand in the butt pocket of Mom's jeans. You
could tell they thought they looked like a
fabulous couple, but the truth was that they
were old people acting like seventh graders
walking down the school hallway. I did my
best to pretend I had never met them before
in my life.

OTHER DISTURBING ISSUES:
I'm feeling paranoid about the idea that
Dolores's ghost could be 'coming after me'
because I yelled out her name on the bridge.
  So far, so good.
  But it's starting to rain outside, and this is
kind of spooky. I can imagine Dolores
Lambert standing outside my window in the
rain right now, just waiting for me.

Sitting behind the wheel of her new SUV, Nikki
Grimaldi drove highway 696 at an alarming speed and
with a little too much confidence, considering the
steady sprinkling of rain that was now becoming a
heavy downpour. Her boyfriend Dinkel slept next to
her in the passenger's seat, wearing a sweatshirt that
declared, 'MICHIGAN KICKS ASS.' Every now and
then, he let out a little snore.
  As she exited the highway, the Eminem song
blaring on the radio became overwhelmed by static.
Fiddling with the radio, Nikki didn't notice that the

cars in front of her had stopped until it was almost too late.

She slammed on the brakes, narrowly avoiding a collision. Nikki braced herself for a deluge of criticism from Dinkel, who woke up grumpy at the best of times, but to her relief, he only snorted in his sleep.

Creeping behind the line of backed-up cars, Nikki glimpsed a homeless person standing on the shoulder of the road, holding a cardboard sign.

Weird, Nikki thought. *It's a girl.*

Something else was strange. The girl stood motionless in the rain. She made no effort to approach car windows; instead, she appeared to be focusing very intently on Nikki's car alone. *Why is she looking at me?* Nikki wondered. *I must be imagining it.*

But as Nikki drew closer to the stoplight, she could still feel the girl looking at her. In fact, she began to have the horrible sense that the girl was actually *inside* the car in some way. She smelled something that reminded her of pine needles and the scent of a wet dog.

Now the girl was right outside Nikki's car window, and Nikki didn't want to look; she didn't want to see the girl's sign, but something forced her to read the words:

NIKKI

I AM SO COLD

PLEASE HELP ME

Now the face was just a few inches away from the car window: the swollen face, the blue eyes – so horribly familiar. The worst thing was that she was not sullen or angry; she was pleading and close to tears. She silently mouthed the words, *Nikki . . . please.*

Nikki slammed her foot down on the gas pedal as the light turned green. Driving on the shoulder of the road, she passed several cars, then swerved onto Woodward Avenue, accelerating in an effort to create as much distance as possible between herself and – and whatever it was she just saw.

She felt queasy and short of breath, as if there suddenly wasn't enough oxygen in the car. *I'm just imagining things*, she told herself. *It was a homeless person.* But why had she seen her own name on the cardboard sign?

She felt sure that she had seen a ghost.

10

The Flood

As her alarm went off at 7:10 Gilda awoke groggily, remembering a bad dream. There had been something about being lost in the maze in the Garden of Contemplation. Tiara was there, trying to lead her somewhere, but someone else kept yelling, 'You're going the wrong way! It's over here!' The frustrating thing was that she couldn't see who was yelling at her. Gilda would have liked to spend more time analyzing her dream, but she was running late.

Gilda had developed a routine that allowed her to squeeze every last second of sleep out of her morning before catching the 7:20 bus to West Bloomfield. The school uniform was crucial to this routine: had she felt the need to *think* about what she might wear, she would never get to school on time.

She jumped out of bed, picked up her uniform where it lay crumpled on the floor, showered, brushed her teeth, de-tangled her hair and stuffed a bagel into her backpack. She was out of the door by 7:19, with one minute left to catch the bus.

The rain had continued all day on Sunday, all night, and into the morning – a persistent thunderstorm with tornado watches throughout the state. Sprinting towards the bus, Gilda ran through the downpour with her untied shoelaces trailing in the mud, her backpack flopping heavily against her leg, and her umbrella violently inverting itself like a frightened octopus.

Stuffed with umbrellas and open newspapers, the bus bristled with the early morning hostility of people on their way to work. The only passenger wearing a school uniform amidst a sea of business attire, Gilda noticed people staring at her bare knees as if offended by their presence. 'Yes, they're *knees*,' she said, chastising a crisp-looking man in a suit whose eyes lingered on her legs too long. 'They're exposed for the purpose of my education.'

The businessman quickly hid behind his newspaper.

Gilda stared out the window at the businesses that sprawled along Woodward Avenue – Starbucks, McDonald's, Wendy's, the Royal Palms Motel, the Fur & Feathers pet store – and thought how strange it was that in a matter of minutes she would be in an environment that looked like a castle. She opened her notebook and wrote:

I should be heading to school with excitement and eagerness to learn, but today I feel only weariness and foreboding. 'Oh, what a rogue and peasant slave am I!' (That's from Hamlet.)

Hamlet fascinated Gilda because the main character of the play was a teenager who spoke to his father's ghost.

'I feel like I have something in common with Hamlet,' Gilda wrote.

For one thing, he obviously misses his dead father. He also can't stand his stepfather, and he's really mad at his mother for going out with him in the first place. Of course, Brad isn't my stepfather yet (thank God!) and of course, he didn't kill my father like Claudius did in Hamlet (as far as I know). Still, I think old Hamlet and I have something in common, especially on a gloomy day like today.

When Gilda stepped off the bus into the rain, she discovered that her umbrella had stopped working completely.

Drawing stares and rueful smiles because of her wet hair and clothes, Gilda made her way towards the freshman locker room, located at the school's basement level. She turned the corner and gagged as she walked into a pungent, mildew-like odour.

'You don't want to go in there!' Ashley splashed through a shallow lake of water, covering her nose with her hand. 'It's totally flooded!'

Curious to see for herself, Gilda took off her shoes and tiptoed through the water towards the locker room.

Inside, a group of freshmen giggled and yelped as they waded barefoot through ankle-deep water to retrieve books, notebooks and sweatshirts from their lockers. 'Gross! It smells like a whole aquarium of fish died in here!' someone complained.

Gilda noticed Sheila purposefully dropping her English paper into the water.

Maybe she's not so dumb after all, Gilda thought. *She knows the flooding is a good excuse for a paper extension.*

A loud scream pierced through the noise in the locker room. The girls fell silent and turned their attention to Tiara, who stood paralyzed, pointing at a spot on the ground.

'I see her,' she said. 'Right . . . there!' She seemed genuinely petrified.

Because of her rebellious insistence on black lipstick and leather accessories, many girls kept a safe distance from Tiara even when she was behaving normally. Now, rather than rushing to see what had terrified her, they simply stared as if they were motorists gazing through glass windows at a car accident.

Propelled by curiosity, Gilda alone hurried over to see what Tiara was looking at.

'It's *her* again!' said Tiara, who seemed close to tears.

'*What is she talking about?*' the girls whispered amongst themselves. 'She's so weird!' someone said a little too loudly.

Gilda stared into the floodwater, but try as she might, she couldn't see anything except the murky liquid in which several ruined, sopping notebooks floated.

Tiara turned to face the other girls in the locker

room. 'I just saw a *ghost*, in case any of you are interested.'

The girls stared at Tiara.

'The ghost of Dolores Lambert – that girl who drowned – is right here in the room with us!'

At this, several girls made a splashing beeline towards the doorway, as if they had just learned that a school of piranhas might be swimming around their feet.

Gilda pulled a small pen torch from her backpack and shone it into the water. 'I still don't see anything, Tiara.'

'Well, I definitely saw something. I *told* you she was after me.'

The room suddenly went dark, and the few girls who had remained to gather their belongings squealed in unison.

'Oh, crap,' Tiara whispered.

Gilda felt a prickling sensation at the back of her neck. *Maybe Tiara is right*, she thought.

The door burst open and one of the school's maintenance workers shouted into the room. 'Ladies! Everybody out!'

The girls left the locker room as Mrs McCracken's voice blared over the P.A. system: 'Ladies, as you can see, we have some flooding. Please remain calm and stay away from the locker rooms for the remainder of the day.'

'I'm going to the nurse's office,' said Tiara, whose face had a greenish hue.

'Are you OK?' Gilda had noticed that Tiara often

asked to go to the nurse's office during class. She wondered what Tiara did there.

'I feel really weird. I have a splitting headache.'

Gilda wanted to ask Tiara more questions about the face she had seen in the water, but Tiara dodged away hastily, making it clear that she was in no mood to talk.

News that Tiara had seen a ghostly face in the freshman locker room spread quickly, and by the end of the day, Dolores Lambert's ghost had made her presence known to several freshmen: she appeared as a mysterious reflection in the glass surface of a vending machine (from which she prevented three candy bars from emerging); she made drinking water taste 'heinous'; she 'put something sticky' in a students' hand; she pulled hair and pinched buttocks.

People are acting very strangely, Gilda thought as she walked past the triplets, who sat outside the nurse's office, crying. *Are they acting this way because the school is haunted, or because they're just having fun being scared?*

Lights continued to turn off without warning throughout the day, and the distraught girls speculated and prayed that they would be sent home. No announcement of school cancellation came, however. They remained stuck at school – trapped in a dark, damp, mildewy castle.

Gilda decided it was time to do some serious research. *I need to know who Dolores Lambert really was*, she thought.

11

Shadows

Gilda felt small and chilled as she wandered under the vaulted ceilings in the school library, amidst carved, dark-wood panelling and shelf after shelf of books. The library was practically empty; nobody studied at long, wooden tables that were dimly illuminated by small lamps.

Gilda rang a little bell at the circulation desk, but nobody appeared. Just as she was about to leave, she spied a long row of books behind the librarian's desk with the title *Our Lady of Sorrows* on each spine. She was in luck; she had found the old school yearbooks.

Gilda snuck behind the circulation desk and swiftly located the book from Dolores Lambert's freshman year. She didn't have to look far for information about Dolores because the first page of the yearbook was dedicated to her:

DOLORES LAMBERT:
WE KNEW YOU ONLY A SHORT TIME, BUT YOUR
SPIRIT LIVES ON WITH US.

There, beneath the dedication, was a picture of Dolores peering out of the yearbook with a hopeful, puppyish smile. She looked as if she expected a pat on the head for co-operating with the photographer. She wore her blonde hair parted in the centre and secured with a plastic barrette over one prominent ear – the last, early-morning touch of a mother who felt compelled to over-accessorize her daughter on picture day. Why didn't Dolores have the sense to rebelliously remove that barrette?

Gilda flipped through the rest of the yearbook, searching for more information about Dolores. The pages of the yearbook made the school seem like a boisterous, happy-go-lucky place – a bubbly contrast with the sombre tone of the opening dedication to a drowned girl. Gilda perused pictures of girls wearing formal gowns at dances, leaning towards the camera like bouquets of colourful flowers. There were pictures of smiling girls throwing snowballs at each other, playing instruments, dressing in costume for the school play, washing cars to raise money for charity, leaning together to share gossip in the lunchroom. Each photograph had a lively caption: *'Having fun the "Our Lady" Way!' 'No "Sorrows" in this bunch!' 'Fun with hats!'* There was a slightly disturbing picture with the caption ' *"Kick the Freshmen" Day! Sophomore Louise Daly gives the boot to Freshman Priscilla Barkley'* – a picture that made Gilda wonder whether it was still a tradition to 'kick the freshmen.' The book culminated with glamorous, professional shots of each girl in the senior class with several pages dedicated to their lists of 'Remember when's':

Remember when Lilly Fontaine had never been in a single car accident?
Remember when we wrote 'WE LOVE YOU' on the black board in Mr Panté's class, and he never even noticed?
Remember when Sonya Roberts DIDN'T have a Mystic tan?
Remember when Cathy Jones tried to paint her white BMW pink using a magic marker?

Where had Dolores Lambert fit into this school? There was little information on the freshman class, and virtually no evidence of Dolores, who apparently hadn't taken advantage of the clubs and extracurricular activities that were photographed. With the exception of her school picture, her identity remained mysterious.

Eager to continue her research, Gilda logged on to a computer and located a newspaper article about Dolores's death:

WEST BLOOMFIELD COMMUNITY SHOCKED BY DROWNING
Students and teachers of Our Lady of Sorrows, a private school in West Bloomfield, are in shock at the news of

Dolores Lambert's death by drowning on the eve of Thanksgiving.

Parents of the deceased girl alerted police when their daughter failed to return home from school. 'She had been really busy working on a big school project, and she often got home late due to her study groups and extracurricular activities, so we didn't really worry until it was too late,' Mrs Frieda Lambert lamented, wiping tears from her eyes. Dolores was the Lamberts' only child.

When officers discovered a break in the ice covering Mermaid Lake – a manmade lake on the school's property – they immediately initiated a search-and-rescue mission.

Divers recovered Dolores's body at approximately 3 a.m.

Police say there were no eyewitnesses of the tragedy to their knowledge. They speculate that Dolores attempted to cross the frozen lake in an effort to take a shortcut to her home in the nearby West Bloomfield neighbourhood – something students who live in the area had been known to do in the past. 'The ice simply wasn't frozen deep enough to support her body weight,' Officer Denzel Jones commented.

'Our whole school community is devastated by this tragedy, and our hearts go out to Dolores's family,' said Headmistress Shirley McCracken, adding that students had been warned to stay off the ice until an official could test its safety. She also indicated that she would be enhancing safety precautions surrounding the lake and considering the construction of a bridge over the body of water.

Students remember a girl who was something of a loner, but who always had a smile. 'I never really got to know her,' freshman Priscilla Barkley commented. 'She kind of kept to herself. But she always smiled at you when she walked down the hallway, and the people I'm friends with don't even do that all the time.'

It sounded as if nobody had known Dolores very well. Clearly, the school had been shocked by her death, but had anyone really *missed* Dolores? Re-reading the article, Gilda noticed an odd detail: Mrs Lambert said her daughter was 'involved in extracurricular activities,' but the school yearbook didn't show her picture in any of the clubs. She wondered if there was some way she could find Dolores's mother and ask her a few questions.

Gilda suddenly realized that she had lost track of time: she was completely alone in the library. She wandered into the hallway and found that the lights were turned off. The school felt unusually quiet and still. Peering into the dim light of the long hallway, Gilda saw the silhouettes of statues that lined the walls like silent soldiers guarding a tomb.

At the end of the hallway, one of the statues *moved*.

Gilda stiffened. For a moment, she felt as if she might faint. Squinting into the dim light, she realized that the moving statue was actually a tall man – a man who stood in the darkness, staring at her.

The man slowly reached for something, and a moment later, the chandelier overhead filled the hallway with light. Blinking in the sudden glare, Gilda took a moment to recognize Keith – one of the school maintenance workers. She had often seen him clumping down the hallway, grimly carrying a toilet plunger or sighing with exasperation as he examined a radiator. Whenever something went wrong in a classroom – windows that wouldn't open, fans that wouldn't work – the teacher always sighed and said, 'I'll call Keith.'

'You gave me a fright, honey,' Keith said, slowly approaching Gilda and dragging a mop and bucket behind him. His voice reminded Gilda of a rusty engine. One of Keith's eyes was surprisingly blue in contrast with his coffee-colored skin; the other resembled an opaque marble due to an untreated cataract. 'I wasn't expecting to see nobody in this hall.'

'Sorry I scared you,' said Gilda, attempting to sound nonchalant. She walked quickly, realizing that she had better hurry if she wanted to catch her bus.

'For a second, I thought you was that lil' ghost girl.'

Gilda stopped. '*Ghost girl*?'

'Sometimes, mainly when it floods up, I see strange things around here. Two times now it's flooded real bad – so bad you got to dry it quick, or you get you some persistent mould and mildew and then the smell will make think somethin' died. You'd wish your nose would stop workin'.' Keith swept his mop across the floor as he spoke.

'You said something about a "ghost girl"?' Gilda persisted.

Keith nodded. He paused and leaned against his mop. 'One time, the pipes burst and they had to shut down the whole school because all them back rooms flooded like Lake Erie. So I was working all day, trying to get all the water out the building, when what do I see but a girl wearing her pink skirt just like you got on right now. And I says to myself: "that's odd, because there ain't school today. I'll be double-damned if one of them students is coming to school on a flood day." So I walk out the boiler room and look down the hallway just in time to see her walk right through a wall.'

A chill passed through Gilda's body as she imagined what it must have been like to see a girl vanish into a wall. She also felt a surge of excitement: here was yet another sighting of Dolores's ghost! She scrutinized Keith's face. He seemed to enjoy having an audience for his ghost story, but Gilda didn't get the sense that he was inventing the plot as he went along. Gilda reflected that janitors and maintenance workers were always at school during odd hours, when nobody else was around. They had to work alone, in obscure places like 'janitor's closets' and 'boiler rooms.' *It makes sense that Keith would see a ghost if the school actually is haunted*, Gilda reasoned. 'Do you see ghosts often?' she asked.

'No, no. Well, lots of times I do see dark shadows sneakin' out the corner of my eye.'

Gilda wondered if Keith's eyes could be trusted, since one eye was obviously blind. On the other hand, Gilda's *Psychic's Handbook* noted that 'it is not the eye that perceives reality; it is the *brain*. This may explain why some people see spirits walking around while others do not, despite their perfect eyesight.'

'How 'bout you?' Keith asked. 'You ever seen a ghost?'

'Sort of.' On impulse, Gilda rummaged in her backpack and handed Keith one of her business cards. 'I investigate paranormal phenomena.'

'You're a watchamacallit – a ghost buster?'

'It's more like being a detective with psychic abilities.'

'Well, well. A card-carrying psychic investigator.'

'If you see any more ghosts around here will you let me know?'

'Okay,' said Keith, winking. 'I see a ghost; I give Gilda Joyce a call.'

12

A Foul Fish

'Dolores Lambert is with the Lord,' said Mrs McCracken. 'She is not in a drinking fountain, in a coke machine, in a wad of chewing gum, and she is most certainly not floating around on the floor of the freshman locker room.'

But she IS lurking in the 'quorn surprise' in the cafeteria, Gilda thought, wishing Wendy Choy was there to share her little joke.

Following the hysteria of the previous school day, Mrs McCracken decided to meet with the entire freshman class in the chapel to 'put out the fire before it gets out of control.' Next to her, Miss Underhill and Bertha Gumm, the ancient school nurse, stood with arms folded. Tiara, who sat a few feet away from Gilda, kept her eyes downcast.

'If you see a ghost, just tell yourself this: "I'm only seeing my own fears." That's right – *your own fears*. Ladies, as much as I'd like to, I just can't explain a tragedy like what happened to Dolores Lambert a few years ago right here on our own school property. I can't explain *why* a dear, sweet person should die such a horrible death, but I can tell you that you are safe here at school. Just have faith, let go of your worries, and be grateful that we're all here, sharing this special day together.'

Something about Mrs McCracken's smooth words made the entire notion of ghosts evaporate – at least for the moment. The girls gazed up at her with grateful eyes.

'Now,' said Mrs McCracken. 'I think we'll all feel better if we all join in and sing the "Our Lady of Sorrows Song" together.'

The freshmen still didn't know the song very well, so they merely listened and looked uncomfortable while Mrs McCracken, Miss Underhill, and Ms Gumm sang enthusiastically.

Gilda was distracted by a disturbance a few feet away – a strange rustling sound. She peered down the length of the pew and saw Tiara convulsed by what seemed to be either a very bad itch or the beginning of an epileptic fit.

'Eeeewww!' The girls sitting directly around Tiara jumped away.

A shriek echoed through the chapel followed by a chorus of surprised, disgusted squeals.

Gilda stood up and craned her neck to see what was going on.

'Where did this come from?' Tiara's hands flew up to her ears, as if she were under arrest. 'She's after me. Please, make her stop!'

On Tiara's lap was a strikingly large, dead goldfish.

Mrs McCracken, Miss Underhill, and Ms Gumm moved towards Tiara swiftly, like a trio of zookeepers moving in to contain a wild animal who was going berserk. Tiara stood up and the fish flopped to the floor.

Moving quickly amidst the commotion, Gilda scooted herself to Tiara's spot in the pew, picked up the cold, slippery fish and stuffed it in her backpack before anyone noticed what she was doing. She had no idea what she was going to DO with the fish – only that it was evidence of some sort.

'Girls!' yelled Mrs McCracken, clapping her hands to capture everyone's attention. 'You are dismissed. Please go to your next class immediately.'

The girls hesitated, staring and whispering as Mrs McCracken and Miss Underhill each took one of Tiara's arms and escorted her from the chapel.

As the day progressed, Gilda almost hoped that the fish in her backpack would mysteriously vanish, but each time she unzipped the backpack, its round eyes and gaping mouth greeted her with a look of unhappy surprise.

Tiara had apparently disappeared; she didn't show up for any of her classes.

I need to consult an expert about this, Gilda thought. She decided to stop at the Fur & Feathers pet store on her way home from school to ask whether there was anything unusual about the dead goldfish.

A teenage boy whose thick, curly hair grew in a flying-saucer-shaped halo regarded Gilda steadily as she removed the dead fish from her backpack and laid it on the counter. 'We don't take returns on dead fish,' he said, pre-emptively.

'I just want your opinion about something.'

'It's definitely dead,' said the boy.

'I *know* it's dead. But can you see anything *unusual* about this fish?'

The boy shrugged. 'It's a pretty big goldfish, but goldfish can get really big if you let them.'

'Could a fish like this live in a lake around here, or would it have to come from a tank?' Gilda reasoned that if the fish came from Mermaid Lake, it might have something to do with Dolores Lambert. If not, then it was more likely Tiara's own doing.

'It could live in either a lake or a tank. Did you over-feed it or something? That's how a lot of people kill their fish.'

'It isn't my fish; I just want to find out where it came from.'

'We don't have any fish this size, if you were trying to replace it for someone. Lots of kids kill their fish because they put them in the wrong temperature water. If temperature changes too fast, it's too much of a shock. I mean, how would you like it if someone just dropped you in a freezing cold swimming pool without letting you get used to the water first?' He gave Gilda a stern look, as if hoping to get through to her so she would stop murdering the innocent fish of the world through her lack of consideration for others.

Gilda wasn't sure why this sales clerk was acting as if she had brought in the dead body of one of his best friends. *Maybe each day, kids come in to replace animals they accidentally killed, and it's started to drive him crazy,* she thought.

The boy poked glumly at the fish. He took a pencil and looked under its gills. 'Did you realize this fish has been breathing a carpet?' he asked, accusingly. 'Just look at this.'

The fish's gills were filled with grey carpet fibres. Gilda suddenly felt a little sorry for the fish.

'Sometimes a fish will jump right out of the tank and then flop around on the floor until it dies. So maybe that's what happened.'

'You mean, it committed suicide?'

The boy looked at Gilda as if trying to remember her face just in case the police asked about her later. 'Fish don't commit suicide,' he said. 'If anything, it probably jumped out of the tank because it was *happy.*'

More than anything, Gilda now wanted to be rid of the fish. Remembering that things like carpet fibres were often important to crime scenes, she pulled a few of the carpet fibres from the fish's gills and put them in a pocket of her backpack. Outside the store, she glanced around to make sure nobody was

looking, hastily stuffed the fish in the garbage can, and
hurried away.

Dear Dad:
Tiara hasn't been back in school for a week,
and nobody seems to know where she is. I
tried calling her house a couple of times, but
nobody answered.

Right now I'm on the bus, riding home
from school. There are only a few other girls
who ride the city bus with me, and I'm
guessing they're also on scholarship. Two of
them – Yolanda and Jill – seem to be close
friends, but they never actually have a
conversation; they just sit together with their
heads buried in their homework.

I take that back: I just overheard the
following conversation:

Jill: What did you get on your math
quiz?

Yolanda: A.

Jill: Me, too! What did you get on your
English

           paper?

Yolanda: A.

Jill: Oh. I only got an A minus. I hope
Ms Peebles has our science projects graded
by tomorrow. I can't wait to find out what I
got!

This conversation indicates that Yolanda and Jill must be near the bottom of the social hierarchy at Our Lady. And where do I fit in? It's becoming clear that I don't really fit in with *any* group at this school. Not that I *mind*. I know the life I've chosen as an undercover psychic detective is *supposed* to be lonely, and I've always tried to see myself as separate from all the cliques and social groups – someone who doesn't mind being independent and different.

On the other hand, I have to admit it: every now and then (like today) I can't help but think it might be nice to have a group of popular, shallow girlfriends who would call me on the phone to gossip about boys. We'd get jealous of each other based on who we're dating. We'd go shopping together for clothes and dress in matching designer sweatpants and rhinestone flip-flop sandals. We'd go on diets together and tell each other everything we had eaten in a single day: 'A bite of cereal, some black coffee, half a grapefruit, a Diet Coke – and that's all!' We'd be as close as sisters. We'd also secretly hate each other and dream of fleeing to some distant island to just be alone, eat Cheetoh's, and read a good book.

Sitting in front of me is a girl named

Maria who also rides the bus. Today, in religion class, I got into an argument with her about 'whether women should be allowed to be priests.' I said yes; she said no. Miss Appleton took Maria's side, of course. She said, 'There's a reason to preserve tradition.' I told Maria I would take matters into my own hands and write a letter directly to the pope. She and Miss Appleton just laughed. Little did they know I was totally serious!

Dear Pope Benedict,
First of all, congrats on the new job! I bet in the old days you often looked up at the 'pope mobile' and secretly wondered, 'When is it going to be MY turn?' Well – now it is!

My name is Gilda Joyce, and I'm a freshman at a Catholic girls' school. You'll be relieved to know that we wear our skirts at a tasteful three inches above the knee. We do have a shortage of serious nuns, however.

I recently got in a little spat with a colleague, so I thought you might be able to settle our dispute. I just wanted to run my idea by you – some 'food for thought.' Here goes:

WOMEN PRIESTS. HOW ABOUT THEM?
PROS:

1. You make your mark as 'a new kind of pope.'

2. MOST of the girls at my school would be
   your biggest fans.
CONS:
NONE! (Well, a few grumpy, elderly men
might disagree. Who needs 'em?)

I bet you've already got this same idea up
your sleeve and you're just waiting to
surprise us all with the news. That would be
just like you!

I'd be happy to discuss this with you any
time.

Liebe GrüBe und Küsse (German for 'love
and kisses'), Gilda Joyce

P. S. Please say a prayer for my father,
Nicholas Joyce (deceased).

13

The Petunia

Large fans still blew into the freshman locker room in an attempt to get rid of the odour of mildew and swamp water, but sightings of Dolores's ghost had ceased for the moment. A weary atmosphere of resignation descended over the school as the girls reluctantly put aside ghost stories and faced the mounting pressure of tests, papers, and school projects.

Gilda entered Ms Peebles' math classroom and found her classmates quietly reading the school newspaper, *The Petunia*. The front-page headline declared, 'Students Cope with Flood!' Curious, Gilda picked up an extra copy of the paper.

A torrential weekend downpour left several rooms on the lower level of the Castle House flooded this week.

'This is definitely the worst Monday of the school year so far,' senior Nikki Grimaldi stated grimly. 'Good thing most of the flooding happened in the freshman locker room instead of the Senior Common Room,' she joked.

'A paper that I stayed up all night to write got totally drenched in my locker,' freshman Sheila Farber complained.

A number of assignments were lost during the day, causing stress to both students and teachers alike.

'The worst thing is the smell!' freshman Ashley Thomas lamented. . .

Gilda felt incensed when she finished reading the article. *There's not a single mention of the fact that Tiara saw a ghost, and that the whole freshman class completely freaked out!*

Gilda had resisted extra-curricular activities in order to save time for her investigation, but now she felt an urge to join the staff of *The Petunia*.

They obviously need my help, she thought.

As its name suggested, the school newspaper at Our Lady of Sorrows was not known for its investigative reporting or relevance to anything that would ordinarily be called news. *The Petunia*, which was sometimes published weekly and sometimes not at all, featured movie reviews, an advice column, a fashion column, and an editorial page open to any member of the student body (most often featuring only one side of the issue discussed). Most of the news in the paper consisted of personal interest stories about students and faculty, along with erratic reports on various school events.

The newspaper staff met at a bank of computers in the school library. Suddenly feeling nervous, Gilda approached the girls who sat at computers, typing busily. Most of the staff members were juniors and seniors: Gilda noted a distinct absence of pink skirts and the presence of lattes from Starbucks that had been smuggled into the computer area without the librarian noticing.

'We're probably not going to be done until the end of this period if you're looking for a computer,' said a senior named Leah whose eyes were rimmed with dark navy eyeliner. Gilda noticed that she wore high-heeled stiletto sandals with her khaki pants.

'I'm actually interested in writing for the paper.'

'Really?' Leah arched her eyebrows. 'We haven't had a single freshman want to join *The Petunia* yet this year.'

'Most of them can hardly write their own names,' said Gilda, eager to be viewed as more sophisticated than the average freshman.

'Then keep them out of here,' said Leah, sardonically. 'We've got enough problems as it is.'

'Don't worry. I doubt they can find their way to the library.' Gilda sat down at a computer, attempting to look as if she felt at home. 'It's such a relief to be around more mature people.'

Leah regarded Gilda with a bemused expression. 'So . . . You're interested in working on *The Petunia*.' She folded her arms and scrutinized Gilda's face. 'Tell me: what's your favourite colour lip gloss?'

'It depends.' Gilda responded without hesitation, as if this were a perfectly predictable question. 'I like "Rootbeer Float" if I'm just wearing it to put myself in a better mood during the school day, and "New York Red" if I need more of a sultry look.'

Leah grinned. It seemed that Gilda had passed some kind of absurd test. 'I'm researching an article called "Our Favourite Shades of Lip Gloss" for the next issue of the paper,' she explained, sitting down next to Gilda. 'Anyway, my name is Leah, and I'm the editor. And, if you haven't noticed, I write the fashion column too.'

'I loved your article, "*It's Not Too Early to Think About a Prom Dress*", said Gilda.

'Based on the hideous outfits I see people wear outside school, I assume *nobody* reads the fashion column.'

'I took *notes*, and I've already decided I'll be going strapless.'

'Fabulous. Let me introduce you to Danielle,' said Leah, rising from her chair and walking with a sinewy, cat-like grace that seemed to belong in a smoky restaurant rather than a girl's school. 'Danielle's great at showing new people the ropes.'

Leah led Gilda to a strikingly pale, dark-haired girl

who stared at a blank screen with her chin resting in her palm.

Gilda recognized the girl who had introduced the Eating Disorders Awareness Club along with several community service clubs with names like 'Helpers for the Homeless' on the first day of school.

'Danielle, this is Gilda Joyce. She's interested in writing for the paper.'

Danielle offered a wan smile.

'Gilda, you'll have to excuse Danielle; she's suffering from writer's block.'

'Among other problems.'

'She's *supposed* to be writing our advice column.'

'*You're* Miss Petunia?' Gilda had been intrigued by *The Petunia's* advice column because it offered a glimpse into the secret problems and worries of girls in the school.

' "Miss Petunia" isn't just one person,' Leah explained. 'The big secret is that we all contribute answers to the questions.'

Gilda had always thought it would be fun to be an advice columnist. 'Could I try answering a few?'

'I don't see why not,' said Leah. 'Danielle, since you have writer's block, maybe you can get Gilda started answering a couple of those questions.'

'Sure, I guess.'

'Just make sure the advice column is interesting, Gilda, because at the moment, we have nothing for this issue except my lip gloss article. Nothing!'

Leah sauntered back to her computer to write about lip gloss.

'What she doesn't realize,' Danielle whispered when Leah was out of earshot, 'is that I haven't even *started* thinking about the advice column for the next issue; I've been trying to write my college entrance essay. That's what's killing me.'

Gilda had overheard seniors talking in the hallway about their college entrance essays – writing assignments that seemed to loom over them like executioners. Gilda had never experienced writer's block herself (her Eigth-grade English teacher had accused her of having 'diarrohea of the pen'), so she had to admit that it was hard for her to understand what they were going through.

'It's just so much pressure,' Danielle complained. 'I'm supposed to tell a "meaningful story about my life," but it's like my whole life is dependent on one or two pages of writing, and I hate talking about myself anyway.' Gilda noticed the dark circles under Danielle's eyes. She had a pensive quality – an aura of sadness.

Danielle opened a file on her computer. 'See? This is all I have so far.'

'An Interesting Life Experience'
By *Danielle Menory*

Throughout my life I have always strived to do my best. In high school, I have worked hard to achieve my goals. I've been active in community service: for example, each week I volunteer in a shelter for the homeless.

'Sounds like a good start,' Gilda lied.

'It does not.'

The platinum charm bracelet on Danielle's wrist jangled as she tapped the 'enter' key on her keyboard nervously. Her fingernails were painfully short stubs.

'Cool bracelet,' said Gilda, noticing that the charms included several crosses, a four-leaf clover, a tennis racket, and a ballet slipper.

'It was a birthday present.' Danielle exhaled a deep sigh of exasperation. 'My parents are hoping I'll follow in their footsteps and go Ivy League, but I'll be lucky to get into community college with this essay.'

Gilda was gratified to hear a popular senior speaking to her in such a confessional tone. 'Maybe you just need to jazz it up a little bit, and maybe throw in some flattery to get the reader on your side,' she suggested. 'I can help you, if you want.'

'That's OK.' Danielle stared morosely at her computer screen.

'It's no problem.' Gilda sat down at the empty computer next to Danielle and began typing at an explosive pace.

Dear Officers and Madams of the College Admissions Board: I salute you! Without the hard work and rigorous standards of admissions officers like yourselves, our universities would be overrun by riff-raff and pseudointellectuals.

As you can see, others may cringe from the dreaded college essay, but not I. Allow me to introduce myself: my name is Daniel Menory.

Don't worry: I'm not about to bore you with the usual story about how I managed to pull straight As while also winning the school's pie-eating contest for the fourth year in a row. I also won't tell you that 'here-we-go-again' anecdote about how I happened upon a cure for my grandmother's bunions while completing a science project on qualitative analysis. You'll be relieved to know that I won't even waste your time playing the 'pity card' with sob stories of my appendicitis or the setback I endured due to my brief time spent in jail. I will simply say this: you don't know it yet, but you need me. Here's a taste of what I offer:

1) My grades range from fine to super-fine.

2) My community service makes Mother Theresa look like a slacker.

3) (Fill in impressive qualification here.)

I'll tell you more about myself when we have a chance to talk in person, preferably over pancakes and a latte.

Eagerly yours,

'Danny'

P.S. Next time you're driving through West Bloomfield, don't hesitate to stop by for a chat!

'How about something like this?' Gilda felt pleased with her ability to crank out a splendid college

114

entrance essay in less than five minutes. She wondered why the seniors were being such babies.

Danielle leaned over to read Gilda's draft of the college entrance essay. She stared at the computer screen with a confused frown. 'I don't know if that's the kind of thing they're looking for either,' she said, tactfully.

'It would get their attention, though.'

'Gilda, you shouldn't be worrying about my problem; we should get you going on some writing for *The Petunia*. Do you have any ideas for stories?'

'I thought the story about the flood in today's paper was interesting.' Gilda spoke cautiously, aware that Danielle had written the story. 'But I thought it would also be interesting to write a story called 'The Mildewed Ghost', about how all the freshmen were freaking out because they thought the school was haunted. I could also investigate the story everyone tells the freshmen — how the ghost of Dolores Lambert is supposed to rise out of the water if you make any noise when you cross the bridge over Mermaid Lake . . .'

Gilda trailed off because Danielle wore a glazed expression that suggested that she found Gilda's idea about as appealing as a plate of raw kidneys.

'You hate the idea.'

'I just don't think we should perpetuate these kinds of ghost stories in the school; it gets everyone all worked up. Dolores Lambert was a real person, not just a ghost or something spooky.'

Gilda felt chastened, but she also sensed something interesting about Danielle's reaction to the story she had pitched – something that triggered what she thought of as her 'psychic radar.'

'So – you must have been good friends with Dolores?'

'Friends?' A fleeting panic crossed Danielle's face. She shook her head quickly. 'Oh, no. I hardly even knew Dolores. I just don't think we should be writing about ghosts is all.'

Gilda was certain that an article about Dolores's ghost would be news-worthy, but she decided to let the subject drop for the time being. After all, it was her first day on the newspaper staff.

'The other idea I have,' Gilda ventured, 'is a story called, "The Senior Common Room: What's *Really* in There?"'

Danielle laughed and seemed to relax. 'That's funny,' she said. 'Believe me; it's not as exciting as I thought it would be.'

'But everyone who *isn't* a senior is so curious. If you published a paper with that as the headline, I guarantee, all the freshmen would be talking about *The Petunia* all week instead of using it as toilet paper.'

'They use it as *toilet paper*?'

'Sometimes,' said Gilda, attempting to liven up the conversation. 'I mean, only in emergencies.'

Danielle regarded Gilda sceptically. 'Letting a freshman into the Senior Common Room would go against school tradition, but I'll see what Leah thinks of the idea. In the meantime, it really would be great if you could write some Q & A for the "Miss Petunia" advice column. And you could also start writing a profile of someone in the school – like a teacher or someone like that. That's usually the first assignment for a new reporter.'

Gilda already knew she wanted to investigate Miss Underhill. She left *The Petunia* with a new feeling of excitement about Our Lady of Sorrows; she was bursting with story ideas that she was certain would infuse some spark into the wilting pages of *The Petunia*.

14

The Interloper

GILDA JOYCE JOINS *THE PETUNIA*!

By *Leah Jones*

Our newest writer on *The Petunia* is Gilda Joyce. Although a mere freshman, Gilda is quite the writer: she has already written more than two novels!

Gilda lives on the east side of Ferndale, so she has quite the bus ride to get here to Our Lady of Sorrows. 'I don't mind buses,' Gilda comments. 'Most of the germs you pick up on the seats wash off,' she adds.

Gilda's favourite things include: 'my typewriter, which was a gift from my dad (now deceased), finding leftover spaghetti in the fridge when I expect to find nothing but a mouldy jar of jalapeño peppers, having a peanut butter-and-banana sandwich on a rainy afternoon, and wearing my pink freshman

118

uniform.' She adds that she is kidding about the last item.

Keep an eye out for Gilda Joyce!

Dear Dad,

Brad is blatantly attempting to buy his way into our lives.

Mom worked the earlier shift this week, which is always nice because she's home for dinner (but also kind of a drag because she doesn't let us watch television while we eat). She and Stephen and I were eating fried chicken in the kitchen, and I was just in the middle of explaining the plot of *Hamlet* when who shows up at the front door uninvited, but Brad Squib.

Mom lit up like a birthday cake when she saw him, and she started touching her hair and face and apologizing for 'looking such a mess.'

'You always look gorgeous, Patty,' he said (but I noticed he wasn't actually looking at her). He had other things on his mind. You could just tell he had come over with some big purpose, and he was twitching and smirking with excitement. 'Stephen,' said Brad, 'I'd like you to step outside here for a moment.'

Stephen shrugged and followed Brad out

the front door. I stayed in the kitchen.

A second later, Mom screamed, 'Brad! No!'

Then I heard Stephen's adolescent grunts
of euphoria: 'Sweet! This is so awesome!'

'Brad, you really shouldn't have,' said
Mom. 'You just shouldn't have.'

Well, now I had to see what was going on. I
should have guessed what it was, but I still
couldn't believe it: Brad had bought a shiny
new car for Stephen. (Well, I guess it isn't
exactly brand *new* – but it's still darned
shiny.)

'Got a great deal on this baby,' said Brad.
'That's one of the perks of my position.'

Mom looked ill. I happen to know that the
idea of Stephen actually driving around in his
own car makes her scared. 'But Stephen
doesn't even have his driver's licence yet,'
she said.

'Mom, I have my Level I driver's licence; I
just need to finish about twenty more hours
of supervised driving.'

'Not like the good ole days when a teenager
was allowed to just crash his car all around
town, right?' Brad grinned and dangled the
car keys in front of Stephen's nose. 'I can
help him get some of those practice hours in,
Patty.'

Stephen climbed into his new car and sat

behind the steering wheel with a silly grin on his face. It reminded me of when he was a little kid pretending to man the controls of an airplane or a rocket ship. I knew I should feel happy for him, but I couldn't help it: something about the whole situation just made me mad, so I walked inside and called Wendy.

You know how sometimes you just want to complain about something to a friend who agrees with everything you say? Well, Wendy isn't that friend. Whatever you do, don't call her if you definitely want someone to agree with you.

WENDY: What's so bad about a guy who buys a car for your brother and helps you get into private school?

ME: He's acting like he's trying to be our new dad or something!

WENDY: Maybe he's just trying to be nice.

ME: Nobody's ever just 'trying to be nice.'

WENDY: You're so bitter!

ME: I'm just being realistic.

WENDY: Your problem is that you think that if you let yourself like this guy even a little bit, you're betraying your father. I'd trade my parents for him in a second.

ME: Wendy, it's not about that. My instincts are telling me there's something about this guy that isn't right. I'm psychic, remember?

WENDY: Yes, you keep telling me that.

NOTE TO SELF: Secretly, I think Wendy might have a point, but that doesn't make me like Brad any better.

PANTÉ UPDATE:

It's obvious that the Triplets have a huge crush on Mr Panté. When he calls on them, they bat their eyelashes, chew on their pencils, and swing their crossed, Mystic-tanned legs. Then, when he turns around to write something on the blackboard, they giggle and lean over to whisper to each other, especially if there's chalk lingering on his butt from leaning against the eraser tray. Sometimes I feel sorry for teachers, because no matter what school they teach in, people are always looking at their butts.

Dear Dad:

STALKER ALERT:

Marcie Dinklemeyer is driving me crazy!

7 a.m.: Call from Marcie reminding me wake up on time for school.

7:30 a.m.: Call from Marcie telling me to 'wear a sweater because it's a little chilly outside.'

8:00 a.m.: Note from Marcie in my locker: 'In your own special way, you'll have a super-great day! Love, your big sister, Marcie!'

9:00 a.m.: Marcie makes me sway back and forth with her during the sing-along portion of 'morning prayers.'

12:00 p.m.: I eat lunch with Marcie in the dining hall. As I eat, she makes little comments: 'Don't you get tired of eating peanut butter and jam so often, Gilda?' and, 'Gee, isn't that can of Coke going to make you really tired later even if it perks you up now?'

12:30 p.m.: Marcie tells me 'a way to iron your school uniform so it doesn't look so wrinkly in the back.'

3:00 p.m.: Marcie informs me that my shoe is untied. I tell her I want it that way, and bend down to untie the other shoe as well. I also roll my socks down around my ankles just to complete the look. 'You're so weird, Gilda!' Marcie says.

4:30: Call from Marcie to find out how my homework is coming along. I tell her I haven't started it; I'm busy having a sugary snack.

7:30: Call from Marcie to ask me if I'm watching a rerun of 'Buffy the Vampire Slayer' instead of doing my homework. I tell her that my brother is showing me how to play a video game called 'Grand Theft Auto' (It's a game he only plays when Mom isn't home, because she can't stand it. Sometimes it's just nice to sit on the couch with Stephen even if that means watching a bunch of things blow up and conversation consisting of phrases like, 'Watch it, Gilda!' and 'You're so bad at this!') Marcie doesn't like the sound of the video game. I tell her I love video games (even though I don't) and that my favourite one is called 'Festival of Violence.'

9:30 p.m.: Marcie informs me that she has just prayed for me. She hopes I don't stay up too late playing video games because I'll be tired the next day and then I'll have to drink lots of Coke at school. She hopes I'll have a good night's sleep despite having too much caffeine during the day. She also reminds me to iron my skirt, not to worry about packing a lunch because it's pizza day

tomorrow, and to make sure I have clean
socks.

I have half a mind to show up at school
tomorrow wearing the smelliest socks I can
find in the Woodward Avenue gutter, and to
pack a lunch composed of nothing but
gumdrops and Coke.

UNSOLVED MYSTERY:
Tiara hasn't been in school for days.

I've called her house about twenty times,
but nobody ever answers the phone or calls
me back. What if the ghost in her house did
something to her family?

Oops – just remembered something: I'm
supposed to turn in a question and answer
for the Miss Petunia column tomorrow. I'd
better get started channeling my inner advice
columnist!

Dear Miss Petunia:

My parents won't allow me to go on any dates without
a chaperone. The problem is that three or more of my
senile relatives are always tagging along whenever a boy
wants to take me out to a movie or something, and they
make dumb comments and ruin everything. How can I
explain to them that four is a crowd?

Signed,

Exasperated

Dear Exasperated,

Try to bring some fun games or other activities like finger puppets for your aging relatives to keep them busy, or better yet, steer the conversation toward topics people of all ages can enjoy, like hair loss and window treatments. Remember: in this day and age, bringing some elders along for a night out simply makes sense.

-Miss Petunia

Dear Dad:

Danielle loved my first advice column installment. I think she also appreciated the help I gave her with her college entrance essay, because tomorrow she's going to take me into the Senior Common Room so I can see what really goes on in there. I'm pinching myself – a senior is actually going to let me into their top-secret hangout!!

15

Mysteries of The Senior Common Room Revealed

The freshman locker rooms were located in the back of the Castle House, an area of the school that was partially underground and prone to flooding, large spiders, and mice. In contrast, the Senior Common Room was located near the front of the school — far enough away from the administrative offices and headmistress's quarters to maintain its relative privacy, but close enough to benefit from being in the most well maintained and elegantly furnished portion of the school building.

'This is it,' said Danielle, her hand resting on the brass doorknob. 'You are officially the first freshman ever to set foot in the Senior Common Room.'

'I'm ready,' said Gilda.

'I'll probably regret this,' Danielle added.

'It's in the interests of good journalism.' Gilda was secretly more focused on appeasing her own curiosity than on finding a story for *The Petunia*. She heard the murmur of conversation punctuated by fits of giggling from behind the door.

When Danielle and Gilda entered, a guarded silence descended over the room. Gilda found herself facing a couch piled high with throw pillows and seven girls who sprawled across each other like a litter of puppies, taking a nap together. They regarded Danielle and Gilda with expressions of sullen, bleary-eyed resentment.

Sensing that she might be kicked out at any moment, Gilda surveyed her surroundings, attempting to take in every detail as quickly as possible.

The room had an atmosphere of unkempt grandeur: there were chaise longues, day beds, and velvet love seats, most of which were stained or torn. A wall of mirrors reflected dressing tables equipped with silver combs and brushes.

Contrasting with the relative luxury of the surroundings was the stale odour of spilled Starbucks coffee and an old pastrami sandwich. Plastic bags of snack foods littered the floor along with a jumble of backpacks.

'A freshman?! Who brought fresh meat in here?'

A stocky girl wearing a University of Michigan sweatshirt rose from her seat on a velvet chaise longues. Her curly, caramel-coloured hair stuck out in two angry-looking pigtails. It was difficult to tell whether she was genuinely outraged or simply aiming for a dramatic effect.

Gilda recognized Nikki Grimaldi; whether or not

you were friends with her, you couldn't miss hearing her voice in the hallway since she usually yelled to her friends from a distance rather than approaching them to have a conversation in a normal tone of voice. Gilda already knew several facts about Nikki: she was president of the Young Republicans Club; her father owned the Grimaldi Ford Dealership '*where only stealing is cheaper!*'; she was an enthusiastic University of Michigan football fan, and she had a long-term boyfriend with the ridiculous name Dinkel.

'Now you've done it,' said Nikki. 'Now we have to kill her.'

The girls lounging on the daybed, giggled, but Danielle didn't laugh.

'Seriously,' said Nikki, 'what's the deal with dragging this frosh in here?'

'My name's Gilda.' Gilda held out her hand to Nikki, attempting to undercut her hostility with a business-like demeanour.

'I prefer the term "fresh meat",' said Nikki.

'Gilda's writing a story for *The Petunia*, and I told her she could take a look in here,' Danielle explained. 'I don't see what the harm is.'

'You don't see what the harm is in what?' A strikingly pretty girl entered the room, flipped her sleek, blonde hair over her shoulder, and tossed her backpack on one of the chairs.

It was Priscilla Barkley – a girl who held a celebrity status at Our Lady of Sorrows. Priscilla's power to attract others was largely the result of her undeniable natural beauty – the dimple that winked from one cheek when she smiled, the toothpaste-commercial teeth, the green eyes and smooth skin as soft and clear as a young child's. She was also popular simply because she seemed to be everywhere at once. She served on student council; she tutored younger students as a member of National Honor Society; she sang in the school chorus; she pirouetted and shimmied on the dance team; she debated on the Trial Lawyers Club; and she always played starring roles in the school play.

'Danielle brought a FRESHMAN in here who's going to write about the Senior Common Room,' Nikki explained.

Priscilla regarded Danielle coolly. 'Nobody except seniors can be in the Senior Common Room. Everybody knows that. It's *tradition.*'

'I know it's tradition,' said Danielle, 'but that's why Gilda thought it would make a good article for the paper, and I agreed.'

The girls all regarded Danielle with stony silence.

'I just can't help but wonder,' said Priscilla, speaking with a quiet violence. 'If you're willing to let a freshman into the Senior Common Room, what *other* secrets are you willing to give away?'

'None. Because I don't *know* any secrets.'

'Good,' said Priscilla. 'I'm glad to hear that.'

'*I* would never give away a secret,' said Gilda, hoping

Priscilla and Danielle would let her in whatever juicy gossip they were alluding to.

'Gilda,' said Priscilla. 'This isn't your fault, but I'm afraid you're going to have to leave.'

'It's OK,' said Gilda, sensing that Danielle was in big trouble with the other seniors. 'I don't think there's much of a story here anyway.'

The girls regarded her with disbelief.

'I mean, it's *nice* in here; don't get me wrong. But it isn't what I was hoping for, and I wouldn't want to disappoint the other freshmen.'

'Are you kidding?!' Nikki yelled. 'It's awesome in here!'

'Where are the tanning beds? Where's the whirlpool? Where's the minibar?'

'We *have* a mini refrigerator right over there, and for your information, there's plenty—'

'Listen,' said Priscilla, interrupting Nikki, 'Freshmen aren't allowed in the Senior Common Room. It's as simple as that. And Gilda, we'd appreciate it if you'd keep quiet about everything you saw here.'

'I was just leaving,' said Gilda. 'Thanks, Danielle; I'll start researching my story about Miss Underhill instead.'

Outside the Senior Common Room, Gilda stopped and pressed her ear against the door. She thought she heard Priscilla saying something about 'secrets.'

Gilda glanced at her watch and saw she only had half an hour left in her free period before her next class. With pen and reporter's notebook in hand, she headed straight down the hallway towards the

131

administrative portion of the school building where Miss Underhill's office was located.

Gilda was surprised to find Miss Underhill's office occupied by a stranger – a young woman who had the formal, uncomfortable look of someone just starting a new job.

'Can I help you?'

'I was looking for Miss Underhill.'

'She's not here. I mean, she doesn't work here any more.'

'She doesn't *work* here anymore?'

'Excuse me,' Mrs McCracken suddenly appeared in the doorway, instantly blasting the room with honeysuckle-scented perfume. 'Susan, would you mind setting up a lunch meeting for me to talk with this girl's parents?' She pointed to a stack of papers in her hand.

'Of course.' Susan was apparently Mrs McCracken's new assistant.

'And how are things going for *you*, Gilda?'

Gilda remembered the intimidating feeling of gazing into the headmistress's fierce eyes. 'Great!' she declared, aware that she should try to stay on Mrs McCracken's good side. 'I'm learning so much in my classes, and I'm writing for *The Petunia* now.'

'Wonderful! And is there anything we can help you with?'

'I'm supposed to be interviewing Miss Underhill for *The Petunia*, but it appears that her employment has been terminated.'

Mrs McCracken stood up a little straighter. 'Unfortunately, Miss Underhill is no longer with us.'

'Why did she leave?' Gilda wondered if Miss Underhill had been fired.

'The circumstances of her departure are private, which is how she wanted it.' Mrs McCracken glanced at Susan, who quickly busied herself with pencilling something in an appointment book. 'Sorry I can't tell you more, Gilda, but just ask me or Susan for help if you need anything.'

Gilda thought fast, hoping to get a bit more information out of Mrs McCracken. 'Mrs McCracken, I've also been wondering what happened to Tiara.'

Mrs McCracken looked surprised. 'You're friends with Tiara?'

'Sort of.' What was the right answer? If she said she was Tiara's close friend, would Mrs McCracken give her more information? 'Tiara hasn't been in school for a while, and I wondered if she was OK.'

Mrs McCracken put an arm around Gilda and guided her towards the doorway. 'Gilda, I know that Tiara's little episode was upsetting for everyone. She has some issues that I've been talking to her parents about, but you don't have to worry because she's doing fine.'

'When is she coming back to school?' Gilda turned to face Mrs McCracken, resisting the headmistress's subtle effort to nudge her out of the office.

'As I said, there are some issues. We're hoping she'll

133

be back in school, but it's a private matter involving Tiara and her parents.' Mrs McCracken glanced at her watch. 'I'm late for a meeting, Gilda, but so glad your school year is going well so far!'

'Susan,' said Mrs McCracken, now halfway out the door, 'please do get that meeting set up for me.'

'Will do,' said Susan, turning to her computer.

Mrs McCracken hurried away.

Gilda hesitated, noticing something on the new assistant's desk that might be very useful – a directory of home addresses for all the school employees. As Susan busied herself with typing, Gilda swiped the handbook and walked quickly from the room.

Gilda looked up Velma Underhill's address in the directory and discovered that she lived in Hamtramck.

Pausing in the hallway, she pulled out her reporter's notebook and scribbled:

People are dropping like flies. This place is just festering with dark secrets!

Is there any link between the disappearance of Tiara and Miss Underhill? Both were kind of 'Goth' looking. Both were telling people that the school is haunted.

Is Mrs McCracken hiding something?

PLAN:
Go to Miss Underhill's house and find out what really happened to her.

16

Miss Underhill's House

Gilda gazed through the bus window at the treeless streets of Detroit, where small lots were stuffed with cars: used cars, trucks, taxi cabs, school buses, junkyards towering with crashed cars and auto parts. She passed liquor stores and small churches where some young man always stood alone, as if waiting for someone to show up; she passed weather-beaten houses and burned-out, boarded-up old factories.

Finally the bus turned down Holbrook Street into the gritty, quirky community of Hamtramck where the streets were lined with rows of pointy little houses with rickety porches and balconies with wrought-iron railings.

Gilda stepped off the bus and walked passed 'Genie's Weinies' and the Our Lady Queen of Apostles Church. Finally, she reached the row of fragile houses where Miss Underhill lived

Miss Underhill greeted her with frank confusion. 'Gilda? What are you doing here?'

Miss Underhill looked softer away from school: she wore faded jeans and house slippers, and her black hair hung over one shoulder in a loose ponytail.

Gilda realized she hadn't thought through exactly what she was going to say. 'I heard you left Our Lady and – and, well, I didn't get a chance to say goodbye.' Gilda knew that her words sounded false; she and Miss Underhill hadn't been the least bit close. Nevertheless, Miss Underhill's face softened.

'That is so nice of you, Gilda! Why don't you come in?'

Inside, Gilda's curiosity was piqued by the sight of a wheelchair in the middle of Miss Underhill's dim, cluttered living room. She followed Miss Underhill into the kitchen, where a tiny, elderly woman moved slowly towards the kitchen table, clutching her walker with rope-veined hands.

'Mother and I were just about to have some tea,' said Miss Underhill, pulling some china cups from a cabinet.

'Your tea taste like pee,' Miss Underhill's mother slurred. She wore dark-red lipstick that bled into the wrinkles and crevices of her lips.

Gilda giggled, and Miss Underhill's mother stared at her with small, watery eyes that gleamed with a mean sparkle. *She looks like a little witch*, Gilda thought.

'Who are YOU?'

'That's Gilda, Mother. She came to say hello. Gilda, this is my mother, Hazel.'

'Nice to meet you,' said Gilda.

'One of them lil' Lady of Sorrows girl-chil'ren?'

'Yes, Mother,' said Miss Underhill, helping her mother sit down and handing her a cup of tea. 'Gilda goes to Our Lady of Sorrows.'

'Rich girl!'

'I'm actually on scholarship.' Gilda felt the need to distinguish herself from the stereotypical Lady of Sorrows 'girl-children.'

'Smart girl,' Miss Underhill declared, pointing a finger directly at Gilda. 'Not like Velma. She drop out of college.'

'And *worked* to help support you,' Miss Underhill snapped. 'Gilda, would you like some tea?'

Gilda didn't have a chance to reply because Miss Underhill's mother began to scream. 'Don't you tell me about money! You've been stealing from me all my life! All of you have!'

With her outburst complete, Hazel glared fiercely at her daughter for a moment, as if waiting for her to respond. When Miss Underhill only continued to dangle a tea bag into a cup, Hazel seemed to give up and crumple inwardly. She crouched quietly, like a small grumpy squirrel, lifting her teacup slowly to her withered lips with two gnarled hands.

Miss Underhill remained eerily calm, and simply placed a plate of shortbread cookies next to her mother.

'Gilda, Mother's having a bad day because she decided to go outside by herself and cross two lanes of traffic in her *walker* – and not at any stop light, mind you, but right in the *middle* of the street – just so she could get to the liquor store. Mother *knows* she's not supposed to be drinking because this is what happens when she drinks.'

'I need my Baileys.'

'You're lucky you're even alive right now, Mother,' said Miss Underhill, sounding increasingly impatient. 'You could have been hit by a car.'

Miss Underhill's mother blew raspberries at Velma.

This was the last straw for Velma. 'Mother, I'm going to have to put you in a home if this keeps up!'

'Put yourself in a home.'

'Put myself in a home? That makes a lot of sense!'

'We should both be in a home for the mentally insane. Then we'll have tea.' Hazel Underhill broke into a raspy laugh.

Gilda began to feel as if she had accidentally wandered onto a stage where a volatile, demented play was in progress. It seemed that both Miss Underhill and her mother were liable to pick up an object and hurl it across the room at any moment.

'I should probably be going,' said Gilda, quietly beginning to back out of the kitchen. 'I have a tonne of homework to do.'

'There's a drowned girl at that school,' said Hazel, looking at Gilda.

This *non sequitur* made Gilda catch her breath. She hesitated, eagerly waiting for Hazel to say more.

'I seen her walking up and down the lake and by the trees when I visited Velma for lunch one time. Lost.'

Gilda stared. 'You *seen* – I mean, you *saw* Dolores Lambert's ghost?'

Hazel merely nodded and sipped her tea in reply.

Miss Underhill gestured to Gilda to follow her from the kitchen toward the living room. 'Gilda,' she said, lowering her voice, 'Mother's been drinking today, and she's suffering from some senior moments, to say the least. She hardly knows what she's saying right now.'

Gilda felt certain that Hazel's words must have *some* meaning. 'But – you *yourself* told me that "if you make any sound when you cross the bridge, Dolores's ghost comes out of the water screaming"!'

Miss Underhill winced as if remembering something she would rather forget. She reached for a package of cigarettes on the mantle. 'Sorry if I scared you. I just don't take chances with stuff like that.' She lit a cigarette and inhaled deeply. 'Call me superstitious,' she said, exhaling toward the ceiling.

Gilda coughed. It was a habit she had developed from the days when her mother smoked; she had often used dramatic displays of poor respiratory health in an attempt to motivate her mother to quit.

'Sorry,' said Velma, waving smoke around with her hand. 'But we're not at school, right?'

'Hey, it's a free country.' Secretly, Gilda was shocked to see the woman who had aggressively handed out detentions about skirt length lighting up right in front of her. She wondered how many of the most strict teachers at school were at home chain smoking right at that moment.

'I'm trying to quit, but I'm just so stressed after the day I've had with Mother. And on top of that, I need to find a job.'

'It's none of my business, but – did you get fired?'

Miss Underhill shook her head. 'I decided to leave.'

'Why?'

'I need a job that pays better, for one thing. Besides, there's something just – *wrong* about that place.' She flicked cigarette ashes into her teacup. 'I think it really is haunted.'

Gilda was fascinated. 'So you saw Dolores's ghost too?'

'Not exactly. But the whole time I was there, I sensed this presence – like someone who was really unhappy about something was always watching me. I think . . .' Miss Underhill shook her head as if she thought better of whatever she was about to say.

'Yes? You think *what*?'

Something crashed in the kitchen, startling both Gilda and Miss Underhill.

'Sounds like mother dropped her teacup again.' Miss Underhill sighed and stubbed out her cigarette. 'Listen, I would drive you home, but I can't leave Mother.'

'But, Miss Underhill, what were you just about to say?'

'Oh, nothing. I can't remember. I have to go now, okay?'

Gilda wanted to ask Miss Underhill and her mother about a hundred more questions, but Miss Underhill made it clear that the conversation was over.

'Good luck, Gilda,' said Miss Underhill, showing the way to the door. 'Be careful, OK?'

When Gilda got home, she found a letter waiting for her in the mailbox. There was no return address, but something looked familiar about the chicken-scratch handwriting.

Dear Gilda,

You're probably wondering where I am. Well, I'm somewhere in Pennsylvania. At the moment, I have no phone, no email – nothing except a pen and paper. I'm at a 'treatment programme for wayward teens,' and now I'm on, like, five different kinds of medication, so if I seem a little different when I finally get back home, that's partly why.

You're probably wondering what happened when I left school.

My parents wanted to send me to a boarding school (Mrs McCracken wanted to kick me out of Our Lady for too many 'disruptions') but I told them that I'd run away if they sent me there. Anyway, they changed their minds and convinced Mrs McCracken to let me come back as soon as I finish this programme 'to everyone's satisfaction.' McCracken probably realized the school needs the tuition money.

My psychiatrist thinks I'm 'very suggestible,' and I

supposedly have a hard time distinguishing fantasy from reality. Once I got the idea that ghosts were after me, I guess I just took it to the extreme. Sometimes I would simply feel compelled to do something — as if someone else was telling me to do it. Like when I found a dead fish lying next to the aquarium in our living room, I really felt that someone told me to pick it up and take it to school. It's hard to explain, but like I said, I'm getting better now.

Anyway, I know you're interested in ghosts, and I wanted to apologize, because I probably was not a very forthcoming and honest subject for your research. For example, when that glass broke against the mirror, that was because of me. I didn't really mean to do it; it was just an impulse I couldn't resist. I'm trying to become more honest with people. I don't see as many weird things now.

I didn't lie about everything, though. For example, it turned out that my dad was having an affair with one of the maids who used to clean our house, and the maid got really jealous of my mom. SHE was actually throwing tomatoes and eggs at things in our house! My mom caught her doing it — and some other things too. Are my parents staying together? Who knows? My life is just so crazy, Gilda! Anyway, if you ask me, I have a couple of pretty big apologies coming my way, since my parents were both so sure I was the reason for all of these weird occurrences.

Hope we can still be friends,
Tiara

Dear Dad:

I'm glad Tiara's OK, but I have to ask myself: what kind of person toys with a séance by throwing a glass against a wall? I know I've stretched the truth from time to time, but I would never do anything like *that*. I feel sorry for Tiara, but I'm almost glad she isn't around at the moment. She's the kind of person who says something just to get a reaction, and then you waste all this energy believing her and trying to help her only to find out that it was all made up.

Dad, if you have any insight into what's really going on at Our Lady of Sorrows, try to send me a message!

Looking forward to hearing from you,
Gilda

17

The Ruins

Gilda looked up at stars that gleamed in a clear, black sky. All around her, a flat sheet of white snow covered the frozen lake.

Her father sat next to her in the warm, yellow glow of a campfire. *I feel completely happy right now*, she thought.

'I'm thinking of doing some ice fishing,' her father said.

A familiar car appeared on the surface of the lake – Brad Squib's black SUV, rolling quickly towards them. Brad stepped out of the car and approached, carrying his fishing pole.

'You're on thin ice,' said Gilda's father.

'It'll hold,' said Brad, nonchalantly.

Gilda wished that Brad and his car would crash through the ice and disappear forever. 'He's ruining everything,' she whispered to her father, and her father looked sad.

Her father pointed to a spot across the lake, and Gilda saw the black leafless trees that surrounded the shadowy ruins. There was also a person — someone who stood eerily still, like a statue.

Gilda awoke and reached for the dream journal she kept by her bed. Her dreams sometimes contained information that aided her psychic investigations, and dreams in which her father appeared were of particular interest. As her *Master Psychic's Handbook* noted:

> If you dream of a dead individual, it may mean that you have actually made contact with him or her. Pay careful attention to such dreams — not only to the words exchanged, but also to details of the surroundings and the general feeling or mood of the dream landscape.

This dream reflects my annoyance with Brad Squib, Gilda wrote in her journal.

But there's something else, too. It seems pretty weird that I had a dream about a frozen lake, when that's exactly where Dolores died. Dad pointed at something I was supposed to look at — something in the ruins on the other side of the lake.

Gilda decided that after school she would sneak down to the lake to check out the ruins.

Standing on the bridge overlooking Mermaid Lake, Gilda watched trees that swayed in colours of crimson, gold, and tangerine. The birds were gathering to plot their winter escape — a sight that always made Gilda feel melancholy: it meant that winter lurked just around the corner. There was a chill in the air and she wished she had worn a warmer jacket.

As Gilda tiptoed silently across the bridge, she glimpsed something sparkling in the mud at the edge of the water. She felt a familiar tickle in her left ear as she knelt down to pull the shiny object from the dirt.

It was Danielle's charm bracelet.

What had Danielle been doing by the lake? Gilda put the bracelet in her pocket and made a mental note to ask Danielle about it. She turned to head toward the crumbling stone walls of the miniature castle.

Inside the ruins, sunlight streamed through the shell of an arched ceiling. Something about the place reminded her of a late afternoon movie she had once watched – a film set in a lonely English village where the sky was low and church bells tolled ominously. Gilda couldn't remember the exact plot of the story, but there had been something about a woman who knew she would be killed at some point during a weekend.

Stop freaking yourself out, Gilda reminded herself.

In one corner, she spied a wooden doorway with a plaque:

Martha Jackson Reading Room
a resting spot for ladies

Gilda was intrigued. Nobody had ever told her that

the ruins contained a 'reading room.' It made her think of an era in history when women wore petticoats and parasols – a time when girls powedered their noses and were encouraged to take afternoon naps.

She turned the doorknob and was stunned when the door swung open easily. *Almost as if someone wanted me to go inside*, she thought, with both excitement and trepidation.

Gilda had an eerie sense of having wandered into another time. She found herself in a small, cottage-like room that looked like the kind of place a group of elegant ladies might meet to have tea and scones together. Faded pink cabbage roses bloomed on the dusty chairs and curtains; china pitchers, teacups, and silver candlesticks cluttered a side table. She half-expected to look up and find a group of women who wore dark-red lipstick and old-fashioned waves in their hair sitting all around her.

Gilda picked up one of the china teacups and discovered something lying at the bottom – a ring with a heart-shaped, pink stone. She put the ring on her finger for a moment, then dropped it back into the teacup.

The room also contained a marble fireplace and a shelf stuffed with old books with titles like *The Compleat Gentlewoman; The Lady's Guide to Ravishing Men* and *Pretty Is as Pretty Does: A Guide for Young Ladies.*

Gilda opened *Pretty Is as Pretty Does* and read: 'By the time your husband comes home from work, make sure you've put on some powder and lipstick, and a figure-flattering frock. Who wants to look at a woman in dungarees and a stained apron after a long day at the office?'

Gilda was about to slam the book shut when something slipped from the pages – several yellowed, handwritten pieces of paper. At first, she thought it was simply an old homework assignment someone had forgotten. But as she skimmed the pages, she realized she had found something far more intriguing and mysterious. She sat down on one of the soft, flowered chairs and began to read.

THE LADIES OF THE LAKE GUIDE FOR PLEDGES
WHO IS A 'LADY OF THE LAKE'?

She is beautiful and confident, and she moves through her life with effortless success in everything she does. When she has a problem, she doesn't worry, because she knows she is never alone. She knows that without even having to ask, her secret best friends (we call them 'mermaids') will be there to assist her in whatever way is needed.

THE LADIES OF THE LAKE IS A SACRED PACT FOR LIFE. IN SHORT, IF YOU MAKE IT INTO THE LADIES OF THE LAKE, YOU'RE 'ALL SET.' YOU'VE GOT IT MADE FOR LIFE!

The Ladies of the Lake is a SECRET society. As a Pledge, you are a potential part of this group. As a Pledge, you also have a sacred duty to uphold the rules and regulations of the LADIES OF THE LAKE.

IF YOU DO NOT THINK YOU ARE UP TO THIS TASK, KINDLY STOP READING RIGHT NOW AND STOP WASTING OUR TIME.

If you are still reading, we assume that you genuinely want to become a member of the Ladies of the Lake.

MEMBERSHIP IS NOT GUARANTEED.

FAILURE TO COMPLY WITH RULES AND REGULATIONS WILL LEAD TO A PENALTY. REPEATED OFFENSES WILL RESULT IN MORE SEVERE PUNISHMENTS OR A FORFEIT OF YOUR OPPORTUNITY TO BECOME A FULL MEMBER OF THIS AWESOME CLUB.

<u>MEMORIZE THE FOLLOWING RULES AND REGULATIONS:</u>

1. The vow of silence. The Society **MUST** remain secret at all costs. Do not tell acquaintances, parents, boyfriends, or even pets about the Ladies of the Lake. Violation of this rule will merit the most severe punishment available.

2. Your best friends are members of the Ladies of the Lake. They are your number one priority.

3. PLEDGES do not speak unless spoken to.

4. **DON'T CALL US; WE'LL CALL YOU.** You will receive instructions, invitations, and any messages necessary from us when the time is right.

5. Your flaws are subject to scrutiny by the Society, which will make recommendations for improvement.

6. Pledges do not eat cookies or brownies.

7. A weekly essay documenting the joys of being a Pledge to the Ladies of the Lake should be submitted by 8:00 a.m. every Monday morning. **NO LATE PAPERS ACCEPTED.**

8. *Respond to all orders from members swiftly and cheerfully.*
9. *Give your heart to the Ladies of the Lake.*
10. *Bury all things you find dead.*

As she contemplated the 'Ladies of the Lake Guide for Pledges,' Gilda felt so excited, she could scarcely contain herself. Were the Ladies of the Lake currently in existence, or was the 'Guide for Pledges' a remnant of some secret society from years past?

Gilda stashed the 'Ladies of the Lake Guide for Pledges' into her backpack. She was certain she had found either a significant clue or, at the very least, a fascinating story for *The Petunia*.

18

Charms and Curses

Danielle skated across a sheet of ice that somehow covered her entire school. She watched herself moving swiftly on sharp blades, doing her homework, turning in assignments, speaking to the Eating Disorders Awareness Club, gliding through mass in the chapel. She was delighted when she looked down and saw the familiar pompoms she used to wear on her figure skates when she was a child, but she didn't like her figure skating costume; it made her feel naked and exposed. She realized she was wearing the short, pink skirt of her freshman uniform. *Why did I wear this? I'm not a freshman any more.* Danielle's legs were cold, and she noticed that everyone looked with great disappointment at the cellulite that jiggled like gelatin on her thighs as she skated through each activity.

'Aren't you afraid you're going to fall?' The girl who spoke had blonde hair and looked somehow familiar, but she had no name.

'Whatever you're doing isn't helping your cellulite.' It was Priscilla Barkley's voice.

Danielle looked for Priscilla, but found that she was alone, standing on frozen Mermaid Lake. There was something ahead – a dark spot on the ice. She knew she should move away from this dark object, but her skates seemed to have a will of their own and they sped perversely towards it.

The spot became clearer; an object protruded from the ice. As she drew closer, she saw that it was half of a person.

With her lower body completely buried in ice that fanned out from her waist like a vast, flat skirt, Dolores Lambert calmly waited for Danielle.

Why isn't she frozen to death? Danielle wondered. *Why isn't she dead?*

Cracks radiated out from her body, criss-crossing the surface of the lake – a web of lines that began to break apart the perfect surface of Danielle's world as she awoke in a sweat.

'How's the college essay going?' Gilda asked, handing Danielle the news article she had written about Miss Underhill. The headline read, 'Underhill Flees Position Due to "Unhappy Presence" – Struggles to Support Dilapidated Mother!'

'Don't ask.' Danielle's eyes looked glassy and sunken, as if she were coming down with a case of the flu.

'Are you OK?'

'Just had a bad night, that's all.'

'Too much partying?'

'No, nothing like that.'

'Bad dreams?'

Danielle flinched. 'I really don't want to talk about it, if you don't mind.'

'OK. Sorry.' Gilda found Danielle's reticence maddening. She sat down and waited for Danielle to read the article about Miss Underhill.

Danielle wrinkled her nose.

'You hate it.'

Danielle shook her head. 'It's interesting. But I thought we already talked about not perpetuating these ghost stories.'

'But Miss Underhill *told* me she thinks the school is haunted; she said she always felt like there was an unhappy spirit watching her.'

Danielle covered her mouth with a child-like fist and chewed on a thumbnail for a moment. 'Mrs McCracken will never let us print the stuff about a ghost.'

'Why not?'

'Well — it freaks people out, for one thing. Then all everyone does is talk and speculate. Before you know it, crazy rumours start circulating around the school, and nobody can get any work done.'

Remembering the hysteria that ensued after Tiara saw a ghost in the Freshman Locker Room, Gilda had to admit she saw Danielle's point. On the other hand, wasn't it her duty as a journalist to tell the whole truth?

'We'll just tone that part down,' said Danielle. 'And

let's get you working on a new story – something more fun.'

'I already have another story idea.'

'Let's hear it.'

'You know the Martha Jackson Reading room – that place in the ruins?'

Danielle seemed to stiffen. 'What about it?'

'I found something there.' Gilda handed Danielle the 'Ladies of the Lake Guide for Pledges.'

Danielle stared at the pages without actually reading them. She rubbed her nose vigorously, as if suddenly allergic to something. 'You aren't supposed to go down to the ruins by yourself,' she said. 'You'll get a detention.'

'I know, but don't you think this is interesting? Have you ever heard of this secret club?'

Danielle bit a hangnail and shook her head. 'It's probably totally made up,' she said. 'I don't think stuff like that goes on at this school.'

'Why would somebody make this up?'

'I'm pretty sure Miss Appleton does an assignment where you have to imagine a really exclusive, mean club and then talk about why we should avoid cliques. I bet it's just someone's old assignment.'

Gilda felt disappointed as she stuffed the 'Ladies of the Lake Guide for Pledges' into her backpack. She had felt certain that she had made a big discovery.

'Oh, I also found something that belongs to you.' Gilda pulled Danielle's charm bracelet from one of the front pockets of her backpack.

Danielle gaped at the bracelet as if Gilda were handing her a dead tarantula.

'I found it by the lake,' said Gilda. 'It's still a little dirty. It is your charm bracelet isn't it?'

Danielle nodded, but didn't reach to reclaim the bracelet. She didn't seem the least bit happy to see it.

'I guess you must have dropped it.'

'Keep it.'

'But – it's your charm bracelet.'

Danielle shook her head. 'I really, really don't want it any more.'

Gilda stared at the charm bracelet. Why was Danielle so repulsed by the piece of jewelry, as if it were something hideous – a gift from someone she now loathed?

There's something very strange about Danielle, Gilda told herself.

When Danielle left the library to walk to her next class, Gilda decided to follow her. Walking behind at a slight distance, she noticed that Danielle shuffled along with a hunched posture, as if protecting herself from some imminent attack.

As Priscilla Barkley approached from the opposite direction, Danielle caught her attention, motioning to her to stop. Turning their bodies away from the crowd of students who now filled the hallways with giggling and shouting, the two seemed to be in a very serious conference about *something*.

Wishing that she could magically attach an

eavesdropping wire to Nikki and Priscilla, Gilda leaned against a doorway and observed as much as she could while pretending to read her dog-eared copy of *Hamlet*. Peeking over her book, she caught a glimpse of Danielle's face. She appeared to be close to tears.

'Hey, Gilda!' With a feeling of annoyance, Gilda turned to see Marcie Dinklemeyer. 'Aren't you going to be late to your next class?'

'Maybe.'

'Well – what are you doing, then?'

'I'm *trying* to eavesdrop on a conversation.' Had Danielle just said something about 'the lake'? *Why wouldn't Marcie mind her own business?*

Marcie giggled. 'You're so funny, Gilda.'

'I'm kind of in the middle of something, Marcie.'

'But you're just standing in the hallway.'

'It *looks* like I'm just standing in the hallway, but I'm actually extremely busy.'

Marcie dismissed these words as if they couldn't possibly make sense. 'Gilda, I'm getting a committee together to help plan the next school dance,' she said, 'and I thought you could be on it!'

'Thanks, Marcie, but I have a tonne of homework to catch up on.' Rejecting Marcie's suggestions had become a habitual response for Gilda. These days, she didn't even pretend to stop to think before saying no.

'But this will be fun!'

'Marcie, you should know by now that I'm not much of a joiner.'

'A joiner?'

'That's right. I don't join things. I stay on the fringe; that way I get more information.'

'More information about *what*?'

Had Priscilla just said the word 'ghost'? How many clues was she missing? Frustrated, Gilda felt the urge to shock Marcie into leaving her alone. 'You want to know the truth, Marcie? I'm actually a psychic investigator.'

Marcie frowned. 'You mean, like an undercover *cop*?'

'I investigate *psychic* phenomena – things involving ghosts and stuff like that.'

Marcie looked blank. 'But I don't really believe in that stuff.'

'Then I guess we must be imagining this whole conversation.'

'What?' Marcie felt confused, but she sensed that she and Gilda might actually be getting in a fight. 'I don't know if you should be getting involved in that sort of thing, Gilda. Maybe you should talk to Miss Appleton about this.'

'Marcie, I don't need to talk to Miss Appleton. I also don't need someone pretending to be my big sister all the time. Do you want to know the truth? You're driving me crazy.'

Marcie's expression wavered, as if a foundation beneath her face had just cracked. Tears threatened to leak out at any moment.

'Then I'll just leave you alone,' she whispered.

'Marcie—'

But it was too late to apologize or attempt to soften the blow; Marcie had already hurried away.

Gilda had a terrible feeling – a kind of nausea combined with euphoria.

I feel guilty, she thought. *I should go run after her and apologize.*

On the other hand, she was finally free.

She turned to see if she could catch any more of the intriguing conversation between Danielle and Priscilla, but they were already gone.

Dear Dad:
A whole evening has gone by without a phone
call from Marcie to see whether I finished
my homework, ate my vegetables, and
watched appropriate television shows. I
almost feel lonely (but not quite so lonely
that I want to call Marcie).

A RIDICULOUS SCENE:
Brad came over after school to help Stephen
practise driving his fancy new car, and
Stephen must have gotten really nervous
because he stepped on the gas when the car
was in reverse. He backed the car over the
hedge that grows at the edge of the
driveway.
    I watched the whole scene from my

bedroom window. Brad and Stephen climbed out of the car and pushed and pushed until their faces looked purple, and Brad kept stopping to put his hands on his hips and shake his head. Stephen just scowled with that look he gets when he feels too bad to say he's sorry. Finally they removed the car from the hedge, which looked totally flattened and kind of offended too, as if it were wondering why the hell it just got run over by a car.

Brad and Stephen scrutinized the car's body paint to look for scratches. I couldn't see anything from my window, but Brad kept pointing to little flaws.

Finally, they climbed back in the car and Stephen started the engine. This is the part where I literally fell down on the floor laughing.

Stephen started the car, stepped on the gas, and KNOCKED OVER THE MAILBOX.

The car stopped, and nothing happened for a whole minute. They just sat there. Finally, Stephen climbed out of the car and glared at the mailbox as if it had thrown itself in front of his car on purpose. I bet you a million dollars Brad was thinking twice about buying him that car.

After I stopped giggling enough to see

straight, I looked out the window and saw
that Brad and Stephen had a hammer and
some nails. They were trying to fix the
mailbox, but at this point, they weren't
saying a single word to each other, as far as
I could tell.

I know you probably wish you were around
to help teach Stephen to drive, so I thought
you'd be happy to know that you aren't
missing much. At least you don't have to
explain the broken mailbox to Mom!

INVESTIGATION UPDATE:
DANIELLE IS HIDING SOMETHING!
In religion class this afternoon, I asked Miss
Appleton, 'When are we going to do the
assignment where we make up a secret club
with mean rules?'

'I've never given an assignment like that
before,' she said.

VERY INTERESTING.

Dear Dad:
Now that Marcie and I are no longer
'siblings,' I eat lunch at a table with Yolanda
and Jill (the 'city bus' girls) at one end and
the Triplets at the other.

I wish I could go to Starbucks for lunch
with the older girls who work on *The*

Petunia, but they never invite me. Freshmen aren't allowed to leave campus. Still, you'd think they'd offer to pick up a mocha frappucino for me, since we're co-workers!

Today, just to keep things interesting, I eavesdropped on the Triplets during lunch. One thing I noticed is that they all have salads every day, and they seem to pay a lot of attention to the food they see each other eating.

'What is THAT?!' Ashley was staring at Lauren's salad as if bugs were crawling all over it. Apparently, Lauren had put too much salad dressing on her salad, and this filled Ashley with disgust.

'Don't you realize dressing has a TONNE of calories?' said Britney.

Lauren kind of stopped eating after that. I felt bad for her, so I asked if she wanted to contribute her leftovers to my 'food sculpture.'

Whenever I buy my lunch at school, I try to leave something entertaining for the octogenarian lunch ladies, just to brighten up their drab days. This amuses everyone, and before you know it, we're all chipping in empty potato chip bags, French fries, Coke cans, and straws to add to the sculpture. When it's as whimsical and precarious as I can make it, I label it with a handwritten title.

Today's sculpture was titled 'Salad Wars!' As I presented it to the lunch ladies, I saw Marcie watching me from across the room, just shaking her head.

CONTINUED ATTEMPTS AT PANTY HUMOUR:
Wendy and I came across an advertisement for 'The Smartest Panty Money Can Buy!' so I left a copy on Mr Panté's classroom desk today, just to see if he would laugh. He hardly looked at it: he just crumpled it up, threw it in the wastebasket, and said, 'Seen it all before!' Then he commented: 'Whoever thinks she's funny needs to take her studies more seriously.'

I got the feeling Mr Panté suspected me. I have a chance to redeem myself, though, because he just gave us a fantastic writing assignment – to create a Gothic story for Halloween! The story I'm writing is just reeking with Gothic atmosphere and macabre twists and turns. Mr Panté is going to be so impressed, he'll forget all about the sentence diagrams I haven't turned in yet. In fact, he'll probably start asking me to join him in the faculty lounge to help him edit his poetry.

19

A Phone Call From a Ghost

'There was this girl who was left home alone while her mom went out drinking with some guy.' Gilda sat on her mother's bed, watching as her mother got ready for a date with Brad. 'When her mom got back, there was nothing left of her daughter but her little finger with a note attached to it. And what do you think the note said?'

'I have no idea, Gilda.' Mrs Joyce calmly continued to apply brown mascara to her otherwise invisible auburn eyelashes.

'Well, duh. It said, "Either give us a million dollars or don't expect to see your daughter again.".'

Mrs Joyce shook a can of hairspray in response.

'Luckily, this girl's mom happened to have a million dollars just lying around the house, so she got her daughter back the next day. I mean, the girl only had little fingers, so she had to quit her piano lessons, but she was otherwise OK. *Some* people wouldn't have been that lucky.'

'Gilda, I know you've been nervous about staying

home by yourself recently,' said Mrs Joyce, adjusting a stray lock of hair. 'Stephen has to work tonight, so I've made arrangements for a babysitter.'

'What?!' Gilda jumped up from the bed, outraged. 'I'm old enough to *be* a babysitter. Wendy Choy has been babysitting Terrance for three years now.'

'Is that why you're telling me stories about girls who have their little fingers cut off when they're left alone?'

'No. I'm just telling you that to make you feel bad.'

'I don't need anything else to feel bad about, Gilda.' Mrs Joyce moved toiletries around on her dressing table, searching for a misplaced earring. 'I asked Grandma Joyce if she wouldn't mind coming over tonight, and she was thrilled.'

This wasn't exactly good news. Grandma Joyce's idea of a fun time was, 'Let's surprise your mom and wash the windows!' Or: 'I bet if we set our minds to it, we can get this room really, really spick and span!'

'She'll probably want to clean all the toilets in the neighbourhood or something,' Gilda complained.

'That would be wonderful,' said Mrs Joyce dabbing off some excess lipstick. 'But I've already told her that I want her to relax. No housework tonight.'

'I'm ready for the slumber party!' said Grandma Joyce, standing at the front door and holding up some microwave popcorn and a video of the movie *Halloween*.

Grandma Joyce was the only woman Gilda knew who not only used sponge rollers, but who wore them outside with a scarf that looked like a lumpy turban around her head.

'Hi, Grandma. Haven't we seen *Halloween* before?' Gilda asked, letting her grandmother in.

'You know how I love the scary shows, and it was the only thing I could find in the video shop.'

Grandma Joyce loved horror movies, but she was a frustrating person to watch them with because what she really enjoyed was the failure of the films to evoke any fear. As she watched, she made frequent comments: 'Now that's just silly. Oh, for heaven's sake, that is just ridiculous!'

'Let's get this popcorn popping!' said Grandma Joyce, heading towards the kitchen.

Grandma Joyce tossed the popcorn into the microwave then started to wash some dishes that had been left in the sink.

'Did Mom tell you that she's going on a *date*?' Gilda wondered what Grandma Joyce knew about Brad Squib. Did she view Mrs Joyce's dating life as a betrayal of her dead son?

'I'm not the meddling type,' Grandma Joyce declared. 'Not like my friend Layla; she's always into her kids' business, and her daughter-in-law's business and then she even tells her grandkids what to do. I tell her, "Layla, give them some space!" She doesn't know when to stop.'

'Mom's boyfriend's name is Brad.'

Grandma Joyce scrubbed a pot vigorously, as if it

165

needed a good thrashing as well as cleaning. 'Nice name.'

'I think it's a stupid name.'

Grandma Joyce paused and looked at Gilda. 'You know, Gilda, your dad would have wanted you mom to find somebody. He really worried about how hard it was going to be for her on her own what with all the bills and college just around the corner and everything you kids were going to need.'

'You're saying she should marry for the money?'

'I wouldn't put it that way.'

'How would you put it?'

'I'm just saying that it's understandable that she wants a companion. Now, I personally don't need a man around to keep me happy because I have my friends and grandkids and church and favourite TV shows and everything, but your mom's still a young person and she doesn't have many hobbies either, so you can't really expect her to spend the rest of her life as a single woman.'

'Maybe we can find her a hobby,' Gilda suggested. 'Some model airplanes or something.' Gilda always felt very impatient with girls who felt that they needed to have a boyfriend at all times, and she wondered if her own mother now fell into that category of weak females.

'I see you've still got that smart mouth.'

'It's not that I don't want Mom to find someone,' Gilda explained, 'it's just — there's something about *this* guy that I don't trust.'

'What don't you trust?'

'I think he's hiding something.'

'I see,' said Grandma Joyce, nodding knowingly. 'You never can tell with some people. Now, my friend Layla gets a call the other day, and next thing she knows, her daughter is getting married to a man in Vegas. Well, come to find out, the man stole her daughter's credit cards and every pair of her tights, and she has never seen him since.'

'He stole her *tights*?'

'There are crazies out there, Gilda. Crazies!'

Grandma Joyce always had a way of bringing every subject back to the troubles encountered by her friend Layla. It was actually a very good technique for changing the subject.

As Gilda and her grandmother sat down to watch the movie, Gilda's mother appeared looking shimmery and polished in a black, knit trouser suit, high heels, and gold jewelry. Her auburn hair was free of stray greys, and she had a new haircut that flattered her face with layers.

Gilda felt a conflicted sense of pride and annoyance with her mother. It was true that her mother looked younger than ever and that her fashion sense had greatly improved. On the other hand, it was irritating that Brad was the inspiration for this makeover.

'My, don't we look spiffy!' Grandma Joyce declared.

'Thank you,' Mrs Joyce grabbed her purse and

looked as if she would like to escape the house quickly. 'I'll be on my way now.'

'Get thee to a nunnery,' Gilda mumbled, staring at the television.

'Excuse me?'

Gilda cleared her throat. 'I said, "Go thy ways to a nunnery".'

'Why are you telling your mother to go to a nunnery, Gilda?' Grandma Joyce asked.

'It's from *Hamlet*. Haven't either of you read Shakespeare?' Gilda had just finished reading *Hamlet*, and had been eager to say this line to someone.

'I don't like your tone one bit, Gilda,' said Mrs Joyce. 'And I think you will apologize right now.'

'What did I say?'

Mrs Joyce stared at Gilda for a moment, as if trying to decide whether forcing an apology was worth the trouble. She had the feeling the line was a reference to something familiar, but she wasn't sure what. At any rate, it sounded rude. She walked to the centre of the room, picked up the remote and clicked off the television.

Grandma Joyce sighed. 'Gilda, will you please apologize to your mother so we can watch the movie?'

'I'm *sorry*,' said Gilda, irritably. 'You know, you send me to school to learn literature, and then you punish me when I actually speak like an educated person.'

'That's right,' said Mrs Joyce. 'I don't like a smart mouth.'

Gilda had never understood the logic of the term 'smart mouth.' Shouldn't someone *want* to have a 'smart mouth'?

Mrs Joyce sighed. 'Well, I can see I'm not wanted around here this evening. I'll be going now.'

'Have fun, dear, and keep your wits about you,' said Grandma Joyce. 'There are crazies out there on the dating scene these days.'

Mrs Joyce raised an eyebrow at Gilda, as if blaming her for this piece of unsolicited advice.

Gilda and her grandmother settled down on opposite ends of the couch with an enormous bowl of popcorn between them. As the movie began, Grandma Joyce began to combat the show's attempt to scare her. 'Oh, pu-lease! You expect me to believe this nonsense?'

The kitchen telephone rang, and Grandma Joyce shrieked.

'You're not scared of the movie, but you scream at the *telephone* ringing?'

'Good grief, that startled me!' Grandma Joyce exclaimed. 'That ringer you have is way too loud. Maybe you should get that, Gilda, in case it's your mom or Stephen.'

Keeping one eye on the television while standing in the kitchen, Gilda picked up the phone. 'Hello?'

Nobody answered.

'Hello?'

A weighted silence was the only response. Gilda

sensed someone on the line, listening.

'Hello?'

'*You will drown . . . in the lake . . .*' a girl's voice whispered.

Gilda felt both confused and terrified. She also sensed the small thrill she got whenever encountering something genuinely mysterious. 'Who *is* this?'

'*I'm dead.*'

A dial tone followed.

Stay calm, Gilda told herself. *Don't panic; think.* She remembered that hitting '*69' would give her the phone number of the last incoming call. A robotic voice provided an innocuous-sounding local number that Gilda quickly dialled. Could a ghost have her own phone number? *You can handle this*, Gilda told herself, listening to the surprisingly ordinary pulsing tone that indicated a phone ringing somewhere.

'Lambert residence.' A woman's hoarse voice answered.

For a moment, Gilda was speechless.

'This is the Lambert residence. Who's there, please?'

'Is this *Dolores* Lambert's house?'

There was a cold silence at the other end of the line. 'It *was* her residence. Who is this, please?'

Is that Dolores's mother? Gilda wondered. 'Mrs Lambert, someone just called me from your phone number.'

'I don't think so.'

'But I just hit "star sixty-nine," and I got your number.'

'I have no idea how that happened, dear. Nobody called you from our house. Good evening.'

The woman hung up. Gilda placed the phone back on the receiver and felt uncomfortably aware of every detail of her surroundings – the creepiness of the vintage cat clock from the 1970s with its moving tail and eyes that twitched away the seconds, the blackness of the windowpane glazed with frost. Every inanimate object looked ominous.

I just received a phone call from a ghost, Gilda thought. She suddenly remembered the blithe advice she had given Tiara: 'Just ask her what she wants.'

'OK, Dolores,' said Gilda, standing in the middle of the kitchen with hands on hips. 'What do you want?'

A hysterical scream from the video playing in the living room was the only response.

20

Dolores Lambert's House

Gilda stood at the front door of Dolores Lambert's house – an enormous Tudor-style home located within walking distance of Our Lady of Sorrows. It had been easy enough to find Dolores's address in an old student directory, but now Gilda felt nervous about actually ringing the doorbell.

A woman who exuded weariness opened the door and peered at Gilda quizzically. Her blue eyes and wide, reddish face faintly resembled the picture of Dolores in the school yearbook.

'Mrs Lambert?'

'Yes?'

'My name is Gilda Joyce, and I go to Our Lady of Sorrows.'

At the mention of Our Lady of Sorrows, Mrs Lambert's face softened. 'I thought that pink skirt looked familiar,' she said, opening the door a bit wider.

'I just wondered if I could ask you a couple of questions.' Gilda felt awkward. There was simply no tactful way to show up at Mrs Lambert's door and ask about a dead daughter who had made a ghostly phone call.

Mrs Lambert looked perplexed, but she gestured for Gilda to step inside. 'Come in,' she said. 'It's already getting so cold out here!'

The house was virtually empty of furniture. Boxes lined the entranceway.

'We're getting ready to move,' Mrs Lambert explained. 'It's going to take us some time to pack everything up.'

'Where to?'

'Hawaii.'

'Awesome! I mean – that sounds nice.'

'My husband and I can't take the cold any more.' She rubbed her arms. 'I guess I'm not getting any younger.'

The atmosphere in the Lambert's house had an icy edge; it was virtually as chilly inside as it had been outside. Gilda remembered reading that 'cold spots or other changes in temperature may be signs of spirit activity.'

'You wanted to ask me something, Gilda?'

'I'm researching a story for the school paper,' Gilda fibbed, thinking it was better not to mention the fact that a ghost had telephoned her from the Lambert's house. 'We might feature a memorial profile of your daughter, since she would have been a senior this year.'

Mrs Lambert's face broke into a quivering smile but her eyebrows arched inwards. A contortion of excruciating pain twisted her face. Despite her blue eyes and fair complexion, Gilda perceived a darkness surrounding Mrs Lambert – a residue of sadness.

'I'm sorry.' Despite her own familiarity with grief, Gilda wasn't sure what to say to Mrs Lambert.

Mrs Lambert shook her head. 'Sometimes, after all this time, something will just set me off.'

Gilda knew the feeling. Sometimes a single, unexpected reference to her father triggered a flood of emotion. *I don't think I've ever seen an expression quite that sad on an anyone's face before*, Gilda thought.

Summoning her courage to gather information from Mrs Lambert, Gilda decided to pretend she was a real detective on official business. 'Mrs Lambert, I wonder if you could show me some things your daughter was interested in,' she suggested. 'Maybe I could take a look at her room?' Gilda knew she was going out on a limb with this request, but it was worth a shot. Dolores's belongings might offer important clues.

Mrs Lambert hesitated. Her eyes moved over Gilda's pink skirt and tattered backpack wistfully. 'Her room is upstairs,' she said, turning to lead Gilda toward the second floor. 'I kept it just the way she left it.'

Upstairs, Mrs Lambert opened the door to reveal a perfect little girl's bedroom where everything was pink and quite literally frozen. 'I need to pack up this room for our move, but I haven't been able to make myself do it yet.'

'It's cold in here,' Gilda observed.

'We closed off the vent in this room. I don't go in here much.'

The pale pink walls in Dolores's room perfectly matched her ruffled pink bedspread. A collection of teddy bears and bunny rabbits huddled together as if trying to stay warm. Girlish posters featuring ballerinas, kittens, and inspirational messages decorated the walls: 'Hang in there!' 'Never give up!' 'Believe in yourself, and reach your goal.' 'Think thin!'

Mrs Lambert waited for Gilda in the doorway, as if entering her daughter's bedroom would break a spell of some kind.

'Was she a dancer?' Gilda eyed a poster of a ballerina posed in an expressive arabesque. '*If you can dream it; you can achieve it. If you can think it; you can become it,*' the poster urged.

'She took a few ballet lessons, but I think she just liked the poster.'

Gilda surveyed the motivational messages blaring from the walls. She herself was intensely goal-oriented, but something about the combination of posters seemed hysterical. 'Dolores must have had some big goal she was working to achieve, right?'

Mrs Lambert cocked her head as if seeing her daughter's posters for the first time. 'I don't know of any big goals. She always wanted to lose a few pounds, but unfortunately, she took after her mom in that department.'

Gilda glanced at Mrs Lambert's figure. She was a

large woman, but her clothes were noticeably baggy, as if she had recently lost a large amount of weight but never bothered to shop for a smaller wardrobe.

'She was on a diet?'

'*I* thought she looked just fine, but she was at that age when she was starting to get really concerned about her weight. She just wanted to get rid of the baby fat. Once, she got so upset I took her to Jenny Craig with me, but it didn't really work. We just ate the diet food for snacks and then went to McDonald's for French fries.'

Mrs Lambert's eyes filled with tears as she surveyed her daughter's belongings. Her skin looked suddenly puffy; it was as if a pool of pain rippled just beneath the surface of her face.

Gilda turned back to the poster, her eyes lingering on the sinewy tendons and muscles of the dancer's body. Something about the pictures made her think of Danielle and the Eating Disorders Awareness Club.

'In your news article, you can say that Dolores's main goal was doing well in school,' Mrs Lambert declared, composing herself. 'I told her, "Dolores, this school is going to be tougher than your old school," but she still wanted to do it. She was just so proud when she got in to Our Lady of Sorrows, so excited about everything—' Mrs Lambert's voice broke. She blinked quickly, fighting tears. 'You know how it is; at a certain age, you just don't want to tell your mother everything?'

'Definitely,' Gilda agreed. 'My mom thinks I'm working at the library right now.'

'She *does*?'

'It's OK.' Gilda wished she hadn't blurted that fact. 'She doesn't want to know all my details.'

Mrs Lambert looked concerned. 'I'm sure your mother wants to know all your details, Gilda.'

'Believe me; she's got enough on her mind as it is.' Gilda pulled open Dolores's desk drawer and found a Hello Kitty notebook and a bunch of pencils with chubby erasers bundled together with a rubber band. 'Would it be OK for me to take a look?' Gilda asked, pointing at the notebook.

'I suppose, but I really should be getting back to my packing.'

'It'll just take a second.'

Gilda flipped open the notebook before Mrs Lambert could protest further, and found Dolores's notes from English class. ' "To be or not to be?" ' Dolores had written at the top of the page in fat, girlish handwriting. 'Hamlet thinks about the value of his own life. He is MELANCHOLY.' Gilda flipped through a few pages of *Hamlet* notes, wishing that she had time to read every page carefully in search of personal messages or other clues. She was uncomfortably aware of Mrs Lambert's presence behind her, watching her every move. Just then, something in the notebook caught her eye — a poem:

> *My friend must be a Bird –*
> *Because it flies!*

Mortal, my friend must be,
Because it dies! . . .

It was the same Emily Dickinson poem Mr Panté had shown Gilda's English class at the beginning of the school year. *That poem is in our poetry textbook, so she must have had some personal reason to copy it in her notebook*, Gilda thought.

'Mrs Lambert, who was Dolores friends with?' Gilda turned abruptly and caught Mrs Lambert scowling behind her.

'She had lots of friends,' said Mrs Lambert, defensively. 'I mean, I think she missed her friends from her old school, but whenever I'd suggest calling them, she'd just tell me she didn't want to see them any more.'

'But did she have many friends at Our Lady of Sorrows?'

Mrs Lambert abruptly walked into the room, took the notebook from Gilda and closed it. She stuffed it back in Dolores's desk drawer. 'I'm sorry, Gilda, but I don't like that poem,' she said. 'There's something so sad about it.'

She doesn't want to think her daughter was unhappy, Gilda thought, noting with interest that Mrs Lambert knew exactly why she was asking about friends. She knew Mrs Lambert was eager for her to leave, but the more time she spent in Dolores's room, the more questions bubbled in her mind.

'So – Dolores *didn't* have friends at Our Lady?'

178

'Well, I don't remember all the names. She told me she was friends with some popular girls.'

Something about this statement rang false, but Gilda decided it would be fruitless to press the issue further with Mrs Lambert.

'Look,' said Mrs Lambert, pulling a photograph of her daughter down from its perch high on a display shelf. 'This is my favourite picture of her.'

The photograph looked very different from the school picture Gilda had seen in the *Our Lady of Sorrows Yearbook*. With her chin resting in the palm of her hand, Dolores looked pretty – less puffy and anxious. One thing really caught Gilda's interest – the pink, heart-shaped stone that gleamed on Dolores's finger. Gilda felt sure it was the same ring she had seen in the bottom of a teacup in the ruins. 'Pretty ring,' Gilda observed, hoping Mrs Lambert would tell her more.

'It was a real amethyst, and it was *gorgeous*. I know Dolores felt so bad when she lost it.'

Gilda's ears perked up at this piece of information. *I bet I know where the ring is*, she thought. 'This might sound like an odd question, Mrs Lambert, but did Dolores ever mention anything about a club called The Ladies of the Lake?'

'I don't remember anything like that. What type of club is it?'

'To be honest, I'm not really sure. I only know that it's a secret club.'

Mrs Lambert shook her head. 'Dolores really wanted

to be popular, so I doubt she'd go for something secret.' She picked up the image of her daughter, rubbed away some dust using her shirtsleeve, then placed it back in the same spot on the shelf with a gesture of finality. She stood for a moment looking up at it, her hands clasped tightly in front of her abdomen. 'Gilda,' she said, 'I think we're done now.'

Mrs Lambert seemed more cheerful as she led Gilda to the door. 'Good luck with your article and your studies,' she said. 'It's always nice to see the girls from Our Lady of Sorrows. Everyone was so thoughtful after the tragedy happened, and if you can believe it, that sweet girl Danielle Menory still stops by to help me with errands.'

Gilda stopped abruptly, as if she had just bumped into a wall. '*Danielle Menory* comes over here?'

'Isn't she *something*? She does it completely out of the kindness of her own heart,' said Mrs Lambert. 'Just last week, I hurt my back and she came over twice to help me put away groceries and pack some boxes. And she won't even let me pay her a dime! She is really something.'

There's definitely something fishy about this, Gilda thought 'Mrs. Lambert, was Danielle here on Friday evening, by any chance?'

'Why, yes, she was. Can you believe that – coming over on a Friday night to help a neighbour?'

'It's impressive,' said Gilda, struggling to contain her

excitement at having discovered another major clue at Mrs Lambert's house. 'And were you *with* Danielle the whole time she was at your house?'

Mrs Lambert gave Gilda a quizzical look.

'I mean, did you let her out of your sight for any length of time?'

'That's an odd question.'

'I'm only asking because I received a phone call from your house on that night, but there was some interference, and I couldn't quite hear who it was. I thought maybe Danielle was the one who called.'

'Oh, so that was you! Well, there you go, Gilda; mystery solved,' said Mrs Lambert cheerfully. 'Danielle was just here for a few minutes; she put away some things in the kitchen, and when I came back down she had already left. I bet she tried to give you a ring while she was here. She does the school paper too, right?'

'Right.' Had it been Danielle's voice on the phone? The idea of soft-spoken Danielle whispering '*You will drown in the lake*' was almost as hard to imagine as the notion of a phone call from a ghost. Still, there was something far too suspicious about the fact that Danielle had been at Mrs Lambert's house on the very night that Gilda received the eerie phone call.

What if I'm on to something really big? Gilda wondered. Then, a more disturbing thought as she remembered the threatening, whispery voice on the phone: *What if my life really is in danger?*

21

Halloween Day

'*Hearing Lord Fangue's evil proclamation, a swarm of bats emerged from a nearby cave and defiled themselves in Dulcia's crimson hair. The end.*'

Gilda looked up to gauge the class's response to her Gothic tale, which she had just read aloud. Her lengthy story described the plight of beautiful, dimwitted Dulcia Schmetterling and her gloomy life in Spinsterloche Castle. In a freakish turn of events, Dulcia's husband is murdered by a loathsome chicken – an 'uncanny, insane hen' who still wanders through the grounds of the castle. Tricked by Lord Tibor Fangue's request for a 'juicy chicken dinner', Dulcia cuts off the vile chicken's head, only to discover that this very hen is actually her husband in disguise! Her husband has been under Lord Fangue's spell all along – and now Dulcia has murdered him by mistake. In the tragic conclusion, Dulcia is forced to marry the hoary-eyebrowed object of her hatred – the wretched Lord Fangue.

Gilda noticed that Mr Panté's face looked pink for

some reason. He seemed to be struggling to control his facial expression. Had the part about the see-through nightdress been too risqué for him to handle? Had the image of Dulcia French-kissing the lips of her dead husband been too graphic?

As she gazed out at her classmates' inscrutable, painted faces, Gilda felt as if she were facing an audience of clowns. It was Halloween day, and at Our Lady of Sorrows, *everyone* came to school in costume – even the freshmen. Wearing a wig with long, black hair and a white silk dress from a vintage clothing store, Gilda was dressed as a 'Lady of the Lake' from Arthurian legend. She loved the romantic feeling of the long, fake hair falling over her shoulders and the silkiness of the dress. Her costume was also a serious part of her investigation: when people asked, 'Who are you supposed to be?' she watched closely for any unusual reactions as she said the phrase 'the *Lady of the Lake.*' So far, no new suspects had emerged.

With a pair of sparkly, purple antennae bouncing on her head, Sheila stood up and applauded. 'Standing ovation,' she said. 'That was the best story I've ever heard in school.'

The other girls politely joined her with more subdued applause.

I was wrong about Sheila, Gilda thought with gratitude. *She's a genius.*

'Thank you, Gilda,' said Mr Panté, smiling a little too broadly. 'Comments, anyone?'

'It was weird!' Ashley complained.

'What do you mean by "weird"?' Mr. Pante asked.

'I don't know. It was kind of icky.'

'Well, sometimes Gothic literature *is* "icky". I thought Gilda certainly captured a Gothic atmosphere, didn't you?'

'It seemed a little wordy,' said Amelia, whose own story had been very spare.

Mr Panté nodded. 'I do agree, Gilda, that you could pare down the adjectives in your writing. Sometimes less is more.'

'And sometimes more is more,' said Gilda.

The girls laughed, but Mr Panté looked annoyed.

Gilda left class feeling disappointed. As she had read her story aloud, she'd imagined Mr Panté slapping her on the back and immediately sending her story off to New York for publication. Later, they would sit in the back of the classroom and secretly split a bottle of champagne to celebrate her literary success. 'You're the most talented student I've ever had in my life,' Mr Panté would whisper.

Instead, Mr Panté had merely pointed out the overuse of adjectives in her writing. *Dad would have loved that story*, Gilda thought, glumly.

The atmosphere in the school hallways was like a carnival. Unlike Gilda's old school, where only a few students dared dress in costume, the girls at Our Lady of Sorrows – particularly the juniors and seniors – had no qualms about looking ridiculous. The costumes had a liberating effect, and the boisterous laughter and shouting between classes was five times as loud as normal.

On the walls, posters announced the annual Halloween Dance that would take place that night: 'Get Spooky! Don't Miss the Halloween Dance! Bring a Date, a Friend, or Just Bring Your Scary Self!'

Gilda decided to put aside her disappointment with Mr Panté's response to her Gothic tale. *I have to stay focused*, she told herself. *I have an investigation in progress.*

Gilda's plan to interrogate Danielle about her suspicious work for Mrs Lambert had been thwarted thus far because Danielle had skipped the last *Petunia* staff meeting. She also seemed to be going out of her way to avoid Gilda in the hallway.

Gilda decided to turn her effort to 'PLAN B.' She would bring Wendy to the Halloween dance as a guest. Then, when nobody was looking, the two of them would sneak down to the ruins to conduct a séance. After all, Gilda reasoned, when could be a more promising time to speak to Dolores's ghost than Halloween night, the very night the spirits of the dead were supposed to intermingle with the living?

Priscilla Barkley twisted her hair into a messy bun. She grabbed the English paper she had just finished writing, the script for the school play, and her Cleopatra Halloween costume and hastily stuffed everything into her backpack. It was nearly 10:30 in

185

the morning, and she had skipped her first two classes of the day to turn in her advanced placement English assignment on time. If she didn't hurry, she would miss yet another class.

With her pink, logo-covered Coach purse in one hand and a mug of bitter coffee in the other, she ran out the door into a surprisingly heavy downpour.

'Crap!' Priscilla yelled, racing towards her car without an umbrella or raincoat.

As she sprinted through wet grass, her open backpack filling with rainwater, an invisible object seemed to place itself in front of Priscilla's shins. Everything went flying. For a moment, Priscilla remained frozen on her hands and knees, trying to absorb the horror of the fact that her khaki pants were now stained with grass and mud and that her cashmere sweater was sopping wet. What really scared her was the feeling that someone had stuck out a mean-spirited foot to trip her *on purpose*. Had she heard an impish giggle in the rain – a split-second of evil laughter at her expense?

Or was she starting to lose her mind just like Danielle and Nikki?

'You're breaking the rules,' Priscilla yelled into the rain as she stood up and attempted to walk with some degree of dignity back to the house to change clothes.

Priscilla liked rules, providing that she was the one who made them up. Until this year, her rules rituals had worked, and Dolores's ghost had left her alone.

Why didn't they work any longer?

What does she want? Priscilla wondered as she went back inside and dropped her backpack and purse on the kitchen floor. *I already gave her a Dior scarf and a Dolce & Gabbana purse and gold earrings from Tiffany's.*

'*But you shoplifted those things,*' a voice in her head replied. '*How could they really matter to you?*'

Maybe that was the problem. She had broken her own rule about giving away something of genuine value, and now she was paying the price. As she trudged upstairs to change clothes, Priscilla decided that they would do the ritual again, and this time it would work. This time, she would sacrifice something that truly mattered to her.

22

The Halloween Dance

'Hey! There are cute boys here!' Wendy exclaimed, causing a group of boys to turn and check out her 'black cat' costume, which included a long tail and a purse constructed from a bag of kitty litter. 'I thought it was just going to be a bunch of nuns!'

'I told you a boys' school was invited,' said Gilda.

The ornate, feminine ballroom at Our Lady of Sorrows had been transformed to look like a nightclub. Music boomed from enormous speakers surrounding the darkened room, and a large screen on the stage pulsed with the bright, fragmented images of music videos.

'OK, let's leave a little more room here, kids!' Gilda observed Miss Appleton shining a flashlight on a group of boys and girls who were touching each other in a manner she considered 'too lewd'.

'You mean we can't freak dance here?' Wendy seemed disappointed.

'Since when do you freak dance?'

'I love it,' said Wendy. 'I've been doing it all year.'

'You have not.'

'Yes, I have.'

'Freak dancing is for people who don't know how to dance.'

'Then you should try it.'

Gilda was just about to give out a scathing comeback when she spied Danielle, Priscilla, and Nikki chatting with two boys in a darkened corner of the room. Even from a distance, Gilda could tell that both boys were fascinated with Priscilla's Cleopatra costume: she wore a gold bustier, heavy bracelets around her bare arms, thick, black eyeliner, and a gold headband shaped like a snake. One of the boys had his arm around Nikki, who appeared to be dressed as an Ohio State football fan who had got beaten up; she had smudged dark eye shadow beneath her eyes to look like bruises. Danielle looked awkward in an angel costume with cumbersome wings and a silver halo that hovered above her head, suspended by a bit of wire.

Gilda was about to move closer to see if she could find a way to insinuate herself into their conversation when Wendy grabbed her arm and pulled her into the middle of the dance floor. 'Hey, it's our favourite song!'

The song was called 'Bits of Love', and Wendy and Gilda had a special dance that went with it. First, they acted out the melodrama of the lyrics, mouthing the story about how 'You chained me, then shamed me; you sent me downtown on the city bus! You claimed me, then you lamed me; you kicked me right in the nu–uts! Thrown on the floor and stomped on; like broken bits, broken bits of love!' Then they bounced around the room to the chorus: 'Broken bits, Broken bits, Broken bits! Little broken bits of loove!'

Gilda usually didn't hesitate to dance as outrageously and ridiculously as she wanted, but something about the proximity of her colleagues from *The Petunia* and the sight of Mr Panté leaning against the wall made her feel self-conscious.

She decided to go say hello to Mr Panté just to be polite. While Wendy was bouncing wildly towards a group of private-school boys, Gilda slipped away from the dance floor and headed for the teacher.

'Don't you just hate these things?' Gilda leaned against the wall next to Mr Panté, who observed the dance with a glazed expression, as if he wished he could magically transport himself to a barstool in some other city.

'Oh, hello, Gilda. Having fun?'

Gilda shrugged. 'I prefer more of a small cocktail party type atmosphere myself.'

Mr Panté chuckled. 'You're too sophisticated for this low culture.'

Is he secretly making fun of me? Gilda realized something annoying: she really wanted Mr Panté to like her. 'I just meant that it must be boring for you to have to sit here watching us act dumb.'

'Yes, the tables are turned for once.'

Sometimes Mr Panté said the strangest things. Gilda didn't have a chance to continue the conversation, because The Triplets suddenly planted themselves in front of Mr Panté and gazed up at him with glittery faces.

'Are you having *fun*, Mr Panty?'

'Loads of fun.'

'Because you look bored!'

'I can't imagine why.'

'Did you see us dancing over there?'

'Yes – yes, I did.'

'Hey, what's the big idea of leaving me out there by myself?'

Gilda turned to find Wendy standing behind her with hands on hips, looking incensed. 'For your information, I totally crashed into that group of boys over there, and they were like, "Watch where you're going, kitty cat!" '

'I thought you wanted to meet boys.'

'I thought *you* wanted to do a séance.' Wendy eyed Mr Panté with interest.

'Did you ever freak dance when you were a kid, Mr Panté?' Britney asked.

'No, can't say that I did.'

Gilda noticed with resentment that The Triplets had managed to steal Mr Panté's attention. She was torn – part of her wanted to stay and see if she could get him to talk about Gothic literature or something. On the other hand, it was the perfect opportunity to slip away.

Across the room, Miss Appleton was busy shining her flashlight on another groping couple.

'OK.' Gilda braced herself to make a run for it. 'Let's go.'

Carrying miniature flashlights and shivering in the cold air, Gilda and Wendy made their way through the trees that surrounded the school. When they reached the bridge overlooking Mermaid Lake, they stopped and gazed over the black surface of the water. Clouds drifted across a full, white moon like smoky dragons wafting across the sky.

'I'm picking up a vibration.' Gilda felt a different sort of anxiety than the usual goose-bumps associated with walking outside in the dark on Halloween night. There was *something* – a presence all around them. If she were an animal she would have lifted her nose in the air and sprinted away, certain that some predator was nearby, observing her. Was it simply her imagination, or was someone watching them?

'Why didn't you tell me about your new boyfriend?' Wendy whispered.

'What boyfriend?'

'You know. Razor stubble boy.'

'Mr Panté?'

'I knew it!'

'Shush!' Gilda whispered fiercely. 'We're supposed to be quiet on this bridge!'

'I knew there was a reason you kept going on and

on about that teacher and his panties!' Wendy lowered her voice to a whispered shout.

'I have not been "going on and on" about him!'

'Sh!'

'Shush yourself.'

'You don't have to be so defensive,' said Wendy. 'I think he's kind of cute.'

Gilda and Wendy fell silent as a surge of wind suddenly roared through the tree branches around them.

'Wendy,' Gilda whispered, 'I really think we should get off this bridge.'

Both girls shivered as they tiptoed quietly across the rest of the bridge then hurried toward the pale ruins that waited for them on the other side of the water.

Inside the reading room, Gilda surveyed the floral patterns of the furniture in the yellow glow of her flashlight. She gasped: *a girl with long hair stood stiffly in a corner.*

'What is it?' Wendy waved her flashlight around wildly.

'Oh.' Gilda realized she had merely glimpsed an old scarf hanging from a coat rack. 'Never mind.'

As Wendy pulled the Ouija board from her kitty litter purse and began to set it up, Gilda found Dolores's ring. 'Look,' she said, handing it to Wendy. 'This belonged to Dolores.'

'Looks like a real amethyst or something.'

'It is real.'

Wendy held up the ring and examined it with her flashlight. 'What's the deal with everyone wearing real jewellery these days? What ever happened to fake stuff?'

'I wear fake stuff all the time.'

'You'll wear anything that glitters.'

Gilda and Wendy sat cross-legged on the ground with the Ouija board resting on their knees so that it balanced between them. They closed their eyes and placed their fingers lightly on the planchette.

'Dolores,' said Gilda, 'give us a sign if you are present with us.'

They heard a sound from outside – the faint murmur of a girl's voice swallowed by wind.

Wendy grabbed Gilda's wrist and squeezed hard.

'Ow!'

'Did you *hear* that?' she whispered.

Gilda nodded and told herself to focus on her breathing, to remain calm.

Wendy placed her hand back on the planchette and bit down on her lower lip.

Gilda was about to question Dolores's spirit again, when they heard faint giggling sounds and the crunching sound of footsteps drawing closer.

'Someone's really out there!'

'Then I told Dinkel, "I can't drive you all over town. You have to get your own car fixed at *some* point.'

Gilda recognized Nikki Grimaldi's voice. She

grabbed Dolores's ring, slammed the Ouija board shut, and gestured frantically at Wendy to hide.

Panic ensued as Gilda and Wendy waved their flashlights wildly and bumped into each other, looking under tables and chairs for a hiding place. Without a second to spare, Gilda managed to conceal herself behind the draperies while Wendy crouched in a dark corner behind a chair.

Gilda heard the door swing open. A flashlight flickered across the room.

'Damn, it's cold out there!' Nikki declared.

Someone shushed Nikki.

Straining to comprehend the murmur of voices, Gilda wished she could will her ears to turn into eyes for just a moment. Who was in the room with Nikki? Had Wendy found a good hiding place? She heard rustling and scraping sounds – pieces of furniture being rearranged. Gilda prayed that nobody would move the draperies.

'No,' someone said. 'Put it over there.'

That sounds like Danielle, Gilda thought.

Then it was all Gilda could do to remain silent when she heard another voice that sounded very familiar – the clear, smooth voice of Priscilla Barkley.

'The Ladies of the Lake are called to order,' Priscilla declared.

23

The Secret Meeting

'We will now recite the sacred oath of the Ladies of the Lake.' Still dressed in her Cleopatra costume, Priscilla perched regally on her chair and regarded her subjects – Danielle Menory and Nikki Grimaldi. Concealed in the shadows of the room, Gilda and Wendy struggled to remain completely motionless though Gilda had managed to position the drapes so that she could peep out a little.

'We *still* have to do that?' Danielle complained.

Priscilla regarded Danielle with a withering gaze. 'Yes, Danielle, we still have to do that. Especially since you're both having so many issues.'

'What's *that* supposed to mean?' Nikki asked.

Ignoring Nikki's question, Priscilla began to recite the secret oath, and the other two girls quickly joined in:

'*The Ladies of the lake pledge to stick by each other no matter what and to remain best friends forever no matter what, to become powerful, popular girls and never to reveal the name, location, meeting times or anything else about the identity of our club to anyone without the full agreement of all members.'*

'The meeting is now called to order,' said Priscilla. 'Have you brought your precious belongings?'

Nikki and Danielle nodded.

'Please display for the group what you have brought to sacrifice to the lake, and explain its value.'

Danielle removed a book from her backpack and placed it in the middle of the floor. 'It's a book of poems by Edna St Vincent Millay,' she said. 'My grandmother gave it to me when I started going to Our Lady, and it was one of her favourite books. I don't know exactly how much it's worth, but it's an early edition, and pretty valuable as far as books go.'

'OK.' Priscilla eyed the book sceptically.

Nikki tossed two tickets into the middle of the floor. 'All I can say is, you know I'm freaking out if I'm giving up these tickets to the Ohio State game. Dinkel is going to totally kill me when I tell him I gave them away. In fact, let me know if you have any ideas for an excuse I can make up, because—'

'Nikki, I don't think we need to hear another saga about Dinkel right now.' Priscilla snapped.

Nikki's mouth hung open in mock surprise at the reprimand. 'Whatever,' she said quietly.

Priscilla unzipped a metallic bag that matched her Cleopatra costume and removed a small, worn teddy bear.

'This is Teddy. He's worth less than some of the

other things I've given away in terms of monetary value, but for me, this is like giving away a member of my family.'

Danielle and Nikki gave each other a knowing glance.

'Teddy has been my best friend since I was a little girl, and he's been with me through every experience in my life, good and bad. This is the most meaningful object I've ever sacrificed.'

The teddy bear lay helplessly on the floor, its sad, glass eyes staring up at the ceiling, as if hoping to be rescued.

'I thought your best friends were the Ladies of the Lake,' said Danielle, observing the stuffed bear coldly.

'You *know* what I meant, Danielle.'

'She means the teddy bear is like a security blanket,' Nikki explained helpfully, 'and those are definitely hard to give up. I had a fanket until I was like, seven years old, and I'd scream if my sister took it away.'

'A *fanket*?'

'My favourite blanket.'

'Can you two save it for the Senior Common Room? Considering the problems you've both been having lately, I would think you'd take this more seriously.'

Danielle stared at the forlorn objects lying in the middle of the floor. 'The problem, Priscilla, is that this *isn't* going to work.'

'Excuse me?'

'I have a gut feeling it's all over.'

It was as if Danielle's words had punctured a hole in an airtight life-support system. Nikki simply gaped at her, and Priscilla observed her with narrowed eyes.

'You're a very destructive person, Danielle.'

'I'm just looking at reality! For one thing, that freshman girl Gilda thinks she's some kind of investigative reporter or something. Who knows what she's already figured out?'

Peering out from behind the draperies, Gilda stifled an urge to cheer for herself.

'I thought you took care of her,' said Priscilla.

'She got a phone call, but that doesn't guarantee that she'll just give up and stop asking questions.'

So Danielle is the one who called me!, Gilda thought. *I knew it.*

'I sincerely doubt a freshman will keep poking around the lake after getting a call from a dead girl. She's probably at home, hiding under her bed right now.'

Gilda couldn't help but let out a very tiny, involuntary snort.

The three girls fell silent. 'Did you *hear* something?' Nikki whispered.

Gilda quickly shut the tiny gap in the drapes and held her breath and bit her lip until it almost bled. *Please don't let them look behind the drapes!*

'I have that feeling again,' said Nikki. 'I feel like someone's in here, watching us.'

'Danielle,' Priscilla whispered, 'you'd better stop undermining us.'

'I was just being honest,' Danielle whispered back. She twisted her arm behind her awkwardly, attempting to scratch an itch beneath her angel wings. 'This costume is driving me crazy!'

'If we keep fighting with each other like this, she'll sense our weakness.'

'How do you *know*, Priscilla?' Danielle's voice grew louder with frustration. 'Sometimes I think you just make up all this stuff!'

'Hey, I agree with Priscilla,' Nikki interjected. 'We've come this far without having anything really bad happen to us, haven't we? If we stick together, the ghost will leave us alone, and that Gilda chick won't get any more information either. Do you realize how totally screwed up our lives would be if someone like Mrs McCracken found out what we did?'

'Nikki!'

'What?'

Priscilla spoke in a low, menacing tone. 'Remember – there's nothing to find out, because we didn't DO anything.'

'Right,' said Nikki. 'Sorry.'

Danielle tore the wire halo from her head angrily. 'Priscilla, you can't possibly believe that what you just said is true.'

'It is true.'

'Just because you *say* something's true doesn't

make it true. It's like you think you're God or something!'

'OK, time out!' Nikki jumped up from her chair and placed herself between Priscilla and Danielle like a referee. 'Just stop it, both of you! OK, so we're not as close as we used to be. We just have to make it through this last year together so we can all graduate and go to great colleges and just move on with our lives!'

Her speech complete, Nikki sat down. Priscilla fixed Danielle with an icy stare, and Danielle kept her eyes downcast, looking sullen and uncomfortable.

'I just have this funny feeling,' said Danielle quietly. 'It's this feeling that her ghost doesn't *want* the ritual any more. What she really wants is for us to finally get caught.'

'I'm beginning to wonder if *you* want us to get caught.'

'We're not going to get caught!' said Nikki. 'Listen, we've already done tonnes of community service, and we're nice to everyone all the time. That makes up for *something*, doesn't it?'

'I don't know,' said Danielle. '*Does* it?'

'I don't know about *you*, Danielle, but this time next year, I'm going to be drinking beers at fraternity parties – not rotting in jail. Call me *weird*, but I don't exactly want my life ruined just because of some stupid thing that happened when I was a freshman!'

'Sometimes I feel like my life is already ruined,' said Danielle.

Neither Priscilla nor Nikki knew how to respond to this comment. It scared them.

'Well, that's why we need to do this ritual, Danielle,' said Priscilla, after a moment of uncomfortable silence. 'You aren't alone with this, you know; the Ladies of the Lake are always here for you.'

'Right,' said Nikki. 'And just a few more months of school to go and then we can finally just *relax*.'

'That's why you're going to be a big success in life, Nikki; you think positively.'

Danielle sighed.

'One thing's for sure. Either we all succeed together, or we all fail together.'

Priscilla and Nikki observed Danielle, waiting to see what she would do. Was she about to give up completely and reveal the secret they had managed to keep for three years?

'OK,' Danielle said quietly.

'OK, what?'

'Let's do the ritual.'

Hurrying before Danielle could change her mind, the girls gathered their offerings from the floor and headed outside into the cold.

'Omigod!' Wendy whispered loudly, emerging from her hiding place behind a chair. 'You go to the weirdest school ever!'

'Wendy, I can't believe how huge this is.'

'They're freaks! I mean, Danielle might be OK, but that one who's the leader of the club is so bitchy.'

Gilda wished she had brought a tape recorder so there would have been some proof of the conversation she had just overheard. *Three of the most popular seniors at Our Lady of Sorrows are in the Ladies of the Lake*, Gilda told herself. She felt almost giddy at the impact of her discovery. 'Wendy,' she whispered, 'it sounds like they *murdered* Dolores Lambert!'

'But they never said they murdered her.'

'Well, they definitely did *something* bad to her, and they're obviously afraid of her ghost. This ritual seems to be some weird attempt to bargain with her spirit.'

'I don't get what they're doing. Why would a ghost care about stuff like a teddy bear or football tickets?'

'I'm not sure,' said Gilda. For some reason, she remembered how, when her father was very sick, she had tried to make deals with herself. *If I can go a whole month without eating a single Twinkie, he won't die.* Or: *If I can go an entire week without saying anything mean to Stephen, he won't die.* None of the deals had worked.

'I bet Dolores's ghost *doesn't* care about a teddy bear or football tickets,' said Gilda, reasonably. 'But *they* care.' She remembered a sixth-grade lesson about the Aztecs, who sacrificed humans to the sun god to protect themselves from natural disasters. 'I bet they made up a ritual to protect themselves,' she suggested. 'If they give away something they care about, Dolores's ghost is supposed to leave them alone.'

'Like I said; you go to the weirdest school.'

'Come on; let's go see what they're doing outside.'

Gilda and Wendy groped along the stone wall of the ruins in the darkness.

Standing on tiptoe, Gilda peeped over the edge of the wall and saw a light flickering on the bridge.

She beckoned, urging Wendy to follow her.

Gilda and Wendy scampered from one pine tree to another, crouching and peering through prickly branches to make sure they weren't spotted. Closer and closer they crept towards the bridge where they could now see the shadowy image of three girls. Huddled together in the darkness, the Ladies of the Lake resembled one lumpish monster with three faces. Priscilla stood in the middle. In the glow of her flashlight, the gold snake on her headband gleamed.

'I wish I could hear what they're saying,' Gilda whispered. 'I bet they're chanting some kind of spell.'

One by one, the girls leaned over the railing of the bridge and each let her 'precious belonging' fall down to the cold water below: a book that sank with a small splash, bits of paper that flew aimlessly into the breeze, then a fluffy bear that floated away without a sound.

The three girls stood and stared mournfully at the water, almost as if they expected someone to rise from the lake and thank them for their gifts.

24

Turmoil

Dear Dad:
Mom didn't have to work today, so she made
us pancakes with maple syrup for breakfast,
just like you used to make. She had gone out
with Brad the night before (and didn't get
home until 2 a.m., incidentally), but I decided
not to say anything about that so we could
just have a nice breakfast together for once.

'Brad is going through a tough time,' she
announced, completely out of the blue.

'Too bad,' I said, reaching for another
pancake.

'He's been laid off from his job,' she said.

Dad, I remember when you were laid off,
and how that was the best summer ever
because you took us to the swimming pool
each afternoon. I guess it's different for
Brad. He *loved* his job. I mean, how will be
able to get through the day without being
able to turn to someone and declare, 'I'm

Director of Regional Sales!'?

'Maybe his co-workers got tired of his stories,' I suggested.

Mom slammed the refrigerator door shut. She looked tired. I bet she was up all night listening to Brad talk about his problems and I guess she was in no mood to take a joke.

'Smoot's dad just got fired too,' said Stephen. 'They might have to move.'

'If Smoot moves, who's going to come over to play video games and throw up on our carpet?'

'Plenty of people.' (Stephen was acting pretty nonchalant, but I bet he'll be devastated if his best friend 'Smoot' really does move.)

'Well, *we* aren't going to move,' I said, just in case Mom was getting any sneaky ideas. 'But *Brad* should be willing to go to whatever state or country will take him. He might want to check out Alaska. Or maybe Afghanistan.'

'Gilda, I've just about had it with your rude comments.'

'What did I say?'

(Of course, I *knew* what I had said. Deep down, I think Mom feels a little guilty about dating Brad, and to be honest, I've been taking advantage of that by dropping mean comments here and there. Up until this morning, I've been able to do it without getting in trouble.)

'After all Brad has done for us, you could at least show a little concern when he loses his job!'

Mom started cleaning the refrigerator the way she does when she's in a bad mood, grabbing old jars and containers and hurling them in the trash as if they're smelly vagrants she just discovered camping out on her property.

As usual, Stephen took this as his cue to take his plate to the sink and leave the room. As usual, I stayed to see what would happen next. It was like Mom was a big thundercloud and at any moment, she was going to burst.

'Why are you so upset just because Brad lost his job?' I asked. 'It's too bad, but why is that *your* problem?'

Mom opened a jar of pickles and made a face.

'Hey, I didn't know we had pickles!'

'Well, now you know we do,' said Mom. 'That's what we have here. Old, smelly, two-year old pickles.'

'My favourite.'

'Some people have beautiful homes and designer clothes and gourmet dinners, but we don't need to worry, Gilda. At the Joyce household, we have pickles.'

Then I knew why Mom was so upset; she expected Brad to marry her and fix all of our financial worries, but now he's unemployed, so that dream has just been flushed down the toilet. I knew it was wrong to feel happy, especially because we need the money, but I admit it: I felt a little bit happy.

'I *like* pickles,' I said.

By now, Mom had practically emptied the entire refrigerator. She stood and just stared into it with the door wide open. 'I'm used to dealing with problems,' she said, as if there was someone else sitting in the refrigerator who was actually listening to her. 'Problems are what I know best.'

I wasn't sure what she meant. 'What *kinds* of problems?' I asked.

'*All* kinds,' Mom snapped. 'I'm just not feeling that great today, Gilda, so if you could cut me some slack that would be great.'

I guess it's true that Mom has faced her share of problems. I mean, she's a nurse, so sometimes people are really rude to her just because they don't feel well, and other times, she'll really start to like one of her patients, and the next thing she knows, they end up dying in surgery or something. I guess she

now has one more problem: Brad Squib needs
a job.

'I noticed they were hiring at McDonald's,'
I said.

'Go do your homework, Gilda.'

<u>NOTE TO SELF</u>: Keep an eye on Brad to make
sure he doesn't steal all our loose change
now that he's unemployed.

<u>LADIES OF THE LAKE UPDATE!</u>:
As if the turmoil in our household isn't
enough, I'm also hot on the trail of a secret
ring of murderers disguised as innocent
schoolgirls!

<u>PROBLEM:</u>
No motive. *Why* would Priscilla, Nikki, and
Danielle kill Dolores Lambert?

I have a gut feeling about one thing: I bet
Dolores was a 'pledge' to their secret club.
And they weren't very nice to her either.

Gilda turned reluctantly to her English homework:
'Please discuss the significance of the "play within a
play" in *Hamlet*'

'Hamlet suspects that his Uncle Claudius
became king illegally, by murdering his

209

brother (Hamlet's father),' Gilda wrote in her notebook. 'Hamlet stages a play about a similar situation and watches Claudius to see if he acts guilty.'

'The play's the thing wherein I'll catch the conscience of the king,' Hamlet says.

Hamlet watches his stepfather's response to the play very closely: King Claudius throws a big hissy fit. Obviously, this guy is guilty! Hamlet now knows his suspicions were correct all along: his stepfather is in fact a murderer.

As Gilda wrote about Hamlet's plot to expose his stepfather, a plot of her own brewed in her mind. 'Our Lady Arts Day' was approaching – an opportunity for students to perform dances, musical compositions, skits and other artistic creations for the rest of the school. Gilda had been toying with the idea of staging a dramatic reading of her 'Gothic Tale,' but now she had a more intriguing idea:

What if I wrote a play that made the Ladies of the Lake reveal what really happened to Dolores? I bet seeing a play about Dolores Lambert would totally freak them out! They'd either confess what happened right away or get really nervous and reveal some incriminating evidence by accident. Danielle might already be on the verge of confessing, so this plan might push her over the edge.

TO DO:
Write, direct, and perform a chilling play about the death of Dolores Lambert, and make sure Nikki, Danielle, and Priscilla see it.

PROBLEM:
I have less than two weeks to complete this task.

25

Cat and Mouse

Gilda discovered a tiny, meticulously folded piece of paper waiting for her at the bottom of her locker. For a moment, she wondered whether Marcie had resumed her old habit of slipping inspirational verses and cheerful messages through the vent in the locker door.

But this note clearly wasn't from Marcie; it had been folded with maddening precision, almost as if the sender wasn't sure whether she wanted it to be read. Finally, Gilda managed to uncover the crinkled message written in neat, anonymous, capital letters:

YOU'RE BEING WATCHED

Gilda looked around, but the locker room was empty. The sound of water dripping from a leaky faucet echoed in the dreary room. The rows of lockers, the long mirror on the wall, the rust-stained sinks – everything suddenly looked sinister and threatening.

Gilda crumpled the note in her fist, slammed her locker shut and threw her backpack over her shoulder. As she walked through the locker room, she felt light-headed. She sat for a moment on a bench, resting her head in her hands. *I wonder if I'm getting the flu*, she thought. *I hope I don't throw up. There's nothing worse than throwing up at school.*

Gazing down at the wadded ball of paper in her palm, Gilda realized something: she felt *afraid*. She wished she could sit down at her typewriter and write a quick letter to her father, since this always made her feel safer. She did the next best thing and pulled out her reporter's notebook and began to write:

Dear Dad,
I admit it: I'm scared. If the Ladies of the Lake really were responsible for Dolores's death, who knows what they're capable of?

Gilda remembered Priscilla's snide comment during the Ladies of the Lake meeting: 'She's probably hiding under her bed right now.'

On the other hand, there are a few things the Ladies of the Lake DON'T know about me:
1. I already know exactly who's in their club.
3. I already know they had something to do with Dolores's death.
Maybe they're the ones who should be scared of *ME*.

Dad, please help protect me if you can. I
need some luck!

With her courage bolstered, Gilda stuffed the note in
her pocket, exited the locker room, and hurried down
the hall towards her next class.

Gilda arrived late to biology class just as Ms Peebles
was setting up her overhead projector. With scarcely a
glance in Gilda's direction, Ms Peebles scribbled a
signature on a detention slip and thrust it at Gilda.
'Tardy,' she said.

Faint titters rippled through the room, but Gilda
hardly noticed because something else caught her
attention. Tiara sat at a desk right in front of her.

At first, Gilda almost didn't recognize Tiara without
her black eyeliner and lipstick. Everything about her
looked softened: her hair had grown out slightly and it
was no longer styled with stiff spikes. The ends were
still bluish black, but an inch of natural chestnut-
coloured hair showed at the roots, leaving her with an
unusual two-toned colour.

Tiara gave Gilda a perfunctory wave hello and went
back to scribbling something in a notebook.

Ms Peebles was one of the few teachers who
arranged her classes in rows, so Gilda took advantage
of the opportunity to slip into a seat directly behind
Tiara where she could observe her more closely. She
noticed that Tiara seemed to have new school supplies,

as if it were the first day of school and she was starting with a resolution to be perfectly well-organized. She was dutifully recording the homework assignment written on the chalkboard – something that she never would have done in the past.

As Ms Peebles began to talk about neurons, synapses and the electrical impulses of the brain, Tiara reached back to scratch the back of her neck and dropped a folded note on Gilda's desk.

So what's new around here? You never called me, by the way.

As Gilda scribbled a reply to Tiara, she suddenly had an urge to tell everything she had discovered about the Ladies of the Lake. Then she remembered Tiara's unpredictability. Who knew what she would do with the information? *I'd better stay undercover*, Gilda told herself. When Ms Peebles' back was turned, Gilda dropped her note over Tiara's shoulder.

You never left me your phone number, so how could I call you?!

How did everything go in Pennsylvania? Your hair looks good, by the way.

We're almost finished reading Hamlet in Vanty's class, and now we're going to read Antigone. It's about a girl who wants to bury her dead brother.

I'm pretty sure 'the triplets' are in a big fight,

215

because lately, I only see Ashley and Britney passing notes to each other, and Lauren has started sitting on the other side of the room. Maybe they're all getting sick of looking exactly alike.

I've been writing for *The Petunia*. I'm also writing a play for 'Our Lady Arts Day.' (I'm going to post an audition notice in the Freshman Locker Room this week.) You should be in it!

Tiara began writing furiously. A minute later, she dropped a wad of paper over her shoulder while pretending to nod with interest as Ms Peebles pointed out the location of the brain stem on a diagram.

I'm growing my hair out, and it's kind of at an awkward stage right now. I'm thinking of dying it again. Maybe I'll try our platinum blonde wig idea. If that doesn't look good, I'll just go bald. Haha.

Pennsylvania wasn't as bad as I thought it would be. I think I learned a lot about myself. Some of the kids in my group kept writing poems about killing people. We played this 'trust' game where you have to let yourself fall back into the arms of other people in your group, and they're supposed to catch you. I couldn't do it for weeks, but then I finally just did it, and when those other kids actually caught me instead of letting me get killed, it was such a good feeling. We'll have to do that game sometime, maybe by the lake. Haha.

Did they stop buying toilet paper for the freshman locker

room? Things have gone downhill since I've been gone!

I will definitely be in your play! I love acting, but since I've been gone so long, I didn't get to audition for the drama club's play. So count me in!

'Gilda?'

Gilda was horrified to realize that Ms Peebles was staring at her. She had completely lost track of the class discussion while reading Tiara's note.

'Gilda, what would your answer be?'

To Gilda's annoyance, Tiara actually turned halfway around in her chair to peer at her, as if she shared Ms Peebles' irritation.

Gilda remembered some talk of the brain and the nervous system before she started passing notes to Tiara. 'How about neurotransmitters?' she ventured.

'How about them?'

The other girls shared amused smirks.

'Who can get along without them?'

Ms Peebles scribbled out another detention and slapped it down on Gilda's desk. 'We're talking about the mystery of consciousness and what happens when a person goes into a coma.'

'Well, *that* sounds interesting.'

'Yes,' said Ms Peebles. 'Had you been paying attention, you might have learned something.'

'*Thanks a lot!*' Gilda whispered into the back of Tiara's neck.

As Ms Peebles began to distribute homework

assignments, Tiara tossed one last note over her shoulder:

I'm trying to do better in school, so don't distract me, OK?

Gilda scribbled one last note:

Excuse me, but you're the one who started passing notes in the first place!
P.S. I'm glad you're back. You should sit at my lunch table today. We could use some new blood over there. Between 'The Triplets' on one side and the 'Straight-A Club' on the other, it's all I can do to stay awake while I eat my macaroni and cheese.
See you at auditions for my play!

As Gilda walked down the hallway after class, she felt a bitter surge of adrenaline as she glimpsed Priscilla Barkley striding towards her. Priscilla chatted with another senior, but as the two drew closer, she eyed Gilda warily. *She wonders if I'm scared*, Gilda thought. Catching Priscilla's eye, Gilda forced herself to smile cheerfully and wave as if she were in an exuberant mood. 'Hey, Priscilla!'

Priscilla responded with a tight, prim smile, but her green eyes scrutinized Gilda with a sober intensity.

She's the one who's watching me, Gilda thought.

26

The Drowned And The Damned

'Why is it set in a nunnery in Transylvania?' Wendy frowned at the pages spread before her. She and Gilda sat on a leather couch in the Choys' immaculate living room. Mrs Choy hated clutter, and no stray toys, books, video games, or magazines filled the room as they did at the Joyce household. Aside from a stuffed Elmo doll propped in a chair, there was virtually no evidence that Wendy's two-year-old brother Terrence lived in the house.

At the moment, Terrence was busy sticking mailing labels all over Gilda's script.

'Cut it out,' said Wendy.

'It's OK,' said Gilda. 'I like stickers.

'Dickers!' yelled Terrence with sudden glee. 'Dickers!'

'Be quiet!' Wendy snapped.

'DICKERS!'

'Here,' Gilda handed Terrence a page of her maths homework. 'Put some stickers on that.'

Terrence took Gilda's maths homework and his

mailing labels and sat down on the carpet to begin a new project.

'What's the deal with all the face slapping in this script?' said Wendy, turning her attention back to Gilda's play. 'And then a *ghost* gets beaten up and dragged across the floor?'

'It's a metaphor. The girls think they can control the ghost, but then she springs back to life and kills *them*. It shows they've lost control of the situation.'

Wendy leaned back in her seat and clasped her knees to her chest. 'Let me get this straight. You're going to stage this little play for the school, and when those girls see it they'll be so overwhelmed with guilt, they'll run down to the headmistress's office to confess?'

'Either that, or they'll freak out and end up revealing themselves by accident. It's a way of putting the pressure on them.'

Wendy wrinkled her nose with scepticism.

'Sea urchins?'

'Excuse you?'

'You say the ghost is covered in 'sea urchins'. Can those even live in a freshwater lake?'

'It's a play, Wendy, not a biology project. Anyway, we can sort out the details during rehearsals.'

'We?'

'You're my assistant director.'

Wendy opened her day planner. 'Take a look at this, Gilda.' The entire month was blackened with music lessons, assignment deadlines, and music competitions. 'There's no way I can do all this.'

'You love it.'

'I hate it.'

'What if I help you babysit Terrence? Maybe you could squeeze in a couple of rehearsals.'

Both girls suddenly realized something: Terrence was nowhere in sight.

'Uh-oh,' said Wendy. 'If he's quiet, he's doing something bad.'

'But you told him to be quiet.'

'Still, he's up to no good.'

'Terrence?' Wendy jumped up from the couch, looking worried. 'Terrence!'

Just as Wendy and Gilda were ready to search the house, Terrence appeared, a proud, silly grin plastered across his face. He was covered from head to toe in sanitary napkins he had taken out of a box in Mrs Choy's bathroom. 'Dickers,' he said, pointing joyfully to the feminine protection stuck to his head.

'Omigod.' Wendy was appalled. 'This is one of the most embarrassing things he's ever done.'

Gilda literally rolled off the couch in a seizure of laughter.

Wendy angrily plucked maxi pads from her little brother, who took obvious delight in making Gilda crack up.

'Dickers,' he said once more, catching Gilda's eye

and pointing to his head. She broke into another
fit of giggles.

'Gilda!'

Gilda gasped for air. 'What?'

'Don't encourage him! So when are you planning to
stage this play?'

'Next week.' Gilda wiped tears from her eyes.

'*Next week?*'

'It's doable.'

'No!' Terrence protested as Wendy plucked the last
few 'stickers' from Terrence's body. 'Leave on!'

'Mom is going to be mad at you, Terrence.'

'I just need to do is find actors, costumes, sets, and
then I'll be all set. Hey, maybe Terrence can be my
costume designer!'

'All I can say is, you'd better get busy.'

'Dickers,' said Terrence.

'And Gilda,' said Wendy, 'you'd better think carefully
about what's going to happen *after* you do this play.'

27

Friends and Enemies

AUDITION NOTICE — OPPORTUNITY
FOR TALENTED ACTORS

THE DROWNED AND THE DAMNED

Don't miss this opportunity to showcase your dramatic range in the most mind-searing play ever to be performed at Our Lady of Sorrows.

PREFERRED: Actors with dancing, singing, martial arts and tumbling skills. Photographic memories strongly preferred.

REQUIRED: Strong stomach for violence and evil. Ability to face the squalid underside of human nature.

AUDITION TODAY AFTER SCHOOL IN MR PANTÉ'S CLASSROOM.

After school, Amelia and Sheila strolled into Mr Panté's classroom singing an enthusiastic, tone-deaf version of a Broadway show song together.

Gilda handed scripts to Amelia and Sheila, and to her relief, both girls immediately stopped singing, sat down at desks, and began to read their scripts as if they had just been asked to prepare for a test.

'Can I just say one thing?' Tiara appeared and planted herself in the classroom doorway, drawing everyone's attention. 'It's my first week back at school, and I have SO MUCH HOMEWORK, IT'S INSANE!'

'Me too,' Sheila complained. 'I shouldn't even be auditioning for this play. I should be writing a history paper that was due three weeks ago.'

'But I *have* to be in this play,' said Tiara, sauntering into the room and picking up a copy of the script. 'I can tell from the title it's just so *me*.'

Amelia wrinkled her nose as she squinted at the script through her round glasses. 'I thought this was supposed to be a musical.'

I knew she'd find something to complain about, Gilda thought.

'Your audition sign said "dancing and singing abilities preferred".'

'That's right.' Gilda prayed that other people would show up to audition so she wouldn't be stuck casting Amelia in the play. 'It also said "martial arts and tumbling" skills, and as you can see, there's a fight scene.'

'But it's not a *musical*, so I don't see why we need to be able to sing.'

'You're a great singer, Mimi-doo,' said Sheila, 'so you don't have to worry.'

224

'Mimi-doo?'

'That's Amelia's nickname,' Sheila explained.

Gilda had always wondered why Amelia, who was one of the most studious girls in the freshman class, had become best friends with Sheila, who was commonly known to be failing most of her classes. Now she understood the attraction: Amelia needed someone to flatter and encourage her – someone who didn't take herself too seriously and who posed no competitive threat.

Tiara squinted at the script with a fierce concentration as she read. Finally, she slammed her hand down on top of the script. 'Awesome play,' she declared. 'Can I be the ghost?'

'Maybe,' said Gilda. 'But I'm sure more people will show up to audition.'

'But everyone else is already in the drama club, rehearsing "The Rat-Catcher",' said Amelia. 'And I'm *also* auditioning for the part of the ghost, by the way.'

'Mimi-doo and I used to be in the drama club,' Sheila explained, 'but Mr Panté would only give us bit parts in the chorus, so we quit.'

Gilda wondered how she was going to stage the play with only three people in her cast. She could do away with the chorus of vampires and owls, but she would still need at least one more cast member, not to mention help with the technical details like lighting and curtains.

Tiara stood up and began to read the ghost's

monologue in a raspy voice: 'The time has come / to rise from my watery grave / To haunt the ladies / Who pushed me in the lake . . .'

Gilda had to admit there was something compelling about the way Tiara read the lines, moving with a serpentine grace as she spoke. It was as if she ceased to be an ordinary teenager with odd, two-toned hair.

Her speech complete, Tiara sat down and casually propped her legs up on a chair across from her, looking pleased with herself.

'*That* was spooky,' said Sheila, oblivious to Amelia's pout of annoyance.

'Tiara,' said Gilda, 'you've got the part.'

'But nobody else has had a chance to audition!' Amelia protested.

'Amelia,' said Gilda, hoping to squelch the argument that was about to ensue, 'you will play the role of Paulina.'

Amelia stared at the script. She was aware that Paulina was the second-best role, but she hated the fact that Tiara had stolen the lead. 'OK. But it still isn't fair.'

'Sheila, you can be Debbie.'

'Okee Dokee.'

'I'll be on the lookout for someone to play Nanette.'

'I just thought of something!' Sheila peered up at Gilda through a fringe of mascara-encrusted lashes. 'Is this supposed to be about that girl who drowned – Dolores Lambkin?'

Gilda stared at the small theatre troupe she had

cobbled together and wondered how much she should tell them about her true motives for staging the play. Did they recognize the thinly disguised representations of three girls in the senior class?

'What do *you* think?' Gilda asked, still unsure how to answer.

'That means, "yes, it's a true story".' Tiara smirked knowingly.

'Ooh!' Sheila shuddered. 'That's creepy!'

Gilda now saw the pitfall of involving a whole cast of students in her strategy to expose the Ladies of the Lake. What if they started blabbing the plot all over school? The crucial element of surprise would be completely ruined. She decided that, for the time being, it was safest to downplay the fact that the play was actually about Dolores Lambert.

'This play shows how being mean to someone can lead to a tragedy — something that could happen to *anyone* at this school,' said Gilda. 'But I don't want people to know what the play's about until we perform it, OK? We want it to grab the audience's attention and surprise them.'

The girls nodded.

Three people in the audience are going to be REALLY surprised, Gilda thought.

REHEARSAL NOTES
TO DO:
   COSTUMES
   STAGE LIGHTS AND SOUND EFFECTS
   SET DESIGN
   STILL NEED A FOURTH CAST MEMBER

   YIKES – I have a lot to do!!!!

Gilda mused that her worries about Dolores Lambert's ghost and the Ladies of the Lake were now overwhelmed by worries about costumes, lighting and whether Sheila would ever be able to stop giggling during the play. As she walked down the school hallway, she spied Marcie taping a large poster to the wall:

Don't be a turkey
and miss the semi-formal Thanksgiving Dance!
Gobble up your tickets in advance!

Gilda had an idea. She knew she might regret the impulse, but she was desperate for help on her play and willing to take a risk.

'Need some help?' Gilda cautiously approached Marcie.

'Oh. Hi, Gilda.' Marcie spoke in the flat, disappointed voice she now used to speak to Gilda. 'That's OK; I can manage.'

'Looks like the dance is going to be fun,' said Gilda, secretly thinking that something about the announcement made her want to stay home and watch horror movies with Grandma Joyce.

Marcie opened her mouth as if she were about to explain something, but then changed her mind.

In the old days, she would have chattered away about why I should get tickets for the dance right now and what kind of dress I should wear, Gilda thought. 'Say, Marcie,' she ventured, 'have you ever done any acting?'

'Why?'

'I thought you might want to play a starring role in a show I'm directing for Our Lady Arts Day.'

The posters tucked under Marcie's arm flopped to the floor. 'Having a hard time finding enough cast members, huh?' She looked red-faced as she stooped to pick up the posters.

'No,' said Gilda, helping Marcie gather her posters and feeling irritated that Marcie had correctly judged her predicament.

'I could have *told* you that would happen if you try to put on a play independently at this time of year.'

'We just need one more cast member.'

'Why should I be in your play? You don't even *like* me.'

Gilda was a little shamed by this naked, direct accusation. 'That's not true.'

'Then why didn't you want me to be your big sister any more?'

Because being around you makes me feel like I have about fifty mosquito bites. Gilda wished she could move time backwards to before the moment when she had impulsively and idiotically approached Marcie. 'It's not that I don't want you to be my big sister,' she said. 'It's just I have a big brother, and sometimes he drives me crazy too.'

'And now I guess you're finding out how tough it can be in this school without someone to show you the ropes.'

'You're absolutely right, Marcie.' Gilda decided there was no point in disagreeing with Marcie, particularly since she had a point; Gilda really did need her help. 'Anyway, we'd love to have your help with this play if you're interested.'

Marcie sighed and looked at her posters. 'I'll think about it,' she said.

Dear Dad:

<u>RED ALERT:</u>

BRAD SQUIB HAS MOVED INTO OUR HOUSE!!!!!!!

<u>A SHOCKING AND PUTRID DISCOVERY:</u>

I came downstairs for breakfast this morning, and there was Brad, sitting at the kitchen table and sipping a cup of coffee as if he weren't loitering on enemy territory.

I've never seen Brad at our house first thing in the morning before. I knew I

shouldn't have been surprised, but I was. Call
me naïve, but I was VERY surprised.

'Good morning, Gilda!' Mom said, a little
too brightly. Did she think a dose of good
cheer was going to make me forget how Brad
was exactly the last person on earth that I
wanted to see sitting at the table, slurping
his coffee?

'Hey there, Gilders,' said Brad.

'My name is *Gilda*.'

'Nice to meet you.'

I *almost* smiled, but stopped myself just in
time.

'Would you like some oatmeal?' Mom asked.

'I just lost my appetite.' Brad is the thick-
skinned type who never even seems to notice
when he's been insulted, so I find myself
saying meaner and meaner things.

'I'd better get cleaned up.' Brad pushed his
chair away from the table. 'I've got to run
out to the car to get my suit.' He washed his
coffee cup and walked out the door.

'What does he need his suit for if he's
unemployed?' I asked Mom.

'Brad has some interviews lined up
downtown, and he's just staying here a few
days or so while he looks for a job. That way,
it's not such a long drive for him. His
apartment lease is up and he may have to

move if he gets a job somewhere, so . . .'

Mom's voice trailed off and she seemed to be concentrating very hard on loading dishes into the dishwasher.

'Excuse me?' I said. 'It sounded like you said Brad was going to be LIVING here. And I know that can't be right. You would have to be crazy to say something like that.'

'Temporarily, Gilda. He's already got some good leads and thinks he'll have something lined up by next week.'

'Get real, Mom! He's going to mooch off you, and then he'll never leave!'

'He's chipping in on expenses while he's here. We'll both save a little money while he's job searching.'

'Interesting reasoning.'

'Every bit helps, Gilda.'

'VERY interesting.'

'Just try to be nice, Gilda.'

NOTE TO SELF:
Worst fears are being realized at home.
Solution: try not to think about home. Just
pretend you're staying here as a kind of
hotel guest – an undercover psychic detective
on the road. Home is nothing but a place to
put your typewriter and make a grilled
cheese sandwich.

Dear Miss Petunia,
I have a weird problem – a phobia of pennies.
Sure, they look like innocent, brown coins just
lying there at the bottom of your purse or sitting
there in a jar, but for me, they are smelly,
loathsome, diseased objects. I cringe from their
touch.

My problem is, I can't seem to avoid them.
Cashiers don't understand that I don't want
small change. My friends think it's funny to
touch me with a penny and see me freak out.

What should I do?
Signed,
Tormented

Dear Tormented,
I myself have a phobia of fifty dollar bills (a
situation that proves awkward when I'm out
shopping for prom dresses), so I can understand
your predicament.

You won't like my advice, but here it is: I
suggest you use *nothing but pennies* in all of
your monetary transactions for the next month.

Only by immersing yourself in the objects of your disgust will you overcome your fear.

As far as your friends are concerned, try to retain your sense of humour. After all, your phobia is ridiculous! You might also keep some slime or hairballs on-hand to return the favour when they decide to 'reach out and touch' you.

Dear Miss Petunia,
Maybe you can help me with a problem. I have two best friends, and we've always been really close. We always have so much fun together. For example, we spent practically the whole summer on the beach together because our families go up north and we just have so much fun. People even say we kind of look alike. One girl even asked if we were sisters, and we thought that was crazy. Then we looked in the mirror and realized 'Hey! We do look like sisters!'

But lately, my two best friends (I'll call them 'Sarah' and 'Jenny') have been acting strange. I know for a fact they've been making plans to do things together without inviting me. The worst part of it is, they aren't just sneaking around behind my back; they actually seem to *want* me to know that I've been left out, just so I'll feel bad. I bet they're talking about me the whole time they're together. It's confusing because they still act like we're all friends at school, but then I hear of these little secret get-togethers they've had without me.

The weird thing is, I can't think of a single reason they've suddenly decided to shut me out. I didn't do anything stupid like get a bad haircut or a perm or try to put highlights in my own hair. I wear cute clothes; I don't have bad breath; I didn't steal anyone's boyfriend; and I don't brag about myself. I've thought and thought about this, but I just can't think of anything – but there must be something I did wrong.

There were a couple of mean postings about me on the Our Lady of Sorrows message board from 'ponygirl' and 'spanky' – screen names I've never seen before – and I'm wondering if 'Sarah' and 'Jenny' are responsible. I asked them point-blank and they said it was probably someone else who's jealous of me. I don't know what to think.

Should I try to talk to them about this? What should I do?

–Confused

Dear Confused,
Based on the screen names 'ponygirl' and 'spanky,' I'm guessing that these two hoodlums *are* in fact your 'best friends,' and that they are indeed having a laugh at your expense. Your choices:

1. Talk to them about your feelings honestly, but be prepared for them to talk behind your back right after you air your many grievances. They'll most likely say you're 'whiney.'
2. My personal preference: fight fire with fire. Post your own reply to 'ponygirl' and 'spanky' – something like, 'Your pornographic screen names aren't fooling anyone, because we all know who you really are. Let's face it: your imbecilic writing style gives you away. Why don't you cut the crap and say it to my face if you have any backbone?' Then, when they do say it to your face, have a squirt gun handy so you can ruin their hairstyles. (I've heard this works well with disciplining cats, too. It will end the friendship, but you'll have a satisfying sense of closure).

REHEARSAL NOTES:

Marcie showed up for rehearsal today. She declared herself 'stage mom' but nobody minded because she brought cupcakes.

She took me aside and said she had some 'concerns' about the subject matter of my play. 'Maybe it's because of that black magic you're dabbling in, Gilda, but I think this story is too frightening for everyone – especially the freshmen.'

I told her that anyone who scares that easily shouldn't be let out of the house each morning.

As far as I can tell, Marcie hasn't picked up on the references to Nikki, Priscilla and Danielle in the script. I bet some people will never believe the truth about the Ladies of the Lake, no matter how much evidence turns up.

After we ran through the play a couple of times, Marcie got everyone working on the sets. She has a friend who takes Mr Panté's tech theatre class who's going to help us with lighting and sound effects.

I never thought I'd say this, but . . .

THREE CHEERS FOR MARCIE!

OTHER NEWS:
The Petunia came out today, and the 'Miss Petunia' column caused quite a stir in English class:

TIARA: Miss Petunia sure is feisty these days!

SHEILA: Who IS Miss Petunia, anyway?

TIARA: I think it's Mr Panté.

AMELIA: No way. Miss Petunia is way too immature to be a teacher.

ME: What do you mean, 'immature?'

AMELIA: A teacher wouldn't tell a student

237

to ruin someone's hairstyle with a squirt gun.

ME: Miss Petunia isn't immature. She has TONNES of life experience.

(Everyone in the room stared at me.)

ME: And she's really good-looking, too.

ASHLEY: Does anyone in here wonder who 'Confused' is? I mean, who do you think wrote the letter to Miss Petunia?

Of course, Ashley knew very well who wrote the letter. Everyone glanced in Lauren's direction. She was pretending to read *Antigone* with great interest, as if it were the Christmas catalogue from Abercrombie & Fitch, but her cheeks were bright red. Britney and Ashley kept whispering back and forth.

Then, out of the blue, Lauren jumped up from her desk and ran from the room. I could tell she was on the verge of tears – that moment when you know you're going to bawl right in front of everyone if you don't leave the room.

It's always weird when something happens right in front of you, but you feel that you're supposed to pretend that you didn't see it at all. I think most of us felt bad for Lauren, but if I'm being totally honest, the truth was that we also found the scene a little

238

entertaining. Mr Panté taught us a German word to describe this feeling: it's *'schadenfreude'* – the secret, happy feeling you have when something bad happens to *someone else*, just because you're glad it isn't happening to YOU. 'Nobody wants to admit it,' said Mr Panté, 'but believe me, everybody has felt it at one time or another.'

I still think Miss Petunia gave Lauren some great advice; the problem is, she'll never use it after what happened in class today.

28

The Play's the Thing

'Looks like we're ready, Gilda!' said Marcie.

'Break a leg, Marcie. Thanks for everything you did to help.'

'Gilda, even if people don't *like* the play, the point is that we *did* it. We pulled the whole thing together in just a week!'

'I don't really care if people like it or not.' But was that the truth? In the process of working on *The Drowned and the Damned*, something had changed. Gilda still wanted to set a trap for the Ladies of the Lake, but she had to admit that she also wanted the audience to *like* her play. Peeking out from behind the curtain, Gilda saw Mr Panté leaning against a wall, his arms folded across his chest as if defying anything onstage to actually entertain him. Would he be impressed with her theatrical debut?

Standing in the wings of the theatre, Gilda felt nervous. Her play was up next, and there had been so many technical details to oversee: the falling of fake snow, the opening and closing of the stage trapdoor, the placement of a crash pad beneath the stage so Tiara didn't hurt herself when she fell through the sheet of Mylar – the shiny mirror-like material that represented ice. There was so much to think about; it would be easy to forget the entire purpose of the performance – to observe the Ladies of the Lake.

Gilda positioned herself strategically where she could monitor the action of her play while also keeping an eye on the senior class sitting in the front rows of the audience. In the second row, Nikki and Priscilla struggled to contain a fit of laughter as the mournful saxophone solo meandering along onstage lapsed into a hysterical squawk. A few seats behind, Danielle appeared to be studying notes from one of her classes.

The saxophone solo ended to the roar of relieved applause, and Marcie, Tiara, Sheila, and Amelia quickly took their positions. Recorded moans of howling wind blasted into the room, and the curtain opened upon a scene of pink-skirted girls frolicking in a landscape of Insta-Snow. The freshmen sitting in the back rows of the audience hooted when Tiara skipped onstage, carrying her pink bunny rabbit. Giggles swelled into little roars of laughter as the actors hammed up the scene of keeping the stuffed animal, mittens, and hat just out of her reach.

They think it's a comedy, Gilda thought, glimpsing wry smirks on Danielle and Priscilla's faces.

Then Tiara plunged through the trapdoor without warning and the audience gasped. Shadows descended on the stage. Thunder cracked and rumbled, echoing throughout the theatre.

Gilda pressed a remote control to turn on the fog machine and activated the small elevator that raised Tiara onto the stage floor. Tiara appeared, her face painted in white stage make-up and long, tangled knots of material resembling water rushes and seaweed draped over her pale shoulders. She looked like a dead water nymph rising from beneath the misty surface of a lake:

> The time has come to rise
> From my watery grave,
> To haunt the ladies
> Who pushed me in the lake –
> The foul skirt-wearers, the loathsome teens;
> The handbag-toting Murderers!
>
> Loitering in toilets,
> Creeping through drainpipes,
> A water serpent I will be;
> Slithering through their glossy locks,
> Poisoning their lip gloss,
> And coiling in their tea.
>
> I'll shake my ghostly chains,
> A surprising rattle snake;
> I'll wait beneath this bridge
> For the Ladies of the Lake.

Priscilla remained stony-faced as she watched the scene. Next to her, Nikki's mouth gaped with disbelief. A few rows back, Danielle stared at a single spot on the chair in front of her, as if the subject matter of the play might change if she simply made an effort to keep staring at something else. It reminded Gilda of the time she had felt seasick while riding on a motorboat. Her mom kept telling her to 'look at a spot on the horizon! Just look straight ahead!'

Nikki leaned over to whisper something to Priscilla, who looked as if some wonderfully horrifying idea was taking shape in her mind, filling her with glee. It seemed that she was looking *through* the action onstage, toward the backstage wings of the theatre. *I feel like she's sending me a message,* Gilda thought. What was the message?

I'm going to get you.

Gilda instinctively backed further into the shadows. *I'm onto them, and now they know it.*

As the play concluded, Gilda braced herself for the audience's response. Dead silence? A contemptuous hurling of spitballs? Had the other seniors guessed that three of their popular classmates had played a role in the drowning of Dolores Lambert?

The velvet curtains closed and then reopened to reveal the four-member cast standing arm-in-arm. They received polite applause, but when Tiara stepped forward to take a separate bow, the freshmen and sophomores in the back rows jumped to their feet with a standing ovation. The upperclassmen gradually took the cue and a few of them stood up and applauded as well. Tiara beckoned enthusiastically to Gilda, urging her to join them onstage.

As she gazed out into the audience, Gilda felt dizzy with euphoria and fear – the rush of applause for a play she had created combined with the uneasy awareness of Priscilla's simmering stare. *Priscilla isn't like Hamlet's stepfather at all*, Gilda thought. In Hamlet, *King Claudius at least felt guilty about killing someone. I get the feeling that Priscilla doesn't even care.*

The rest of the afternoon was maddening in its sheer ordinariness. A few people smiled at Gilda in the hallway and said, 'Good play!' but nobody seemed outraged or shocked. No tearful confessions ensued.

Tiara grabbed Gilda by the shoulders and jumped up and down in the hallway like an exuberant child. 'Everyone loved my performance!' she crowed. 'I am so into this acting thing now!'

'Great,' said Gilda, slightly annoyed that Tiara was only focusing on her own performance. 'What are people saying about the play in general?'

Tiara shrugged. 'They thought it was OK.'

'You haven't heard anything else?'

'I think they got the whole "don't be mean to people" thing, but what they really liked were all the costumes and special effects.'

Gilda suddenly felt vulnerable and alone. The play

apparently remained a private message between herself and the Ladies of the Lake. While she had patched things up with Marcie and helped Tiara rediscover her love of acting, the performance had accomplished little for her investigation. If anything, she had merely tipped her hand so the Ladies of the Lake now *knew* her suspicions.

Dear Dad,
Balthazar Frobenius says that 'a true psychic does her work solely as a gift to others-not for money or for glory.'

Based on the way things have turned out so far, I wonder if, deep down, I put on this play to try to impress everyone – to try to *be somebody* at this school. All of my work is so invisible and secret. Sure, it's exciting, but after a while, I find myself wishing I could have just a little bit of recognition from someone. It's tough to go to a school where day after day, nobody knows who you *really* are.

Was I honestly trying to make the Ladies of the Lake confess what they did, or was I just trying to prove something to them? I know it sounds dumb, but on some level, I think I wanted them to be impressed with me. I wanted them to realize: 'Hey, this Gilda kid really IS smart enough to figure out what

we did! Not only that – she's not even scared
of us at all!'

There's just one problem. Now I AM scared
of them.

The memory of the evil delight on Priscilla's face
made Gilda feel queasy. A nagging thought
occasionally popped into her mind: *what if Priscilla is
actually quite dangerous?*

29

The Threat

'Gilda, can I see you for a moment?'

Mr Panté beckoned, and Gilda's heart beat faster. Throughout English class, she had wondered what Mr Panté thought of her play.

Other students lingered, hoping to overhear something interesting, but Mr Panté waited for them to leave, then closed the door.

Gilda hoped she didn't have bad breath from the salami sandwich she had eaten at lunch. *'I've never seen such a moving play produced at lightning speed, yet with such a commitment to excellence,'* she imagined Mr Panté saying. He would grab her shoulders and press his lips against hers for a brief, ecstatic moment. Then he would tear himself away, sit down at his desk, and weep with tormented frustration because of his forbidden love. They would begin a secret affair, and she would help him grade his papers. Amelia would end up with a C minus instead of an A in his class. Eventually, Mr Panté would be sent to prison as a result of their scandalous affair.

'That was an interesting performance today,' Mr Panté said.

'Interesting' wasn't the kind of compliment Gilda was hoping to hear, but it was a start. 'Thanks,' said Gilda.

'Something about it made me curious.'

Gilda smiled winningly. *I'm interesting enough to make Mr Panté curious.*

'Was there some real-life inspiration for your play?'

Gilda had expected Mr Panté to comment on the influence of Shakespeare in her language or to praise her successful operation of the under-stage elevator. Could she confide in Mr Panté? She felt eager to share her secret with someone other than Wendy Choy, and particularly eager to say something interesting to Mr Panté.

'I know who was responsible for Dolores Lambert's death,' she blurted. Gilda had a momentary sensation of unreality. Had she actually said these bizarre words to a teacher?

Mr Panté frowned. 'That's what worries me. Something reminded me of the play-within-a-play we studied in *Hamlet* – almost as if you were staging an accusation against other students.'

'I have very good reasons for my theory.'

'Such as?'

'I overheard three of the seniors talking – Nikki, Priscilla and Danielle. They have a secret club.'

'I see.'

248

'They do a weird ritual to keep Dolores's ghost away because they know it's their fault she's dead.'

Mr Panté stood with hands on hips. His eyes clouded as if he suspected he was listening to a series of fabrications that he didn't want to hear.

'Gilda, I think you have potential to be a very good writer. But you have to be careful to keep fiction separate from truth in your mind.'

Gilda was speechless. She didn't know whether to be more offended by Mr. Panté's implication that she was fibbing or the meaning in his words '*potential* to be a very good writer.'

Mr Panté leaned against his desk and folded his arms across his chest. 'I'm sure you've been exposed to the ghost stories that circulate around the school.'

'But—'

Mr Panté raised a finger. 'Let me give you a little background about this situation. When Dolores Lambert died, the whole school was in a state of shock, we're still haunted by what happened. None of us can make sense of an accident like that, but in my mind, one thing is certain. Not a single one of the girls you've just pointed the finger at could be capable of the kind of behaviour your theatre group acted out.'

'But, Mr Panté—'

'Priscilla Barkley, for example, is in the drama club, and I know her well. She's an amazing talent and just a spectacular girl. Normally, I appreciate your imagination, Gilda, but I hate to see anyone falsely accused.'

'But I wouldn't falsely accuse anyone—'

'My theory – and it's shared by some of the other teachers – is that Dolores knew *exactly* what she was doing when she walked across the ice on the lake.'

Gilda paused. 'You think it was a suicide?'

'In the words of Sigmund Freud, "There are no accidents".' Mr Panté proceeded to patiently explain how, 'when a person does something "by accident", it's possible that her unconscious mind may have wanted to do that very thing *on purpose*.' He pressed his palms to the air in a cautionary gesture. 'Now, I would never make an issue of this because there's absolutely no way to prove it. And of course, Dolores's parents are devastated enough as it is, so there's nothing to be gained by spreading this idea around.'

Gilda felt deflated. Mr Panté's explanation for Dolores's death was so dreary. To make matters worse, he seemed to view Gilda as someone with hysterical, careless ideas. If he was right, what could explain the things she had overheard during the Ladies of the Lake meeting?

There's no way I'd let him kiss me now, Gilda thought.

Gilda made her way past a chain of mini-vans that hovered in the after-school parking lot like shiny buzzards. The girls who normally stood with her at the bus stop were absent from school; today she waited alone, bracing herself against a chilly wind.

Winter had arrived suddenly, and the trees were

now completely stripped of leaves. Something about the way their black branches splayed against the grey sky reminded Gilda of illustrations of blood vessels and capillaries in her biology textbook. She felt relieved to see the bus approaching.

Relief turned to shock when Gilda glanced behind and saw Priscilla and Nikki marching quickly towards her.

Wearing white, furry boots, a matching fur poncho and white earmuffs, Priscilla looked like an angry snow bunny. Nikki slouched along wearing a shapeless black overcoat that she left unbuttoned. She carried a crumpled bag of Doritos in one hand. The swiftness of the girls' appearance just as the bus arrived made Gilda suspect that they had been watching her like predators for some time. Gilda knew that neither Priscilla nor Nikki ever took the bus: both owned cars.

With brakes whining, the bus came to a stop, and Gilda climbed the steps with Nikki and Priscilla close at her heels. *Stay calm*, she told herself. She could practically feel Nikki's nacho cheese-tainted breath on the back of her neck as she surveyed the seats in front of her. Gilda decided to sit close to the front where a group of elderly people were clustered together. She reasoned that it would be more difficult for Nikki and Priscilla to harass her near the bus driver.

Gilda scooted into a seat next to a rotund lady who shifted her shopping bags begrudgingly and made about three inches of room available. Nikki and

Priscilla were forced to move to a seat further back.

Gilda put on her cat-eye sunglasses because they made her feel safer, opened her notebook, and scribbled hastily:

TO THE PERSON DISCOVERING MY DEAD BODY:

Priscilla Barkley and Nikki Grimaldi are the ones who did it. They go to Our Lady of Sorrows. I know it's hard to believe because they look cute, but it's true. They followed me home on the bus, so it was definitely premeditated. They also killed Dolores Lambert three years ago, by the way.

Mr Panté, I hope this has convinced you.

She folded up the note and stuck it in the pocket of her coat. Turning to another page in her notebook, she wrote:

URGENT (AND POSSIBLY TOO LATE) NOTES TO SELF:

1. Take some self-defence classes – karate or guerrilla warfare training.
2. Start carrying something that can be used as a weapon. Maybe a miniature dagger, shaped like a cross.
3. Grow nails longer for lethal scratching.
4. Get a pet that has some dangerous quality, like a tarantula that I could keep in my purse for emergencies.

The woman sitting next to Gilda kept letting out little huffs of exasperation at Gilda's decision to cramp her space.

'Someone's trailing me back there,' Gilda whispered.

The woman merely shook her head and gazed out the window.

Gilda pulled her heart-shaped compact mirror from her backpack and carefully applied lip gloss while attempting to get a view of Nikki and Priscilla in the back of the bus.

Both girls watched her with blank, unwavering patience, like cats observing a tiny rodent.

What were they planning?

At each stop, several elderly people exited the bus. Under normal circumstances, Gilda would have been delighted to say goodbye to the large, irritable woman with whom she shared her seat, but now she felt a pang of disappointment as her travelling companion gathered her belongings and heaved herself down the aisle.

To Gilda's disappointment, the people sitting in the seat behind her also left the bus.

Gilda peered into her mirror again and felt a prickling sensation at the back of her neck as Nikki and Priscilla stealthily made their way towards the front of the bus. She steeled herself as they slid into the seat directly behind her. She caught a whiff of Priscilla's smell – the scent of baby powder mixed with something that reminded her of Halloween candy.

People are like animals, Gilda reminded herself. *If they smell fear; they'll attack.*

'Something smells,' said Nikki.

'You're right,' said Priscilla. 'Something really reeks.'

Priscilla and Nikki expected her to sit silently, cringing from their barbs.

Summoning all her courage, Gilda turned her body sideways and put her feet up on the seat nonchalantly. 'Maybe the two of you should start taking showers now and then.' She forced herself to gaze directly into Priscilla's cat eyes. 'By the way, that perfume smells like someone puked candy corn.'

Priscilla curled her lip in response.

'Why don't *you* take a shower,' Nikki blurted.

'Because I already *did* take one,' said Gilda, beginning to enjoy the inanity of the exchange.

'Then why don't you go take another—'

'Oh, shut up.' Priscilla stared evenly at Gilda for a moment. 'Your play sucked,' she said, switching subjects.

For a split second, Gilda was caught off-guard; Priscilla had managed to hit a nerve.

'Is that why it got a standing ovation?' Gilda countered.

'At Our Lady of Sorrows, everything gets a standing ovation – especially if the audience hates it.'

'Besides, the whole thing was total B.S. All lies,' said Nikki.

'Of course it was lies. It's a play, right?' *Maybe if I use*

254

reverse psychology, I'll trap them into confessing something, Gilda thought.

'But you seemed to be *implying* something about us,' said Nikki.

'Gee, that sounds a little self-centred.'

'You know what I mean.'

'Do tell.'

'You know exactly what you were doing.'

'What Nikki is trying to say,' said Priscilla, sensing that she and Nikki were losing control, 'is that we simply hate seeing crap on the Our Lady of Sorrows stage. As an actress, I find it personally offensive.'

'Do you find yourself personally offensive?'

Priscilla rolled her eyes. 'That response is so public school. You know, Nikki, Mrs McCracken really let standards decline when it comes to this year's freshmen class.'

'It's so true,' said Nikki. 'She was really scraping the bottom of the barrel with this batch of freshmen.'

'Listen, Priscilla,' said Gilda, now crouching on her knees and leaning against the back of her seat. It wasn't exactly a threatening position, but she felt she needed to face her adversaries as directly as possible. 'You and I both know that you killed Dolores Lambert three years ago. I admit I don't know exactly *how* you did it, but I know all about the Ladies of the Lake, and I know you guys did something awful to her.'

Something behind Priscilla's eyes seemed to flinch. Was she actually afraid? Close up Gilda saw that her skin was perfect, without a single zit or even a freckle. But her eyes were very green, and her pupils were tiny with hatred.

Gilda noticed the familiar Woodward Avenue landmarks signalling the approach of her bus stop. She reached up cautiously to pull the overhead wire, wondering if Nikki and Priscilla were planning to follow her home. *Run fast when you get off the bus*, she told herself.

'If what you're saying is really true,' said Priscilla, 'then Nikki and I could go to the electric chair. Are you so sure you want to be responsible for killing *us*?'

Gilda wasn't sure how to respond. Would kids like Nikki and Priscilla actually get the *electric chair* if they were convicted? Weren't they too young?

The bus stopped and Gilda jumped up quickly.

'Think about what I said, Gilda.'

'Yeah, and mind your own business for a change,' Nikki added.

Fighting an urge to break into a sprint, Gilda forced herself to walk calmly down the aisle and down the stairs of the bus. She breathed a sigh of relief as the bus pulled away, taking Nikki and Priscilla with it.

Gilda approached the comfort of her familiar street, where children's plastic toys and a combination of Halloween and Christmas decorations littered front lawns, porches, and trees. For once, Brad's car wasn't in the driveway, which meant she might actually have a quiet house all to herself. She wished she could simply go inside, make a peanut butter, banana and chocolate sandwich, call Wendy Choy, and forget about the Ladies of the Lake entirely. Instead, she trudged straight upstairs to her bedroom, tossed her backpack on her bed, and immediately sat down at her typewriter.

Dear Dad,
It looks like the Ladies of the Lake aren't about to confess anything.
     I never thought I'd say this, but I might be in over my head. Maybe it's time for me to tell Mrs McCracken about this.
     PROBLEM: I have no hard evidence, and the three of them would obviously deny everything. Who would take my word against three of the most popular seniors at school?
     Sometimes I can't help but think that my life would be a lot easier if I just spent my time doing my homework, going shopping, and talking about boys like a normal girl.

The unfriendly exchanges Gilda had experienced with Nikki, Priscilla, and Mr Panté had left her feeling unusually glum and ambivalent. Hoping Balthazar Frobenius might have some words of encouragement or advice, Gilda opened her dog-eared *Master Psychic's Handbook* to a section with the heading 'Psychics and the Justice System':

257

As a psychic who helps detectives investigate crimes, my role is to help put the justice system on an investigative track. I tell detectives what I perceive, and if hard evidence backs up my theory, an indictment may eventually follow. Note, dear reader, that there have been more than a handful of cases in which a person I know to be guilty walks free to this day for lack of hard evidence against him or her. This is always frustrating — sometimes even devastating — for the psychic who feels helpless. But this is as it must be, for it would be a more dangerous situation for the testimony of any psychic to stand in court as 'evidence'; there are far too many false psychics who might use their own prejudices to put people in jail.

Maybe I'll never have enough hard evidence to really prove what the Ladies of the Lake did, Gilda thought. *Maybe I should just go to the police and hope for justice.*

The sight of her overstuffed backpack reminded Gilda that the Ladies of the Lake weren't her only problem. She had neglected her homework while working on *The Drowned and the Damned*, and now, as Gilda contemplated a long list of papers and assignments, she wondered whether it was even possible to catch up with her studies. Digging through the mess of folders and papers, she discovered a mysterious typed note in her backpack.

Dear Gilda:
Your play really freaked me out.
I think you need to understand what really happened with Dolores. It was a long time ago, and it was more complicated than you realize. NOBODY ELSE can see what I'm leaving for you to read, please.

Just a secret between friends, OK? Call me after you read this.

   – Danielle

It was like finding a winning lottery ticket in the pocket of an old pair of jeans. Attached to the note were several handwritten pages entitled 'Minutes of the Ladies of the Lake.'

30

The Final Test

MINUTES OF THE LADIES OF THE LAKE MEETING NOTES TAKEN BY DANIELLE MENORY, SECRETARY

The Ladies of the Lake met today at our fantastic, secret location in the ruins. Nobody has any idea we go here. Ladies in attendance were Priscilla Barkley (President), Nikki Grimaldi (Activities Director), and Danielle Menory (Secretary).

Priscilla says we should take notes on our official meetings, just like in a real sorority.

SUBJECTS DISCUSSED:

1. Who has the best hair in school
2. Should Nikki call a guy named 'Dinkel' or wait for him to call her?
3. A dream Priscilla had that she was famous

COMPLAINTS:

1. Nikki had a zit (which we couldn't see)
2. Too much homework!
3. The sophomores are mean

4. People kicked too hard on 'kick the freshmen' day

OUR SECRET CLUB:
'It's not just a secret club we're forming,' Priscilla said;
'it's going to be like an exclusive sorority.' Eventually,
we'll invite certain people to 'rush' the Ladies of the
Lake and then the three of us will pick the girls we like
to be part of the group. We'll have fabulous parties
with the cute boys. 'In order for a club to have
prestige, there will have to be some people who don't
make it as members,' Priscilla explained.

A SOLEMN OATH:
'The Ladies of the lake pledge to stick by each other
no matter what and to remain best friends for ever
no matter what; to become awesome, popular girls;
and never to reveal the name, location, meeting
times or anything else about the identity of our club
to anyone without the full agreement of all members.'

LADIES OF THE LAKE MEETING:
ACTIVITY:
We each wrote our names at the top of a piece of
paper, then handed it to the 'lady' sitting next to us in
the circle.
 Priscilla told us to write 'good qualities and faults'
of the individual named on the page, then pass it on.
'Be totally, brutally honest.'
 RESULTS (see attached):

Priscilla Barkley:

Super pretty! Could practically be a model. Smart, but kind of bossy sometimes.

Gorgeous, talented, and a good singer. A little pushy and judgmental. Sometimes has stinky breath.

Nikki Grimaldi:

Fun and funny! Very blunt and honest. Cute with cute freckles ☺. Boy crazy! Very knowledgeable about cars.

Hair is kind of frizzy and needs some highlights or something. Try straightening with a flat iron. Clothing style is a little butch. Muscular build but a little too big. Voice is too loud sometimes; you should tone it down. Pick better guys to like.

Danielle:

Pretty but needs a new haircut. and highlights. Good skin, but too pale. Thin but more muscle tone is needed. Nice clothes but a little boring. Studious and too serious.

Super smart! Will probably go to Harvard or Yale and do great career-wise. Sometimes looks worried about something. Lighten up!

The meeting ended on a sour note.

LADIES OF THE LAKE MEETING:

1. Feelings hurt at our last meeting.
2. It's annoying when the sophomores call us 'fresh meat.'

3. How amazing it's going to be when we're seniors.
4. What does Mr Panté's wife look like?
5. Why we hate Dolores Lambert.

COMPLAINTS:
Dolores has been following Priscilla around the school
'like a puppy dog who copies every single thing I do.'

REASONS DOLORES IS ANNOYING:
1. smiles too much (fake)
2. wears tacky plastic barrettes in hair
3. never understands jokes
4. whiney voice
5. ten to twenty extra pounds of baby fat
6. can't take a hint
7. copies what other people say
8. tries to tell funny stories that always come out
   sounding dumb
9. yells out 'Nuh!' after trying to say something
   funny – a word which has no meaning
   whatsoever
10. always says she's on a diet but never sticks to
    one
11. tells obvious lies about 'a boyfriend she had in
    Wisconsin'
12. her mom leaves extra cookies and stupid notes
    in her lunch
13. shows off her gaudy heart-shaped amethyst,
    which her mom bought her, and that is so lame

14. immature: gets excited about dumb things like having pizza for lunch or watching a movie during class, or knowing that 'Saturday is only two days away.'
15. face looks puffy
16. sticks retarded decorations to the ends of her pencils
17. brags about her grades

THE MOST FUN LADIES OF THE LAKE MEETING YET WAS TODAY!

LADIES OF THE LAKE MEETING:

SUBJECTS DISCUSSED:
Dolores Lambert saw a note about our meeting place in the ruins. Now she knows where we meet and wants to be part of the club.
PROBLEM: Should we find a new secret place to meet?

A PROPOSAL:
Let Dolores join the Ladies of the Lake on a conditional basis – as our first pledge. 'Then she'll have an incentive to keep our meeting place secret,' Priscilla said. 'Besides, it might be fun.'

PROBLEM:
I didn't like this idea. I wanted our club to be a secret

kept between three friends – a place to get away from everything. But Nikki and Priscilla like the idea of having their own sorority.

VOTE:
2 TO 1: Dolores will attend some meetings on a conditional basis.

LADIES OF THE LAKE
FIRST MEETING ATTENDED BY DOLORES
LAMBERT (PLEDGE)

Dolores read the 'Guidelines for Pledges.'

'What does "Bury all things you find dead" mean?' she asked.

'It means what it says,' Priscilla replied.

'But there are dead things everywhere,' Dolores argued. 'Like, what about dead leaves? It would be impossible for one person to bury all of them.'

'Use your best judgment,' said Priscilla.

'And what does "Give your heart to the Ladies of the Lake" mean?'

The President explained that members must all be willing to give up something close to them for the sake of the group, so the Pledge agreed that she would not wear her amethyst ring. It was confiscated and kept in a safe place in the ruino.

'What did the rest of you give up?' Dolores asked.

'That's our concern,' said Priscilla.

Nikki asked Dolores to kiss the shoes of each

265

member, and she complied without even hesitating.

'Dolores,' said Priscilla, 'your progress will be monitored. You'll endure a probation period before you can be considered a full member of the club.'

The Pledge said that she understood.

LADIES OF THE LAKE MEETING

Dolores brought homemade brownies and chocolate chips to our meeting, but wasn't allowed to eat more than one of each. (The rest of us ate numerous brownies and cookies apiece.)

When Dolores snuck an extra cookie, Priscilla declared that she must be punished. 'The Pledge must eat a small lump of dirt.'

We giggled, but then we saw that Priscilla was completely serious.

Nikki went outside and retrieved an enormous clump of soil that contained a worm.

'That's too much dirt for anyone to eat,' said Priscilla (as if a little bit of dirt might be a good snack for some people). She picked a marble-sized clump of mud from the clod of earth and handed it to Dolores.

'What if I get sick from eating that?' the Pledge asked. 'It might have germs.'

In response, the President handed her a larger piece of dirt.

The Pledge took the hint and asked if she could 'have anything to wash it down with.'

Members debated whether Dolores should be

allowed to have any beverage with her dirt.

We finally let her have a sip of Diet Coke, and she managed to swallow the dirt with a gross amount of gagging.

LADIES OF THE LAKE MEETING

The Pledge complained that she was allowed to eat lunch with us, but never allowed to speak unless spoken to first.

The President asked her what it was that she would like to say.

The Pledge couldn't think of anything. 'It's not fair because you're putting me on the spot,' the Pledge complained.

The President reminded her that she was 'getting close to becoming a full member, and then she would be treated as an equal.' The group agreed to offer Dolores up to three opportunities for conversation during lunches, but she would be cut off if her discussion became tedious.

The Pledge submitted an essay assignment to the group, which she read aloud (see attached):

'Why I Want to Be a Member of the Ladies of the Lake'
By Dolores Lambert, Pledge

Being a pledge to the Ladies of the Lake is probably going to be one of the hardest things I have ever done, but I know it will pay off in the end. When I see the members of the Ladies of the Lake laughing in the hallways and passing notes in class, I know that I will soon be sharing secrets with them, and it's so great to know that we'll always be there for each other in life.

The Ladies of the Lake is challenging me to be my best. I am trying to lose weight and keep up my grades and follow all the rules. There are a lot of rules! But sometimes it's kind of nice to have other people tell me my main goals because I know I'm not alone as I face these tough challenges.

I know there's a reason behind the plan, and I trust the Ladies of the Lake because they know what is best for me. I will always be a loyal member no matter what.

As a reward, the Pledge received a group hug.

LADIES OF THE LAKE – SPECIAL UPDATE

A deceased spider lay on the floor in the freshman locker room, and the Pledge was reprimanded for shirking her burial duties.

The Pledge protested that she would be late to class if she took time to bury the spider, but the President reminded her of this important rule.

The Pledge scooped up the stiff, black spider with a piece of paper and disappeared from the room. She returned a minute later and the President asked if she had actually buried the spider.

'I don't have a shovel or anything to bury it with,' the Pledge protested.

The President responded that she should always have 'a spoon, trowel, or other compact burial implement' in her purse in the event a grave is needed, and that her neglect of such tools indicates a 'lack of attention to detail and planning.'

The Pledge questioned the rule. 'Animals in the wild don't get buried,' she said.

The President countered that the expired spider was not in the wild; it was in school, and therefore must be buried. She ordered the Pledge to go back outside and bury the spider using a stick or her bare hands if necessary.

The Secretary complained of a severe stomach pain and ceased taking notes.

LADIES OF THE LAKE – SPECIAL MEETING

The President observed that the Pledge had gained weight instead of losing it, as had been recommended.

The President explained an activity to help Dolores with her lack of self-motivation. 'Sororities sometimes do this,' she said.

We told the Pledge to remove all of her clothing except her underwear.

'But I'll be cold.'

The Pledge was asked again to remove her clothing, and she complied.

We told the Pledge to stand on a chair while we documented her 'areas for improvement,' writing on her skin with markers.

The Pledge giggled because the pens tickled. Areas for improvement were noted:

'Cellulite here→'

'Jiggles here→'

'Can of lard lurking here→'

'Two rolls of fat→'

'Boobs small compared to waist→'

'Butt sagging→'

'Fat knees→'

'Remove this mole→'

'Hairy legs – eew!'

'When you go home and look in the mirror,' said the President, 'remember that the Ladies of the Lake are here to help you become the best person you can be. Other friends will simply tell you what you *want* to hear; the Ladies of the Lake tell you what you *need* to hear.'

The Pledge thanked us, but she looked shaky as she put her clothes back on. She left the meeting early because it was getting dark and very cold, and she had to walk all the way home.

<u>LADIES OF THE LAKE – SPECIAL MEETING</u>

The Pledge was not in attendance.

SUBJECTS DISCUSSED:

1. Dolores was spotted at the Jenny Craig diet centre with her mother.
2. Members complained that they were beginning to feel guilty about certain group activities.

   'Why?' the President asked. 'Can't you see that she *loves* it? She loves being told what to do. She's the kind of person who can't think for herself.'

   'But – maybe it's getting too mean,' I said.
3. The President proposed a final test to determine whether Dolores would become a full member of the Ladies of the Lake. 'To be fair, we have to give her one last chance,' said Priscilla. 'After this, the game will be over.'

THE PLAN:
We'll meet in the Garden of Prayer and Contemplation after school tomorrow.

<u>LADIES OF THE LAKE – FINAL ENTRY</u>
Thanksgiving day. Horrible, horrible, horrible.

10:00 a.m.: Priscilla calls, telling me to turn on the news. Dolores's body was dragged from Mermaid Lake last night.

I feel nauseated and unreal. How can she sound so calm and matter-of-fact as she tells me this news?

'That can't be right,' I say. 'That's not what was supposed to happen.'

'Danielle,' she says, 'This is important. You have to to destroy all the minutes to our meetings right now.'

'But shouldn't we tell someone what happened last night?'

'We didn't do anything.'

'But she probably wouldn't have drowned in the lake if it wasn't for us,' I say. 'She would have been at home, doing her homework or something.'

'Maybe she was a little depressed lately. She might have done it on purpose, you know.'

'And if she was depressed, whose fault was that?'

'Destroy all the records to our meetings, Danielle.'

'But if we didn't do anything wrong, why are you asking me to get rid of evidence?'

'Don't talk about it; just do it.'

But I have to write this down. Writing down the truth is the only thing that keeps me from feeling like I might be going crazy.

We met after school in the Garden of Prayer and Contemplation. It was around 4:30, and already getting dark. The sky was a weird colour – kind of purple – and there was an icy wind. I remember looking at the tree branches and having this really bad feeling because they reminded me of bony fingers scratching at the sky.

I really just wanted to go home. I think we all did. Nothing about what we were doing was even fun any more; it was just something we kept doing together like a bad habit that nobody knew how to stop. And because we did it together, no single person was ever to blame, so none of us ever really felt that bad.

It's easy to blame the whole thing on Priscilla, but the truth is, I was right there, participating in every single thing we did.

I'll be honest: the truth is that some of it was fun. Every time we gave some silly, mean task to Dolores, it made the *next* thing we did seem like less of a big deal. Of course, we were all starting to feel that things were getting a little out of hand, and we really were ready to put a stop to it. But the game had certain rules, and we had to keep playing by those rules.

'Dolores, this is your final test,' said Priscilla. 'If you succeed, you will become a full member. If you fail, you will leave immediately and we will go our separate ways forever more.'

Dolores said she was ready, and we blindfolded her with a pink silk scarf that belonged to Priscilla. It was freezing cold, and she still wore her pink uniform skirt with no tights or sweatpants to cover her legs. She didn't even have gloves. I was wearing gloves, but I didn't give them to her. Why didn't I at least give her my stupid gloves?

I wondered why she didn't just walk away. You can't possibly succeed, Dolores, I kept thinking. Why don't you just leave?

But Priscilla has this way of making you feel that you have to do something, and that no matter how weird it is, it's the *right* thing to do. In fact, you should be proud of yourself for doing it. She should become an army general, or something.

'Dolores,' Priscilla said, 'If something is meant to be, it will be. If you are a true Lady of the Lake, you are meant to find your way to our meeting place in the ruins. Your heart and body will be your eyes despite this blindfold. And of course, it goes without saying that a true Lady of the Lake would never cheat.'

We took her arms and spun her slowly around – once, twice, three times, then released her.

'Good luck, Dolores!'

We quietly scampered away and watched for a moment, giggling amongst ourselves as she groped along the hedges, making her way slowly through the maze of hedges in the garden. I remember how she stuck her tongue out like a little kid who's concentrating really hard, trying to do something difficult. It hurts to think of that now – the image of her tongue sticking out that way.

She didn't call out to us for help. Even after we stood in the cold spying on her for about twenty minutes, she didn't even try to lift her blindfold once. It was really horrible that she had such complete trust in us – like she couldn't even TRY to cheat. I think that was the first moment we were all scared at what we had done to her.7

'What if she actually makes it all the way to the ruins?' Nikki whispered. 'She'll pass the test.'

'Then she'll become a member of the club, just like we promised,' said Priscilla.

'Are you serious?'

'There's no way she's going to make it.'

After a while, we started getting bored with the whole game. Besides, it was really cold outside. When we saw Dolores turn the wrong direction and head towards the school instead of the path that circled the lake and led to the ruins, we figured she would give up soon. Our own fingers and toes were growing numb, so how could she stand being outside for long? Any sensible person would give up. Besides, we really wanted to go home.

I know one thing: we definitely didn't set out to kill her.

On the other hand, she wouldn't be dead now if it wasn't for us.

So are we murderers?

I'm having a hard time breathing right now. Maybe I'm getting the flu or something. I just need to get through the rest of this day. If I can make it through this one day, maybe I'll survive. Maybe there will be a time when I won't feel sick, and everything will seem normal again.

But I doubt it.

31

The Dark Side

Danielle sat at the dining room table and tore open the letter from Georgetown University. She read the opening line with a feeling of doom in her heart:

Dear Danielle Menory:
The Admissions Officers of Georgetown University are pleased to grant you admission into the freshman class at Georgetown University in Washington, D.C. . . .

Danielle re-read the words with disbelief. She had been granted early admission into her top-choice school – Georgetown University! Somehow, she hadn't believed this was possible. She had been certain that the admissions officers would find her college entrance essay tedious. They would realize that her grades and community service activities didn't quite measure up to those of her peers. Or, most disturbing of all, they would somehow perceive her secret guilt. Instead, they had found her worthy of admission. *Maybe I do deserve to get something I want*, Danielle thought. Deserved or not, she felt happy for the first time in ages.

Danielle's parents stood together, watching from the doorway with innocent, hopeful eyes.

'I got in,' she said quietly.

'Oh, Danielle!' They rushed to hug her, and for a moment, she was safe, floating on the buoyant life-raft of their pride.

I never want to disappoint them, Danielle thought.

Then, with a hot feeling in her gut, she remembered something unpleasant. She knew she had better call Gilda Joyce right away.

'Gilda!' Stephen yelled up the stairs from the living room. 'Phone!'

As if in a daze, Gilda trudged downstairs and found the phone left off the hook in the kitchen. She still felt slightly chilled after reading the detailed account of Dolores Lambert's hazing by the Ladies of the Lake. 'Hello?'

'Gilda? This is Danielle.'

Gilda glanced out the kitchen window, half-expecting to see the three Ladies of the Lake waiting for her threateningly in the leaf-covered back yard. She noticed Brad's SUV pulling into the driveway.

'Gilda? Are you there?'

'Yes – I'm here.' Gilda felt caught off-guard. She hadn't had time to reflect on all the information she had just read. What was she supposed to say to

Danielle? Why had Danielle shared these secrets?

'I guess you read that stuff I left for you.'

'I just read it a minute ago.'

'Well, what are you doing this evening?'

Gilda looked around at her mundane surroundings and picked up a cheese grater that was lying on the counter next to one of Brad's motivational books entitled *Send Your Sales Into the Stratosphere!* In the next room, Stephen sprawled on the couch, watching some bizarre Japanese cartoon. 'We're having cocktail hour at the moment,' she lied, 'and then I might go out. I'm not sure yet.'

'I was wondering if we could meet for coffee or something. I think we need to talk.'

'OK, I guess.'

'You live in Ferndale, right?'

Gilda and Danielle agreed to meet at a nearby café. As Gilda hung up the phone, she wondered what she should wear. Despite the horror she had felt while reading Danielle's notes only minutes before, she couldn't help feeling flattered by Danielle's invitation for coffee. After all, it was nearly unheard of for a senior to ask one of the freshman girls to do anything social outside of school.

Gilda ran up to her bedroom, and stared at her closet as if she scarcely recognized her own clothes. She was about to pair a knit skirt with black tights with lavender heels (a look she called 'Paris café') but then changed her mind and decided to aim for something more conservative – something that Danielle would approve of. She pulled on khaki pants, a sweater and boots, then grabbed her favourite black trench coat from the front closet. Glancing in the mirror, she noted with satisfaction that she resembled a young FBI agent. She grabbed her notebook and pen in case she needed to take notes and her dark sunglasses in case she needed a quick disguise. As she skipped downstairs to wait for Danielle, a disturbing thought stopped her: *What if this is a trap? What if she's secretly planning to bring Nikki and Priscilla along?*

Remembering her resolution to begin carrying a weapon, Gilda ran back upstairs. In her mother's bedroom, she found an economy-size can of hairspray which she stuffed into her large shoulder bag, figuring that it could function as a weapon if necessary. She noticed Brad's razor and toothbrush sitting on the counter, looking very entitled. '*Yeah, we LIVE here now,*' they seemed to sneer. '*So what? Wanna make something of it?*'

Something about the sight of Brad's belongings made her glad that Danielle was picking her up to go out, even if Danielle *was* partly responsible for Dolores's death. Downstairs, she heard her mother's voice and the slamming of cupboard doors as she and Brad unloaded groceries.

'That doesn't go there!' her mother snapped. 'More kielbasa? Why did you get *these*?' She was obviously in a bad mood for some reason.

I need to get out of here, Gilda thought. She headed downstairs to wait for her ride.

'I'll have an extra large triple espresso with chocolate syrup,' said Gilda. She and Danielle leaned against the counter at a trendy coffee shop near Gilda's house. Gilda wanted to ask Danielle a million questions about the notes she had read only an hour ago, but something about Danielle's cool, sophisticated demeanour made Gilda feel cautious.

'You're having a *triple espresso* at this time of day?'

'It's my usual.'

'That would keep me up for days. Oh, I'll have a decaf skinny latte, please,' said Danielle, placing her order.

Danielle sat down at a table in the corner table while Gilda doused her espresso with cocoa powder. After she had embellished her drink, Gilda sat down at the table and observed Danielle, who was methodically opening and emptying several packages of Sweet & Lo into her latte. She wore a white angora sweater with long sleeves that partially concealed her slender, nervous fingers.

Danielle grimaced as she took a sip of her coffee. 'This is awful.' She fidgeted with the long scarf she wore wrapped around her neck, as if she were sitting outside in freezing weather.

'Maybe it needs more Sweet & Lo.'

Danielle wasn't amused. 'Gilda, I have to say that for a freshman, you're pretty smart.'

'What do you mean, "for a freshman"?'

'You're pretty smart, period.'

'Thank you.'

'I don't know *how* you figured out the things you seem to know. I guess you're one impressive investigative reporter.'

Gilda felt a rush of gratitude. It was high time someone realized she was impressive! 'I'm actually a *psychic* investigator,' she blurted.

Danielle's eyes grew wide. For a split second, Gilda thought she looked scared. 'You're *psychic*?'

'I investigate psychic phenomena,' said Gilda, feeling that it still might be a bit of an exaggeration to call herself a full-blown psychic. 'Ghosts and things like that.'

'So *that's* how you figured stuff out about the Ladies of the Lake?' She lowered her voice to a whisper. 'You got a vision, or something like that?'

'Kind of.' Gilda decided not to reveal the fact that she and Wendy Choy had spied on a Ladies of the Lake meeting.

Danielle began to tear her packets of Sweet & Lo into little pieces. 'Gilda, I feel so much better now that I've been able to share what really happened with you. I know it's kind of weird for me to be sitting here telling my problems to a freshman.'

'What's so weird about that?'

'You just seem so much more mature than the rest of the freshman class.'

Gilda wished some of her classmates had been around to hear that comment.

'Maybe it's because of your psychic abilities or something.'

A tiny voice in Gilda's head protested that this might be sheer flattery. *She might be manipulating you.* Gilda decided to ignore the thought. Finally, someone appreciated her psychic abilities!

'Keeping this whole thing a secret has just been so tough to deal with,' Danielle continued. 'Half the time, I can't even sleep at night.' She lowered her voice and leaned forward confidentially. 'And – just between you and me – I don't even really *like* Nikki and Priscilla any more, but the three of us are stuck together like this horrible dysfunctional family. I guess Nikki still idolizes Priscilla, but the only thing we all really have in common any more is this horrible secret about something that happened three years ago.'

Gilda watched as Danielle pushed pink shreds of paper into a little mound that resembled a pile of wood shavings in a gerbil cage.

'You must think I'm a terrible person,' said Danielle, a bit coyly.

'Of course not.'

Danielle seemed to be two different people: the girl who had participated in a mean game three years ago, and the distraught girl who now sat in front of her tearing Sweet & Lo packets into bits. For some reason, Gilda wanted to say something that would make her feel better. 'You were just a kid back then, right?'

'*You're* a freshman right now, and I bet you'd never do anything like that.'

Gilda secretly agreed, if only because she would have found Priscilla's rules too annoying to cooperate with. On the other hand, she was aware that you never knew what you *might* do given the opportunity. Years ago, she and Wendy had scared a scrawny girl named Debbie on the playground by threatening to prick her with a safety pin that would give her 'a magic fat injection.' When Debbie burst into tears, they had taken sadistic delight in the fact that Debbie had believed the absurd threat. It was hard not to want to repeat the episode during recess the next day even though they knew it was wrong.

'You never know,' said Gilda. 'Give me half a chance, and I might dunk someone in Mermaid Lake tomorrow.' Her hand shook as she took another gulp of her extra-strong coffee. She felt jumpy.

'We *didn't* dunk her in the lake!'

'Oh. Right.' Gilda remembered how Danielle had called her from Mrs Lambert's house pretending to be a ghost. *The same girl who said 'You will drown in the lake' is sitting right across from you.* Still, Gilda couldn't quite get over the fact that she was out having coffee with a popular senior. She kept hoping that someone she knew would walk into the café.

Danielle sighed. 'I'm so stressed out.'

'Don't take this the wrong way,' Gilda ventured, 'but

have you ever considered telling anyone about what happened?'

'I just explained everything to you, didn't I?'

'But have you ever thought about telling Mrs McCracken – or someone like that?'

Danielle blinked very quickly. 'It's impossible.'

'Maybe you'd feel better.'

Danielle shook her head. 'It would kill my parents.' She covered her face with her hands and blew her nose into a napkin. Her eyes looked small and red. 'I just found out that I got into Georgetown University.'

Gilda wondered why Danielle conveyed this news as if it she had just found out she was scheduled for surgery. 'So I guess you got that college essay written after all, huh?'

'My parents are so thrilled, and if the story about what we did to Dolores three years ago came out now, I could get expelled or, who knows, maybe go to jail . . .' Danielle's face contorted with silent tears. 'It would just be so disappointing and *awful* for everyone!'

Gilda noticed two boys waving at Danielle. 'Hey! Danielle!' They smiled as they picked up their drinks from the counter.

Danielle wiped her eyes with a napkin and composed herself. 'Oh, hey,' she said, greeting them with a weak smile as they approached the table. 'What are you guys doing in Ferndale?'

'Getting coffee. What are you doing here?'

'We're just having a meeting about the school paper.'

Both boys were tall with longish hair that hung in their eyes with a kind of calculated messiness. Gilda recognized Nikki's boyfriend Dinkel from the Halloween dance.

'School paper, huh?' They stood next to the table awkwardly, not sure whether to simply say hello and get their own table, or pull up chairs to join the girls. Then Dinkel noticed Danielle's red eyes. 'Hey, what's wrong? Have you been crying or something?'

Danielle shook her head and waved her hand dismissively. 'It's nothing.'

'Boy problems?'

'Hardly.'

'Come on. You can tell us.'

'She doesn't like her latte,' said Gilda.

The boys seemed to notice Gilda for the first time. 'She doesn't like her *latte*? How bad can it be?' Dinkel picked it up and took a sip. 'Oh, that is bad. What's in here, like twenty packets of sugar or something?'

'Sweet & Lo.'

'I can see why you're crying.'

'I told her not to drink it,' said Gilda, wanting the boys to pay more attention to her.

'She *shouldn't* drink it.'

'I'm Gilda.' Gilda extended her hand, deciding that she might as well introduce herself if Danielle wasn't going to.

'Sorry,' said Danielle. 'Gilda, these are my friends Dinkel and Shane.'

'We're interchangeable,' said Shane. 'It doesn't matter which is which.'

'You're Dinkel, right?' said Gilda, pointing to Nikki's boyfriend.

'How do you know? Have we met?'

'She's psychic,' said Danielle.

'Psychic, huh?' Dinkel pulled up a chair and Shane followed suit. 'So tell me what number I'm thinking of right now.'

'Fifty-seven.'

'Totally wrong. I was thinking of the colour blue.' He eyed her blue sweater.

Wendy was right, Gilda thought; *these boys are totally cute.* Gilda wasn't sure whether it was the espresso or the prospect of actually having a conversation with older boys that was making her feel jittery. She giggled a little too loudly and accidentally knocked over the remains of her coffee.

'Looks like someone's overcaffeinated,' said Dinkel.

'Did I tell you guys that I got into Georgetown on early admission?'

Dinkel and Shane looked dumbstruck. 'You got into Georgetown,' said Dinkel.

'Right.'

'And you're crying,' said Shane. 'Boo hoo! I got into Harvard and Yale! Waaa!'

'And – and Shane, that's not even the *worst* part,'

Dinkel added with mock earnestness. 'My latte is just too *sweet*!'

'Oh, shut up.'

'Well, congratulations,' said Shane.

'Thanks.'

'Some people have all the luck. How about you, Gilda? Have you done your applications yet?'

Was he kidding, or did he really think she might be old enough to apply to college? 'I'm probably going to Oxford,' she said.

'Gilda is a freshman,' Danielle interjected.

'A freshman?! No wonder she looks young.'

'In fact, it's probably about dinner time, so I should probably be giving you a ride home about now, right, Gilda?'

'It's OK,' said Gilda. 'I like to stay out as late as possible.'

'Well, *I* should be getting home,' said Danielle. 'We'll catch you guys later, OK?'

'We can take a hint,' said Shane.

'Nice meeting you,' said Gilda.

'Good luck with your applications to Oxford.'

Gilda thought she heard sniggering as she left, but decided to ignore it.

'Thanks for listening to all my worries,' said Danielle, dropping Gilda off in front of her house. 'I know this goes without saying, but I can trust you with this, right?'

'Sure.' *She means I'd better not tell anyone*, Gilda thought, opening the car door.

'Oh, and Gilda, do you have the notes I gave you about the Ladies of the Lake? I kind of need to get those back.'

The notes were stashed under Gilda's pillow. *The notes are the only hard evidence I have to prove what they did*, Gilda thought, remembering with an uneasy feeling the psychic investigation she now felt half ready to ditch. 'I'll bring them to school.'

'Don't forget, OK? Priscilla would kill me if they got into the wrong hands.'

At the mention of Priscilla's name, Gilda hesitated. 'Danielle,' she said, 'did you know that Nikki and Priscilla followed me home on the bus today?'

'No.'

'They were acting a little thuggish.'

'Sluggish?'

'*Thuggish*. Mean and threatening.'

Danielle rolled her eyes. 'They are so dumb sometimes. Believe me, Gilda, you don't have any reason to be scared of them.'

'Are you sure?'

'I'll set them straight. Nikki and Priscilla thought you were trying to get us in trouble with your play and everything, but they don't realize that you just can't *help* knowing things because you're psychic, right?' Danielle looked at Gilda imploringly. 'I promise I'll talk to them, OK?'

Danielle had a sad, unconventionally pretty face that reminded Gilda of paintings of the Madonna. A kind face.

'OK,' said Gilda. 'Don't worry, Danielle; you can trust me.'

Dear Dad,
I had the best day ever at school, but now I feel rotten about it.

I was on my way to the dining hall when Danielle came up to me and asked if I wanted to come with her to Starbucks.

I said yes, of course.

'Nikki and Priscilla are going too.'

'Oh.'

'Don't worry; I talked to them, and they feel bad about being mean on the bus.'

Freshmen aren't supposed to leave campus at all, so the opportunity to sneak away for a coffee break with the Ladies of the Lake was a major violation and way too exciting to pass up. I told myself I would be observing them undercover.

At Starbucks, I ordered a triple espresso (a 'Trippio'!), and you would have thought the four of us were best friends. I mean, they kept telling me how they would never risk taking any of the other freshmen out for coffee, but I was 'old for my age' so I could handle it.

They also didn't seem to care that I was listening to all their gossip.

I found out that Priscilla can't stand her stepfather (she calls him 'Tom') because he bosses her around all the time.

'All Tom does is criticize me and eavesdrop on my phone conversations,' she said. 'And he gives me the creeps; he's always looking at my boobs.'

'That is so messed up,' said Danielle.

'Oh, I forgot,' said Priscilla. 'Danielle is easily offended because she has the perfect family.'

'Who said I have a perfect family?'

'You did,' said Priscilla. 'You're always implying it.'

'Play nice, you two!' said Nikki. 'Geez, you'd think you'd both be a better example to the youngster here.' She poked a thumb in my direction.

'I don't mind,' I said, wishing Nikki hadn't interrupted the conversation. 'I love a good fight.'

'We weren't fighting,' said Danielle.

'Well, my mom's boyfriend drives me crazy too,' I said, hoping to get Priscilla to reveal more about herself. I told them how Brad makes greasy kielbasa dinners and then sits on the couch for hours, playing video games.

I told them about his books with titles like
Go! Go! Go! and *Shut Up and Find Success!*

Priscilla said she could totally relate to my
situation. It's pretty interesting to discover
that she and I actually have *something* in
common (although, to be honest, Priscilla's
stepfather makes Brad seem OK by
comparison).

In fact, the more time I spent around
Priscilla, the more I could understand how
the Ladies of the Lake wanted to follow all
the rules she made up back when she was a
freshman. There's just something about her
that makes you want her to like you even
though you know very well that she was
mean to you just the other day. If she had
turned to me and said, 'Hey, Gilda; could you
do me a favour and bury that dead tarantula
over there?' I actually might have done it.

Danielle complained that Shane keeps
calling her even though she doesn't like him
any more. I guess they used to go out.

'But he's so cute!' Nikki said.

I agreed with Nikki. 'He can give ME a call
anytime,' I said. This made them laugh for
some reason.

They asked if I had a boyfriend, and I
made up something about 'a boyfriend at
camp over the summer' and how we still

write each other. 'He lives in Ohio, so we don't get to see each other much,' I said. 'We're open to dating other people.'

You would think this would be the end of the conversation, but instead they asked about a million questions. 'What's his name?' 'Is he cute?' 'Does your mom like him?' 'How did you meet?' 'What was your first kiss like?' 'Are you going to go visit him?' Consequently, I was forced to invent a long-distance boyfriend named Huey who's six feet tall and plays on the varsity basketball team and lives on a farm so he doesn't have much time for phone conversations. 'He slobbers a lot every time he kisses me,' I said, 'but he always has minty fresh breath.' I also told them that Huey drives a pick-up truck that breaks down all the time, so that's why he can't come all the way up to Michigan to visit very often.

'Hey, we should take you to visit Huey!' Nikki exclaimed.

'I'm thinking of breaking up with him.' (As you can imagine, I was desperate to get off the subject of the non-existent Huey.) 'In his letters, he's been talking about "separating the hogs with fever" and I'm kind of afraid I'm going to catch something from him if we keep going out.'

This finally shut them up, and they stopped trying to get me to marry old farm-boy Huey.

'I bet we can find you a guy,' said Priscilla. 'Doesn't Dinkel have a younger brother, Nikki?'

'But he's only in sixth grade.'

'Well, Gilda is the coolest girl in the freshman class, so she's probably going to have loads of boyfriends, right?'

As you can imagine, the combination of this compliment along with the caffeine buzz kept me flying high for the rest of the afternoon.

And as if this wasn't enough, Priscilla and Nikki gave me a ride home from school. As we drove past the bus stop, I saw those poor scholarship girls standing there waiting for the bus, and I thought how that used to be me just the day before. It was so much nicer sitting up in Nikki's car where everything is newly upholstered. I admit it: at that moment, I really didn't care about the Ladies of the Lake or Dolores Lambert or anything. Why bother with the hard, lonely life of a psychic investigator when I could be living the good life with the Ladies of the Lake?

Then I got home and made the mistake of calling Wendy to tell her about my amazing day.

'They're obviously manipulating you,' she said. 'They don't want you to tell the headmistress what you know.'

'It *started* that way,' I said, 'but you should have seen how much fun we were having together, Wendy. I know it sounds like I'm bragging, but I think they honestly believe I'm the coolest girl in the freshman class.'

'As long as you don't *tell* on them, you're the coolest girl.'

'Wendy, I've never thought of you as the jealous type before.'

'And I've never thought of you as a sell-out.'

'Start thinking of me as a sell-out who'll be going out with some of the best-looking guys in the metro Detroit area.'

'Omigod, I never knew you could be this gullible.'

'I'm just trying to enjoy my life for once.'

'I thought you were better than that.'

'Well, I'm not.'

'Call me when you figure out where you misplaced your ethics.'

Then Wendy had to go because Terrence was squirting the cat with a squirt gun.

Now, after talking to Wendy, my perfect

day is ruined. She's obviously jealous that a group of seniors are paying so much attention to me.

On the other hand, I have to admit it's pretty suspicious that they're being so nice. After all, if they accept me as part of their popular group, I'll have less incentive to turn them in.

Maybe Wendy is right. Maybe Danielle is being very strategic. It's a good strategy because it's working. The truth is, it feels good to be part of their group.

Gilda turned out the light and closed her eyes. As she drifted into sleep, a disturbing image popped into her mind — a face blurred by sadness. She didn't want to see what was *behind* the aging, puffy eyes — the unbearable emptiness and loss.

It was Mrs Lambert's face.

32

The Bedpost Ghost

As Gilda strolled along the edge of Mermaid Lake, she felt happy. She had just discovered something: Mrs McCracken had opened a Starbucks for students right on school grounds. The coffee shop had been built into the structure of the ruins. Nailed to the crumbling walls, familiar bold letters announced the promise of caffeine: Starbucks!

Wendy Choy appeared. 'Aren't you forgetting something?' she asked.

'You're right,' said Gilda. 'I'm late!' She had almost forgotten that she was actually supposed to be *working* at Starbucks to help earn her tuition money, and now she was late for her shift.

Standing behind the Starbucks counter, Gilda put on her green polyester apron and made herself a Trippio, but accidentally knocked it over as Danielle walked into the shop, carrying something wrapped in tissue paper.

'Want a latte?' Gilda offered.

'I really just want to get rid of this,' said Danielle,

handing Gilda something that felt like some lunchmeat wrapped in paper.

The tissue paper was printed with pink hearts. Gilda opened it and discovered a large goldfish inside.

Something wasn't right about this exchange, but Gilda didn't want to let on that it wasn't her job to get rid of a goldfish. Danielle was a customer and she was supposed to make her happy. 'I'll need to weigh it first,' she explained, turning to the counter behind her, where old–fashioned scales sat next to the coffee grinder. She put the fish on a scale and found that it was far heavier than she had expected. 'Too heavy,' she said.

Danielle handed her a book. 'See if this balances it out,' she said. Danielle held the *Master Psychic's Handbook* in her hand. 'I trust you, Gilda.'

As Gilda placed the book on the opposite scale, she realized that something horrible had just happened. The floor of the shop had flooded with slushy water, and the goldfish had transformed into a girl – a girl with tangled gold hair and puffy, scaly skin. She wore a pink skirt and lay on the ground like a dead mermaid stranded on a beach. Motionless, she gaped at Gilda with blind, colourless eyes.

'Gilda, please help me,' she said. 'I'm so cold.'

Gilda awoke with a feeling of unease. She had the distinct sensation that someone had just been standing at the foot of her bed, watching her.

She watched long, finger-like shadows that moved across her ceiling as a car passed by on the road outside, then jumped out of bed and flipped on the light.

It was 3 a.m. Gilda impulsively decided to call Wendy Choy on her cell phone.

At first, Wendy simply answered the phone and hung up, so Gilda dialled her number again.

'What?!' Wendy's hoarse voice whispered into the phone.

'I think I saw a ghost, Wendy.'

'Hmmm.'

'Wendy? Did you *hear* me?'

Wendy yawned. 'Good. Good.'

'I think it was a "bedpost ghost." I've read about those things – they're ghosts that come stand by your bed, and they have a message for you while you're dreaming.'

'What time is it?'

'I don't know. I think it's about eleven o'clock.' It was actually after 3 a.m.

'But I went to bed at midnight.'

'Wendy, did you hear what I said?'

'You shaw a ghost,' Wendy slurred.

'I'm not sure whether I actually *saw* something, but I definitely *felt* a presence. There was definitely somebody there.'

'Mmm.'

'I had this dream that I was working at Starbucks,

298

and out of the blue, a dead mermaid appeared. She looked right at me with these spooky eyes.'

Wendy snorted.

'Isn't that weird?'

'Yup.'

'I think the dead mermaid represents Dolores.'

'Duh.'

'She wants me to help her.'

'And instead, you're chugging sippios with the people who killed her.'

'Trippios,' said Gilda, slightly startled by Wendy's sudden ability to form a complete sentence.

She remembered a disturbing feeling she had experienced in the dream: the sense that she was supposed to be doing something important – something she had misplaced.

'I think I'm supposed to tell someone about the Ladies of the Lake, Wendy.'

'What are you waiting for?'

'It feels really weird to tell on someone. *I'm* usually the one getting in trouble.'

'You'll get in trouble soon enough.'

Gilda heard Wendy moving something around on her nightstand.

'Omigod! You're such a jerk! It's after three in the morning!'

'It is?' Gilda feigned surprise.

'I have three quizzes tomorrow, Gilda, and now I'm going to be exhausted.'

'Try having an espresso before class; it really helps.'
Wendy hung up.
Gilda opened her dream journal and wrote:

Dear Dolores,
I got your message.
Don't worry; I'm going to help you.

33

Mrs McCracken's Nightmare

Although less ornate than her luncheon room, Mrs McCracken's office was similarly swathed in shades of pink. Gilda peered through the doorway and found the headmistress sitting at her desk behind a large bouquet of silk roses. She cradled the telephone under her chin while holding a china teacup and saucer in her hands.

'We'll all be praying for her,' Mrs McCracken was saying, beckoning to Gilda with a pink talon.

'OK, Ethel.' She slurped her tea loudly into the telephone receiver. 'Excuse me, sweetie! I'm just having some tea. OK, love to your family, sweetie pie. Bye-bye.'

Gilda entered the office and sat down on a plush pink chair that was significantly lower than Mrs McCracken's desk.

'Hello, Miss Gilda! What brings you all the way down to this neck of the woods?'

Mrs McCracken appeared to be in a jovial mood – a mood that somehow made it more difficult to bring up the subject of the Ladies of the Lake.

'I just wanted to talk to you about something,' said Gilda.

'What's that, sugar? You can tell me anything.'

'It's kind of serious.'

'Oh?'

'It's about Dolores Lambert.'

Mrs McCracken frowned and sat up straighter. 'A terrible tragedy,' she said. 'Just terrible!'

Gilda pulled the Minutes of the Ladies of the Lake from her back pack and placed it in front of Mrs McCracken, who regarded the handwritten pages as if they were something Gilda had pulled out of a trash can.

'Danielle Menory is such a lovely girl,' Mrs McCracken cooed, noticing Danielle's name. Her expression soured as she squinted at the handwriting in front of her. 'Sweetie, I don't have my glasses on. Summarize, please.' She gave the paper a little spanking with her puffy, manicured hand.

Gilda told Mrs McCracken about the Ladies of the Lake. She explained how they made Dolores Lambert a pledge to their secret club. She described the final test in which Dolores was blindfolded and left to find her way to the ruins all alone.

As Gilda mentioned each of the seniors involved, she sensed something: the last thing Mrs McCracken wanted to believe was that these girls had anything to do with Dolores Lambert's death.

'So let me get this straight, Gilda,' said Mrs McCracken, leaning back in her chair and squinting fiercely. 'Danielle Menory gave you these notes about this supposed secret club?'

'Yes.'

'Why?'

'I don't know why. I guess she wanted to tell someone what really happened.'

'Why didn't she come to me directly?'

'I guess she didn't want to get in trouble.'

'So it's *your* job to get her in trouble?'

This wasn't the reaction Gilda had expected. 'I just thought you should know about this. I think the reason this school is haunted—'

Mrs McCracken shook her head. 'No, no, no. This school is not haunted!'

'Keith thinks it's haunted, and so did Miss Underhill.'

'Both Velma and Keith have some personal problems.'

Gilda couldn't see why personal problems had anything to do with Dolores's ghost. 'Anyway,' Gilda continued, 'the people who are *really* haunted are Priscilla, Danielle and Nikki. They even do a ritual to try to keep Dolores's ghost away because they feel so guilty.'

Mrs McCracken's face looked more grim and aged than it had when Gilda first walked into the room. She regarded Gilda steadily, then seized the edge of her desk with both hands and shifted her weight around in her chair as if her clothes suddenly felt very itchy.

'Gilda, if what you're telling me about this supposed hazing incident is true, it's a very serious offence. I would be absolutely shocked if this is true. The girls in this senior class have been such role models.'

'Maybe they were different when they were freshmen.' Mrs McCracken grimaced.

'I know they feel really bad about what they did, Mrs McCracken. At least, Danielle seems to.'

Mrs McCracken watched Gilda, as if waiting for her to say more.

'I think that's part of the reason she does so much community service – to make up for it.'

Mrs McCracken pursed her lips.

'I'm not so sure about Nikki and Priscilla, though.' Gilda sensed that Mrs McCracken was somehow making her dig a hole for herself by sitting there silently, saying nothing while Gilda continued to talk. *I'm not going to say another word until she says something*, Gilda told herself. The two stared at each other for a moment.

Finally, Mrs McCracken sighed deeply. 'I'll look into this, sweetie.' She clasped her hands and rested her chin on her knuckles. 'And, aside from this issue, how are things going for *you*, Gilda?'

'Pretty well.'

'Finding some interesting activities to get involved with here?'

'I've been doing the school paper.'

'And how are your grades?'

'Grades?'

'Yes, grades.'

Gilda squirmed. The truth was, she wasn't sure how her grades were. She had a sneaking suspicion that they might have fallen below the requirement needed to maintain her scholarship, because she had just received a 'C minus' on a math quiz. *Isn't the truth about what happened to a drowned girl more important than my grades?* Gilda fumed. *Mrs McCracken doesn't even seem grateful to me for telling her what's really going on at this school. If anything, she seems mad at me!*

'Things have been pretty busy lately.' Gilda sensed that Mrs McCracken was scrutinizing her and forming a judgment. 'I got a little behind, but I'm definitely catching up.'

Mrs McCracken nodded, as if making some silent decision. She stood up abruptly, signalling that Gilda's time was up. 'Gilda, sweetie, I'm so glad you came in to talk to me. You know my door is always open to you.' She extended a squishy hand and Gilda shook it. 'Don't worry about a thing. Just go have a wonderful day, and good luck with your studies.'

Gilda left Mrs McCracken's office with an uneasy feeling. *Something about that handshake seemed final,* Gilda thought.

After Gilda left her office, Mrs McCracken reluctantly

called Priscilla Barkley, Danielle Menory, and Nikki Grimaldi out of their classrooms. One by one, they came into her office, and she did her best to tease out the truth while secretly hoping that Gilda had fabricated this distasteful story.

But Danielle confessed almost immediately. *Yes, those pages of notes were in her handwriting*, she admitted, looking paler than ever. *Yes, she had been there when Dolores Lambert was blindfolded.*

'But why did you keep it a secret for so long, Danielle? It must have been torture for you to live with this burden, sweetie.'

'I didn't want to disappoint everyone.'

Mrs McCracken held Danielle's hand and she began to cry. 'I've just been admitted to Georgetown, and now I've ruined everything.' But even as tears rolled down her cheeks, she looked as if a weight had been lifted. She looked relieved as Mrs McCracken said a prayer for her.

Nikki Grimaldi confessed, but only after learning that Mrs McCracken had written evidence in hand and that Danielle had already admitted her own involvement.

'But Danielle was supposed to get rid of those notes a long time ago,' Nikki blurted without thinking.

'Are you saying she shouldn't have told me the truth?'

'No.'

'Then what do you mean?'

Nikki quickly switched tactics. 'You have to keep in mind how really young we were back then, Mrs McCracken!' she protested. 'We've obviously changed. Look how much community service we do!'

'The problem, darling,' Mrs McCracken drawled sweetly, 'is that what you did to Dolores is called hazing, and it's against school policy. It's also illegal in this state. What you did could actually be considered a criminal offence.'

Ironically, Nikki's tears stopped flowing at the impact of this hard fact. She regarded Mrs McCracken with disappointed, bloodshot eyes.

'So what are you going to do?'

'Technically, I'm supposed to notify the authorities.'

'The *police*?'

'I understand the serious repercussions this could have for you girls, so I need to think this over very carefully and do what's fair. I'll have to talk to your parents, of course.'

'Will we get expelled?'

'I don't know, Nikki. I'll need to think about this.' Mrs McCracken could practically see Nikki's mind at work, searching for loopholes and escape clauses – hidden trap doors to the cage in which she suddenly found herself locked.

'I don't remember anything in the school handbook about hazing,' Nikki said, narrowing her eyes.

'It's there.'

'Was it there when we were *freshmen*?'

Mrs McCracken hesitated. The hazing rule had been added more recently, to reflect state law. 'What you did was wrong, Nikki.'

Mrs McCracken knew that it was likely that Nikki's parents would do everything possible to make the incident the fault of the school rather than the fault of the girls.

And what about Dolores's parents? She had heard they had moved to Hawaii, but once they got wind of the truth, the long-avoided lawsuit would surely materialize.

Wearing a bright fuchsia bathrobe and matching lipstick, Mrs McCracken sat at her bedroom dressing table and peered into an ornate mirror. The high backrest of her chair was carved in the shape of a cross that hovered just above her colourful reflection. An enormous, Gothic bed loomed behind her, its headboard carved to resemble a church pulpit.

Normally, Shirley McCracken felt at peace with herself and with the world as she methodically pulled a small army of bobby pins from her hair and unwound her long, yellow ponytail from its perch upon a heavily teased blond hairpiece (the secret foundation of her beehive hairdo). But tonight she felt decidedly uneasy because she had a terrible decision to make. She looked in the mirror, and her eyes met the gaze of twenty pairs of glass eyes sitting behind her – the collection of antique dolls that sat at the foot of her bed, watching her like a silent jury of porcelain little girls.

'*The sorrow of losing Dolores is a sorrow we all share – the loss of a member of our community and family,*' Mrs McCracken had once written in a note to Mrs Lambert. '*With the help of God, we will get through this.*'

After Dolores Lambert's death, Mrs McCracken had made sure that the Lamberts remained in the bosom of the Our Lady of Sorrows community: she organized a special mass for Dolores, she sent roses to the bereaved couple's home every year, she invited the Lamberts to the school for all special events just as if their daughter were still alive.

While treating the Lamberts like cherished family members, the headmistress simultaneously braced herself for the onslaught of their lawsuit. 'In these situations, the parents usually sue anybody they can,' her lawyer warned. 'They'll argue that you were negligent of your duties in *loco parentis*. The best we can do is show that you did warn the girls to keep off the ice and that you're now making efforts to make the school safer.'

But the dreaded lawsuit never materialized, and Mrs McCracken had given thanks. And up until this horrible day, the senior class had been the symbol of her success as a headmistress: polite, high academic achievers, model citizens to the other girls. Now, she had to face this horrible revelation that Dolores's death was actually connected to mean-spirited behaviour on the part of three of her favourite girls.

How ungrateful of this new girl, Gilda Joyce! How dare she come in from the outside and tarnish the school's reputation!

Although, deep down, Mrs McCracken knew that it wasn't fair to blame Gilda, she resented the truth and wished she could simply turn back time to the day before, when she had been happy and confident in her ignorance.

Mrs McCracken wedged herself between sheets that were starched and folded beneath the mattress so tightly, her bed resembled a large envelope. She clicked off her bedside lamp and folded her hands peacefully, as if she were lying in a casket.

In the dark, she was disturbed by another disconcerting thought: *Priscilla did not confess.*

'I've never seen these notes before in my life,' Priscilla protested, staring directly into Mrs McCracken's eyes with a wide, unblinking gaze. 'I don't know where you found this or who gave this to you, Mrs McCracken, but it's obviously someone who's very jealous, or who's demented in some way.'

'Danielle and Nikki have already told me what happened, Priscilla.'

'Maybe the two of them were involved in this, but I don't know anything about it.'

Priscilla was a good liar. She refrained from the twitches, fidgeting, overacting, excessive talking, embellishment, rubbing of the nose, and broken eye contact – the telltale signs Mrs McCracken had learned to recognize in her years as a school administrator.

Priscilla clasped her hands neatly on her lap. 'Why would I do something that horrible, Mrs McCracken?'

She's lying, Mrs McCracken thought. 'You tell me, sweet cakes. Your name is all over this document.'

'Mrs McCracken, I don't know why my name is on it, but my feelings are really hurt right now.' Priscilla gazed at Mrs McCracken with beseeching eyes. 'First I find out that two of my best friends have decided to *frame* me for some reason, then I find out that you don't trust me either. I think I've been a pretty good student, and you would think I'd get some benefit of the doubt.'

'That's why this is so hard, darlin'. Because I am so very, very disappointed to have to have this conversation with you.'

'Then stop having it.'

Mrs McCracken was stunned. Priscilla had occasionally been a bit overconfident, but she had never been disrespectful in the past. 'Watch your mouth, Miss Firecracker.'

'But I'm being falsely accused!'

'You have one more chance to tell the truth.'

'I'm not going to confess, because I didn't do anything.'

⋆ ⋆ ⋆

Mrs McCracken extracted herself from her covers and kneeled at her bedside. She rested her forehead on her folded hands — the prayer position she assumed when something particularly urgent was at stake.

But instead of praying, she found herself thinking of her two grown daughters, Cheryl and Beth, who lived far away in Baton Rouge. How would she feel if she were in Mrs Lambert's position and discovered that one of her own children had been blindfolded before she fell through ice to her death? Would Mrs Lambert want to know that in Dolores's last moments, she had been a pawn in a mean, pointless game? Poor Dolores! Poor, poor Mrs Lambert!

This could become public, with sensational stories in the paper and on television, Mrs McCracken thought. Long-suffering Mrs Lambert would have to suffer all over again.

I don't think I could bear it if I were in her position, she thought. *I have to protect her. I have to protect everyone. That's my job.*

34

Surveillance

Dear Dad:

Brad has been getting up early in the
morning to put on a business suit and
aftershave that smells of gasoline and burnt
sausages. He doesn't have a job, so I don't
know what he's trying to prove. He keeps
saying he has 'breakfast meetings' about
some 'big opportunities.'

Why am I so sceptical? For one thing,
when I come home from school, Brad is
usually lurking about wearing jeans and an
old sweatshirt, just sitting there playing video
games by himself. I think he's hooked on
'Grand Theft Auto' because he plays it even
when nobody else is home, and as you can
imagine, this drives Mom crazy. Anyway,
whenever I ask Brad how his 'big breakfast
opportunity meeting' was, he always looks
confused for a second, as if he doesn't know
what I'm talking about.

To be fair, he's tried to make himself useful by fixing a bunch of things in the house in his spare time. For example, there has been a hole in the shower curtain for about two years, and Brad covered it with duct tape. He also fixed the toaster by emptying a decade's worth of dried crumbs, and then he organized the entire garage and untangled fifty feet of garden hose. You would think Mom would be in heaven about that stuff, but instead, she's been really grumpy. Maybe he's starting to get on her nerves. To be honest, I feel kind of sorry for Brad right now.

Still, something's fishy about his 'big opportunity' meetings.

NOTE TO SELF:
TRAIL BRAD AND FIND OUT WHAT HE'S REALLY UP TO.

To: Gilda Joyce
From: Gilda Joyce
RE: SURVEILLANCE REPORT
SUBJECT: Bradley ('Brad') Squib

OUTCOME: Disturbing.
Acting on a strong hunch, the investigator (Me) convinces her gawky, adolescent

colleague-for-the day (Mr Stephen Joyce) to 'play hooky' from morning classes and accompany her on a surveillance mission. The suspect: Mr Brad Squib. The bribe: I'm doing my colleague's chores for the week.

8:40 a.m. The lead investigator and her pubescent driver follow Mr Squib's SUV at a reasonable distance.

8:41 Stephen worries that Brad will spot us in his rearview mirror. He weaves around the road prissily.
'Step on it, Grandma!' I tell him.

8:51 Brad pulls into Dunkin' Donuts. Stephen and I argue about whether we can also stop for doughnuts without being spotted. We stay in the car.

9:00 Brad emerges carrying a large cup of coffee and a chocolate doughnut with colourful sprinkles. It looks like the kind of doughnut you'd buy a four-year-old. I guess Brad is trying to cheer himself up.

9:10 Large wad of chewing gum flies from window of Brad's car. Who chews gum while also eating a doughnut?

9:15 I attempt to change radio station and am told, 'Don't touch anything in the car.'

9:16 Bad smell in Stephen's car. Odiferous boy denies responsibility.

9:30 Brad parks and walks into a bookstore. I follow him, wearing my sunglasses and trench coat. I carry a newspaper that I can also use as a disguise by opening it up and pretending to read the business section.

9:40 Brad spotted heading towards the 'self-help' section.

9:50 Titles I catch Brad skimming: *What to do when the Train of Life Heads Off the Tracks* and *Act Happy; Feel Better!*

10:13 Brad buys a newspaper and leaves the store. He climbs back into his car, and drives away.

10:30 Stephen and I watch as Brad heads towards a park bench and pulls open the classified section of the newspaper. He reads for a minute, then takes out his cell phone.

10:55 I cautiously creep up behind the bench to eavesdrop on Brad:

BRAD: 'Hey, Chuck – Squib here! BRAD Squib. Not "Squid" – Squib! S-Q-U-I-B! Don't you remember? I sold you a car a couple of years ago? Great deal. Oh. Well, sorry to hear that. If I were still at the dealership, I would get that fixed for you, but . . . Oh, sure, sure. I understand; you're busy. I'm on the run myself. Say, Chuck, if you ever hear of any hiring over there at your office . . . Oh, I know how it is. Tough everywhere, right? Oh, I've got lots of opportunities, Chuck. NO worries on my end. Take care, buddy.'

(Brad dials another number)

'Hey Larry – Squib here! Brad Squib? That's right; the car guy! Oh, sure – sure I can hold . . .'

11:00 Brad falls silent after making seven phone calls. I'm concealed by a tree just behind his park bench, so I can't see his face, but I sense that he's glum. Nobody he called wants to talk to him about a job.

11:10 I realize something! Brad isn't the person I thought he was. I assumed he was simply brash, arrogant and overconfident, and that whatever he was hiding was something shady – something like cheating on Mom with his ex-wife or compulsive gambling. But now I understand why he wanted to come over to our household acting like a big hero who was helping us out and solving our problems. Sure, he wants to help, but deep down, he's sad. In fact, I get the sense he doesn't know who he is without his job. Suddenly, this surveillance activity isn't as much fun any more.

Dear Dad,
Something has happened. I haven't seen Danielle, Nikki, or Priscilla in school all week.

I went down to Mrs McCracken's office to ask her about it, but she wouldn't tell me anything. 'This is a private matter between me, the girls, and their parents,' she said. 'I suggest you focus on your studies, sweet darlin' pie.'

I wanted to remind her: 'Listen, sweet potato cakes! I was the one who brought this whole matter to your attention in the first place! I think I have a right to know, you marshmallow-shaped hairdo in a dress!'

Luckily, I kept my cool and left her office without saying anything rash.

I wonder if they've shipped the Ladies of the Lake to a harsh juvenile detention facility where the uniforms are made of orange polyester that doesn't breathe in the humidity, and there's nothing to eat but pork rinds and tepid water. How will they survive without iced lattes from Starbucks?

On the other hand, would old McCracken really call the cops on her favourite students? If there's one thing I've learned about people, it's that they HATE having to change their minds.

35

The Runaway

When Mrs McCracken informed Priscilla that she was about to be expelled for 'gross misconduct' and lying, Priscilla became eerily calm.

'Then we have nothing more to say to each other, Mrs McCracken,' she said.

'I'll be talking to your parents soon, so I just wanted to prepare you.'

I'll be gone by the time you speak to my parents, Priscilla thought.

Priscilla walked calmly to her car, drove home, then went straight up to her bedroom, where she sat on her bed and thought systematically about her options. As she surveyed her girlish surroundings – the clutter of nail polish and perfume on her dresser, the Our Lady of Sorrows throw pillows, the high-heeled, shoplifted shoes that dotted the landscape of her floor like pointy little islands – Priscilla reflected that everything around her already seemed like a superficial movie set that would soon be dismantled because the story was over. The person who had lived in this bedroom – the girl who was about to play the lead in the school play, who tutored her peers as a National Honour Society member, who received As in advanced placement courses and was probably going to attend an elite college in some exotic location: this girl had to disappear fast. There was no use mourning her; it was simply over.

Priscilla had to reinvent herself. Now she had to become someone who was on the run.

There was no point in attempting to convince her mother and Tom to argue her case with Mrs McCracken or asking them to get a lawyer – the approach Nikki and Danielle would almost certainly take. For one thing, Priscilla suspected that her stepfather had secretly *hoped* that something like this would happen to her all along. He would lecture her sternly about moral values while secretly gloating about her misfortune. And her real father was no help at all: the last she had heard, he was either in Switzerland or the South of France, and she didn't expect to hear from him until Christmas time when he would probably send a package of gifts from overseas. This time, she wouldn't be around to open it.

Acting on an impulse to get moving, Priscilla jumped up, opened her closet door, and began stuffing pants and sweaters into a duffel bag. Rummaging in her closet, she pulled out her favourite winter and summer clothes – shorts, sundresses, a Calvin Klein bikini. As she dropped the clothes into the bag, ideas began to take shape – a vision of herself to replace the identity she had just lost.

I'm a star, she told herself. *I should be in Hollywood.*

She imagined the story they would write about her in *People* magazine someday: 'After being kicked out of a Catholic girls' school in Michigan, Priscilla Barkley threw her shoplifted Marc Jacobs pumps in the backseat of her car and made her way west – to Los Angeles. Within a week she was spotted by a director who decided to take a risk on an unknown talent, casting her as the lead in his new film *Runaway Hottie.* All we can say is, thank you, thank you Our Lady of Sorrows for expelling Priscilla Barkley so we can admire her where she belongs – on the big screen!'

Within fifteen minutes, Priscilla was all packed for her new life. She headed downstairs, dragging her overstuffed duffel bag behind her.

To her annoyance, Tom appeared at the foot of the stairs. What was her stepfather doing home from work so early? He stood aside and made a rather annoying production of waiting for her to pass.

'Running away?' he joked.

'These are just costumes for the drama club,' Priscilla lied. 'We have rehearsal tonight.'

When she reached the foot of the stairs, she noticed her mother's purse perched in its usual spot on a side table amidst an assortment of scarves and gloves.

Priscilla heard her mother talking on the phone in the kitchen. Glancing around to make sure Tom was out of sight, she carefully removed her mother's wallet from her purse. She was in luck: her mother had been to the cash machine that day. Priscilla hastily grabbed a wad of twenty dollar bills and a Visa card and stuffed them in her pocket. She imagined the argument that would ensue between Tom and her mother: Tom would want to file a police report for theft. Her mother would protest, saying, 'I'd rather have my daughter steal from me than from someone else. She could end up in jail!' Her stepfather would eventually win the argument, but by then she would already be well on her way into her new life in Hollywood.

Priscilla left the house hastily and discovered that the weather had turned cold and winterish. A sleety mix of ice and rain pelted her face as she made her way to her car.

She opened the door of her ageing Ford, tossed her duffel bag in the back seat, turned on the windshield wipers, and left her house without a backward glance.

She already felt free. She had to leave this place – this loser state with its icy rain and depressing grey skies and bad memories.

For a moment, Priscilla contemplated calling Nikki, but then changed her mind. The last she had heard from Nikki was a terse message that said, 'I'm not allowed to talk to anyone right now. I'm totally grounded. Danielle and I are both suspended from school.'

Priscilla knew that she herself had received the harshest discipline from Mrs McCracken – not so much for what she did, but for the fact that she *lied* about it. True, she had lied – but didn't it mean anything to Nikki and Danielle that they had promised *never* to reveal anything about their secret club? At the first hint of pressure, they had caved. Neither one of them had a backbone.

Spoilt losers, Priscilla thought, bitterly. *Their parents have probably already hired about five lawyers apiece. They'll probably slip a 'special school donation' into Mrs McCracken's hand to make sure she doesn't turn them in to the police.*

Nikki and Danielle had betrayed her, and Priscilla was done with them. She told herself that she would never again think about the Ladies of the Lake.

But as she headed down traffic-clogged Woodward Avenue, Priscilla felt something disturbing – the momentary, but intensely creepy, sense that reality was merely a movie projected through her eyes – that if she turned around too quickly to see where she had just been, there might be nothing behind her but the cold blackness of space.

'Stop it!' She reprimanded herself aloud, turning on the radio to distract herself from her own thoughts. 'Get a grip, Priscilla.'

In her haste to leave town, she had forgotten something important. She had no itinerary. Priscilla knew she was heading west, but that was about it. Remembering that her mother had stashed a US highway map somewhere in the car, she opened the glove compartment, located a tattered, multicoloured US highway map, and shook it open.

A small, papery object landed on the seat with a soft thud. Priscilla gasped.

It was a large, dead moth whose desiccated body had probably been lying in the folds of the map for years.

Bury all things you find dead.

Three years ago, when Priscilla had made up the rule 'Bury all things you find dead' for Dolores Lambert's benefit, it had been partly a joke and partly a self-serving whim. She didn't understand *why* being in an enclosed space with a dead creature – *any* dead creature – gave her panic attacks, but she was sick of seeing dead spiders lying around the freshman locker room, and making Dolores bury them was both sadistic and useful. Now Priscilla felt ironically compelled to carry out her own little ritual whenever she found herself sitting near a dead creature – a fly on a windowsill or a moth on a car seat. Something about the tiny, motionless bodies filled her with irrational revulsion. Lately, it was all she could do to make herself drive past the squashed raccoons and squirrels that often decorated the shoulder of the highway without pulling over to drag them off the pavement and cover them with dirt.

The moth lay brown and vulnerable upon the charcoal velour car seat, and Priscilla felt a familiar light-headed, nauseous sensation. She abruptly turned off Woodward Avenue and pulled into the parking lot of a grocery store just as a mixture of ice and rain drummed against the windshield.

With a shaking hand, she gripped one of the moth's thin, lifeless wings between her fingernails. When she attempted to lift it from the seat, the desiccated wing detached from the moth's body. For a second, Priscilla felt as if she might retch all over the steering wheel, so she pushed open the car door and burst out into the rain, where a cold downpour upon her scalp shocked her out of her panic.

I've got to get out of here, she thought.

Braced and numbed by the cold, Priscilla reached back into the car and grabbed the moth's body and amputated wing. She walked to a strip of grass between the parking lot and sidewalk, where she knelt down, raked her manicured fingernails through the wet dirt, and slapped the crushed moth down into the earth. After covering its body with dirt and bits of grass, she looked up into the blurry, electric eyes of the rush-hour traffic. *I wonder if anyone from school is sitting there, watching me right at this moment,* she thought. *I wonder if Mom has realized I'm gone yet.*

Despite the fact that she was now chilled and soaking wet, Priscilla felt better now that the moth was buried. For the moment, she was safe — ready to continue her journey into her new life.

Priscilla walked back to her car, turned the ignition, and slowly disappeared into the black river of traffic.

36

A Nasty Surprise

'I had no idea you're a nurse, Mrs Joyce,' Mrs McCracken said jovially. 'My mama was a nurse, so I considered that profession myself. But get me around a needle, and I faint right splat on the floor.'

Gilda pictured Mrs McCracken lying unconscious on a hospital floor with a syringe in her hand. Mrs Joyce offered a polite, rueful chuckle at the anecdote. She still wore her olive green hospital scrubs and hospital ID badge, having just rushed over to Our Lady of Sorrows from work.

'I told myself, "Shirley, you are not going to do a patient any good if you are unconscious!" Keep me away from the needles is all I can say!'

Neither Gilda nor her mother were particularly happy to be sitting in the headmistress's office after school. Mrs McCracken had given no reason for requesting a meeting at such short notice, and Gilda crossed her fingers that it had something to do with thanking her for her investigative work concerning the Ladies of the Lake.

Mrs McCracken clapped her hands together as if signalling that the time for small talk had ended. She pulled open a file labelled JOYCE, GILDA.

Gilda sensed that something bad was afoot. Perhaps it was Mrs McCracken's sudden serious demeanour that made her suspect that this might turn out to be a meeting about some unpleasant disciplinary matter rather than an exciting session filled with gossip and admiration for Gilda's investigative skills.

'Gilda, sweetie,' Mrs McCracken drawled, 'there have been a few concerns about your performance in school recently.'

Gilda's stomach tightened. Mrs Joyce turned her head slowly to regard her daughter with an expression of calm horror.

'Now before anyone gets upset, let me point out that Gilda's grades are just fine for any average student here at Our Lady of Sorrows.'

'Average?' Gilda hated the word 'average.' It would be better to be called 'abominable' or 'a spectacular failure.' She would prefer to watch Mrs McCracken hurl her file across the room in a fit of disgust and outrage than to be labelled with the reassuring insult, 'average student.'

'That's a little reassuring,' said Mrs Joyce, oblivious to the fact that Gilda was seething.

'The problem,' Mrs McCracken continued, 'is with Gilda's scholarship. You remember that in order to maintain this scholarship, the student's grades must never fall below a B plus average.'

Gilda and her mother were silent for a moment. 'I don't actually recall that you mentioned that,' said Mrs Joyce.

'I'm certain that I did. It's also in the documents you signed when you first came to the school.'

Gilda vaguely recalled seeing something about a 'B plus average' written somewhere, but at the time she had ignored it, assuming that it wouldn't be hard to maintain B pluses at Our Lady of Sorrows.

'Grades for the first trimester have just been turned in, and I see here that Gilda has a C plus average.'

Gilda felt a wave of irritation. Didn't Mrs McCracken realize she had been investigating a crime while simultaneously reading *Hamlet* and studying the Pythagorean theorem?

'So she just needs to study harder and bring her grades up,' said Mrs Joyce hopefully.

'There are a few other performance issue notes in her file,' Mrs McCracken continued. 'Mr Panté says she needs to work more closely with a teacher if she wants to stage any plays in the future.'

'Gilda staged a play?'

'You didn't know that?'

'Gilda never said anything to me about it.' Mrs Joyce glanced at her daughter, and her voice became very quiet. 'I would have been interested in hearing about that.'

'It wasn't your kind of thing,' said Gilda, realizing

that her mother was furious and wishing they could change the subject.

'Gilda has also received detentions for passing notes during science class, wearing her skirt too short, and playing "hooky" from her morning classes.'

Mrs Joyce's face turned pink. Gilda knew from past experience that her mother felt uncomfortable around authority figures like Mrs McCracken, and that more than anything, she hated being called into the office to hear that one of her children had misbehaved in school. Of course, Stephen never misbehaved; it was always Gilda.

'*When* did Gilda play "hooky" from her classes exactly?' Mrs Joyce asked through clenched teeth.

'Let's see. There are actually two instances here. One was at the beginning of the school year when she failed to come back to the classroom with her English class, and the other, more serious one was just a few days ago.'

'A few days ago? Where were you, Gilda?'

'If I can just say something on my own behalf,' Gilda ventured. '*Everyone* at school wears their uniform too short, so I'm really just keeping up with fashion in that department.'

Mrs Joyce glared at Gilda. Her face was rigid with rage.

'Mrs Joyce, I truly am glad to have Gilda here with us at Our Lady of Sorrows. But with a record like this, I'm simply afraid that we won't be able to continue her scholarship.'

'Just because her grade point average dropped for the first trimester?'

'Along with these other items in her file, yes. It's a very clear stipulation of the scholarship. It doesn't mean she can't continue her education here. We just need to make those funds available to students who are the true *academic* leaders in the community.'

'But there's no way we can afford this school if she isn't on scholarship!'

Mrs McCracken folded her hands and looked down at the papers in front of her apologetically.

Gilda decided she had nothing to lose by speaking up. 'Mrs McCracken,' she said, attempting to sound as adult as possible, 'I think we know what this is *really* about.'

Mrs Joyce shot Gilda a horrified look.

'Oh?'

'You know very well why I have a C plus average instead of my usual A pluses.'

Mrs McCracken flipped through some pages in Gilda's file. 'I don't see that you ever had a straight-A average in the past, Miss Gilda.'

Gilda stood up to face Mrs. McCracken as if she were a prosecutor in a courtroom. 'The *reason* I have a C plus average is because I've been working my tail off solving the biggest mystery this school has ever seen.'

Mrs Joyce looked as if she were about to grab Gilda's arm and drag her from the room.

'Mrs McCracken, you and I both know that this school has been haunted for the past three years, and I'm the one who figured out why. I'm the one who uncovered what happened to Dolores Lambert at the hands of a little group called the Ladies of the Lake, and, if I recall correctly, I told you about it just a few days ago.' Gilda paused for effect and realized that she had begun to speak in a slight southern accent that sounded as if she were mimicking Mrs McCracken's voice. 'Funny timing to take away my scholarship, don't you think?'

Mrs McCracken held up a flat palm, as if signalling a traffic stop. 'Hang on there, Miss Fancypants.' She shot Gilda a blue-eyed, fierce look that warned, *I'll direct this conversation, thank you very much.*

' "Miss Fancypants"?'

'I appreciate that you shared what you knew about the so-called "Ladies of the Lake," and I assure you, it's being handled. But that is not *your* concern. Your concern right now should be your own studies, not the problems of other students.'

'You're telling me to go mind my own business when we're talking about murder?'

'We *aren't* talking about murder. Not even close.'

'What's going on here?' Mrs Joyce looked from Gilda to Mrs McCracken, bewildered.

'Mrs Joyce, your daughter seems to see herself as something of a police officer, and I appreciate that. I really do. I have some law enforcement professionals in my own family, and they always need to keep tabs on everyone.'

'I do NOT see myself as a police officer.'

'Excuse me, Gilda. May I finish? As I was saying, Mrs Joyce: from what I've heard, Gilda is very good at spying on the other girls and talking about their problems, but she needs a little improvement in the area of taking care of her own issues.'

Gilda felt completely misunderstood and humiliated. She had an urge to pick up Mrs McCracken's stapler and throw it at her.

'I'm confused,' said Mrs Joyce. 'What is this "mystery" that Gilda supposedly solved?'

'Mrs Joyce, it's a disciplinary matter involving other girls, and the situation is confidential at this point. Out of consideration for the girls and their parents, I can't discuss it. I called this meeting to talk about Gilda – not about other students.'

'But it sounds like it must be something important.'

'Mrs Joyce, do you mind if I make an observation?'

Gilda's mother shifted uncomfortably in her chair. She obviously dreaded hearing Mrs McCracken's observation.

'I believe Gilda needs more discipline and structure at home. In my opinion, she exhibits attention-seeking behaviour, and she seems to be avoiding her own responsibilities as a student.'

'That's a load of horse crap,' Gilda blurted. 'I didn't

solve this mystery to get attention; I solved it because I wanted to get to the truth.'

'You see what I mean, Mrs Joyce? This kind of talk is disrespectful and shows a lack of self-control.'

'But Mrs McCracken—'

'Gilda, please be quiet.' Mrs Joyce spoke in a voice Gilda recognized – her 'this-is-the-final-warning-and-you'd-better-not-say-another-word' voice.

Gilda knew that some kids had parents who *always* took their side in arguments with the school principal, no matter what the circumstances. She wished her mother was one of them. Mrs Joyce tended to take the opposite approach: she assumed that if her children got in trouble at school, they must be completely at fault.

Gilda felt deflated. All the effort she had put into her investigation had only resulted in criticism and resentment. To make matters worse, she had to admit (grudgingly) that Mrs McCracken had a point: it was true that she had neglected her schoolwork and failed to take her scholarship seriously enough. She had accomplished her goal by solving a mystery, but for some reason, it wasn't a goal anybody else seemed to share or value in the least.

In the future, people will really appreciate it when I solve a mystery, and then I'll look back on this day and laugh, Gilda told herself. But at the moment, it was hard to imagine that that day would ever come.

★ ★ ★

Gilda trailed behind her mother, who walked through the school parking lot at a brisk, unfriendly pace.

'We should park our emotions outside the car for the sake of driving safety,' Gilda reminded her mother when the two of them reached the car. *Park your emotions outside the car!* was a phrase Gilda had seen on several of Stephen's driver's education pamphlets.

Ignoring Gilda's advice, Mrs Joyce climbed into the car, slammed the door, and stuck the key into the ignition. 'What were you *thinking* in there, speaking to Mrs McCracken that way?'

'Mom, if you'll—'

'Do you realize what this means for us? We cannot *afford* to send you to school here any more, Gilda!'

'I know, but—'

'Do you think opportunities like this grow on trees? Do you think other schools are just going to knock on your door and offer you scholarships willy nilly—'

'Mom! Mrs McCracken is trying to get rid of me because she knows I'm onto her.'

Mrs. Joyce tapped the side of her head with an index finger. 'Gilda, I'm starting to worry that you don't know the difference between reality and things you make up in your head.'

'Then why don't you just drop me off at the psychiatric ward right now? I'll get myself fitted into a little straight jacket, and you, Brad and Mrs McCracken can get together for a little tea party while I get a lobotomy—'

As a group of students walked past the car, Gilda quickly smiled and offered a cheerful little 'hello' wave.

'OK, Gilda.' Mrs Joyce turned to face her daughter. '*Why* do you think Mrs McCracken is out to get you?'

'Because I figured out that three of the most popular girls in the school murdered somebody.'

'They *murdered* somebody?'

'Well, they harassed a girl and made her do a weird initiation ritual, and she ended up drowning in the lake by accident. It was three years ago.'

Mrs Joyce gazed into her daughter's face intently, as if searching for evidence that the story was fabricated. 'Are you telling the truth?'

'Of course I'm telling the truth! The whole reason I wanted to come to this school was because I knew there was something weird going on. Based on what I've uncovered, my time here has actually been a huge success.'

'Losing your scholarship is not what I call a huge success.'

'Mom, I figured out what really happened to Dolores Lambert! But after I told Mrs McCracken about it, she would hardly talk to me any more. I bet you a million dollars she's worried I'll discover some other dark secrets about the school, so she wants me to leave.'

Mrs Joyce noticed Mrs McCracken exiting the school and quickly turned the key in the ignition.

'Gilda,' she said, backing out of her parking space, 'why didn't you tell me about this right away?'

'I should be able to handle this sort of thing on my own, Mom.' Gilda had never even considered talking to her mother about the Ladies of the Lake. What self-respecting psychic investigator would need help from her mother? 'It's supposed to be my job.'

'It's *NOT* your job! Your job is to be a good student.'

'Mom, did you even hear what I told you? I actually solved this case!'

Mrs Joyce shook her head. 'Gilda, if what you're saying is true, we should be talking to the police.'

For Gilda, going to the police meant acknowledging two uncomfortable truths: 1) deserved or not, three of her peers might actually get in serious trouble 2) she would have to admit that she was actually finished working on the case. After all, the police would hardly view her as a fellow investigator.

'Mrs McCracken would probably just deny the whole thing and say I have some "personal problems" ' she said, glumly.

They drove through the tidy neighbourhoods of West Bloomfield in silence. Gilda glanced out the window and saw the Lambert's large, Tudor-style house. A heavy-set woman she didn't recognize was unloading something from a car parked in the driveway. *Looks like the Lamberts are already in Hawaii,* Gilda thought. She pictured Dolores's bedraggled ghost standing under the tree in the front yard, wondering why her familiar pink bedroom had disappeared.

'Gilda, I have to go finish my shift at work, but we need to have a serious talk about all of this when I get home. I can tell you right now that you're definitely grounded for cutting classes. I still can't believe you would do something that dumb.'

Gilda was about to tell her mother to ground Stephen while she was at it, but then she remembered the sight of Brad sitting on the park bench, making calls to people who didn't want to talk to him. It was bad enough for her mother to discover that she had cut class without also learning that Brad's 'breakfast meetings' were completely fabricated.

Inside, Gilda found Brad sitting on the couch. Surprisingly, he was watching the local news instead of playing 'Grand Theft Auto.'

'Hey, Gilders,' he said. 'How was your day?'

'Well, Brad,' said Gilda, dumping her backpack on a chair, 'it was probably the worst day anyone could ever have.'

Brad bared his teeth in a broad grin. 'I bet I can top you on that one. What happened, anyway? Something I shouldn't know?'

'Mrs McCracken took away my scholarship, for one thing.'

Brad's mouth fell open. 'What'd you do?'

'I didn't do anything.'

'You must have done *something*. Shirley might act

tough, but from what I remember at the car dealership, she's a big teddy bear.'

'A teddy bear with claws and fangs.'

Brad vibrated with silent giggles. 'A teddy bear with fangs. That's funny.'

'It's not *that* funny.'

'I bet you made a joke about her hair or her girdle – something like that.'

'That would be dumb.'

'But I could understand it if you did.'

'I actually figured out the *real* story about what happened to that girl who drowned in the lake, and 'Shirley' resents me because she's afraid I'm going to get her and the whole school in trouble with the law.'

Brad hurled his body against the throw pillows on the couch in a pantomime of exaggerated surprise. 'I was *not* expecting you to say that.'

'It's true.' *I can't believe I'm telling Brad this stuff*, Gilda thought. *But what do I have to lose at this point?*

'. . . So she's playing hardball with you,' said Brad after Gilda told him the whole story of the Ladies of the Lake. He rubbed his hands together. 'This is going to be the most fun I've had all month.'

'What's going to be fun?'

'Tell you what we'll do. Tomorrow morning I'll put on my power suit with the lucky red tie, and we'll both go into old Shirley's office. And I'll say, "Look, lady, pony up the scholarship money, or expect to find a lawsuit on your desk after we go talk to the drowned girl's mother, and tell her everything we know".'

Gilda had to admit she found the idea appealing. 'I think Mrs Lambert already moved to Hawaii,' she pointed out.

'Easy enough to find her.'

'Wouldn't that be *blackmailing* Mrs McCracken?'

'Just a little negotiation tactic.'

Gilda suddenly liked Brad more than usual. Maybe they actually had something in common: they were both people who loved their work, but were either unappreciated or unemployed.

'To be honest, I'm not even sure I *want* to keep going to school at Our Lady of Sorrows.'

Just then, something on television caught Gilda's attention. Priscilla Barkley was on the local news. Rather, Priscilla's senior picture illuminated the television screen.

'A West Bloomfield teenager is missing today,' the news anchorwoman announced in a nasal monotone. 'Lisa Fallows brings us the report.'

'Police are seeking information concerning the whereabouts of Priscilla Barkley, a senior at Our Lady of Sorrows in West Bloomfield. Priscilla was last seen heading to play practice at school. Her worried parents contacted the police when their seventeen-year-old daughter failed to return home.

'Priscilla Barkley has blonde hair and green eyes. She's five feet, five inches tall and weighs approximately 120 pounds. She was last seen in her car,

340

a 2003 Ford Escort, which was found abandoned at the intersection of Woodward Avenue and Highway 696.

'If you have any information that might be of use in the search for Priscilla Barkley, please contact the West Bloomfield Police Department.'

Gilda felt stunned. Why was Priscilla missing? The image of her abandoned car at the edge of the highway was eerie.

'You know that girl?' Brad asked, noticing Gilda's shocked response.

Gilda nodded, still taken aback by the sight of Priscilla's picture on television. 'That's the girl I was telling you about – the girl who's president of the Ladies of the Lake!'

'Pretty girl.'

'What does that have to do with anything?'

Brad shrugged. 'Just stating a fact.'

A commercial for Puppy Chow blared into the room, undercutting the sombre news of Priscilla's disappearance.

'Well, you can bet the police will be talking to old Shirley now,' said Brad.

Gilda had a sense of foreboding – a feeling that somebody was in danger. She knew there was no more time to waste: she had to go to the police herself.

37

The Detective

At the West Bloomfield police station, Gilda and her mother were led to a messy office where a short man with a broad grin jumped up to greet them. 'Hi, there!' he said, shaking hands with Gilda and her mother cheerfully. 'Mrs Joyce? Gilda? I'm Detective Latmos.'

I've never met such a happy police officer, Gilda thought.

'I spoke with someone on the phone about a situation at my daughter's school,' said Mrs Joyce. 'It concerns that girl who's missing, Priscilla Barkley.'

Detective Latmos held up his hand as if he were directing traffic. 'Mind if I talk to Gilda alone for a minute, Mrs Joyce? Sometimes works better that way.'

'But Gilda's already told me everything.'

'It'll just take a minute.'

'Take a seat, Mom,' said Gilda pointing to a chair outside the door.

Detective Latmos giggled. 'You always talk to your mother that way, Gilda?'

'Just when she's being disobedient with the police.'

'The answer is yes,' said Mrs Joyce sitting down in a plastic chair outside the door. 'She often talks to me that way.'

'Something happens when they becomes teenagers, doesn't it?' The detective gestured for Gilda to take a seat in his office. 'I have a fifteen-year-old and a seven-year-old, and which one do you think is nicer to me?'

'The seven-year-old?' Gilda asked.

'You got it.'

Stacks of paper littered Detective Latmos's desk. A photograph of a boy sticking out his tongue was perched next to his computer. Gilda wondered why they were wasting time talking about the Detective's kids when Priscilla Barkley was missing. Wasn't every second crucial to finding her?

Detective Latmos perched on the edge of his desk and reached for a bag of pretzels. 'You friends with Priscilla?'

'Not exactly.'

The detective frowned and reached into his pretzel bag. 'Well, maybe you'll still be happy to know that we just found her.' He delivered the news in an understated tone, as if he were just telling Gilda that he had just found a pair of gloves he had misplaced.

'You just *found* her?'

'S'right,' said the detective, munching a pretzel.

'Is she alive?'

'Any reason she *wouldn't* be alive?' he offered the bag of pretzels to Gilda.

'It just seems like whenever you hear of someone going missing, it ends up being bad news.' Gilda stared at the bag of pretzels and wondered if she should take one. Maybe it was rude to refuse a snack from a police officer. Gilda reached into the bag and grabbed a pretzel.

'This time, there's a happy ending, Gilda. We picked her up hitchhiking near the Ohio border.'

It was hard to imagine Priscilla standing at the edge of the highway with her thumb stuck out.

'Lucky for her, it was a police officer who offered her a ride.'

'I wonder why she was hitchhiking.'

'Runaway,' said the detective, crunching another mouthful of pretzels and swinging his short legs back and forth like a young child sitting in a shopping cart. 'Well, she *tried* to run away, but then her car broke down and she had to hitchhike.'

'Oh.'

'So I take it you must know something about why she was running away. You kids in some kind of trouble?'

'Sort of,' said Gilda. 'Priscilla and two other girls at my school did something a few years ago – something that ended up getting someone killed.'

Detective Latmos stopped swinging his legs and the half-smile on his face faded. He leaned forward to listen to the story of the Ladies of the Lake with keen interest.

As Gilda spoke, a series of worst-case scenarios ran through the detective's mind. This was obviously a hazing incident, but could it also be considered negligent homicide? He began to take notes, writing names and details and envisioning the series of interviews he would conduct. He would start with the headmistress and teachers, then gradually circle in on the three girls involved. By then, a civil lawsuit would probably be filed by the drowned girl's parents. It had the potential to become a big, interesting mess. For the first time in months, he felt excited about delving into a case.

'And how do you *know* all this, Gilda?' It seemed to Detective Latmos that she was telling the truth, but how could a freshman be so certain about something that happened three years ago, during a time when she didn't even attend the school?

Gilda handed one of her psychic investigator business cards to Detective Latmos, who frowned at it sceptically, as if he suddenly wondered whether he had just wasted the last thirty minutes.

'Is this a joke, Gilda?'

'Of course not. I've been working on this case ever since school started.'

'You're telling me you're a *psychic*?'

'Yes.' Gilda sensed the detective's scepticism, but she didn't care. After all, she had solved the case all on her own, hadn't she? Hadn't she earned her professional title?

'You mean, you just saw this whole story in your crystal ball or something?'

'Well, just because I'm psychic doesn't mean I don't use my *brain*. I also searched for evidence.'

Detective Latmos laughed. 'So you're saying you have a strong *intuition* about things like this.' He preferred the word 'intuition' to 'psychic.'

'That's right.'

'Sounds like you might make a good detective.' He popped another pretzel in his mouth.

'Call me any time if you get stumped on a case.'

The detective had a coughing fit, and for a second, Gilda wondered whether she was going to need to rush over and slap him on the back. 'Sorry,' he said, reaching for a bottle of water. 'Choked.' He brushed some crumbs from his pants and stood up to shake Gilda's hand. 'Thank you for bringing this to my attention, Gilda. And you never know what will come up with this case. We just might need to give you a call.'

As Gilda shook Detective Latmos's hand and met his twinkling gaze, she felt that her work had finally been acknowledged and appreciated. She hadn't expected to leave the police station feeling happy.

38

The Break-Up

Dear Dad:

Big news: Mom broke up with Brad. Stephen
and I helped him load his stuff back into his
SUV this afternoon.

It's funny when you finally get something
that you wished for, but by the time it's
actually happening, it no longer seems so
great. Now, instead of feeling happy or
relieved, I just feel bad.

For one thing, he actually seemed sad to
leave us.

'Stephen,' he said, 'Keep that car in good
shape, OK?'

'I will.'

'Gilders, keep up the detective work. I'll
expect to read about you in the papers.'

'Don't worry,' I said, 'I will.'

'And take good care of your Mom.'

'What are you going to do now?' Stephen
asked.

'I've got lots of opportunities,' said Brad.
'Lots. I'm not one bit worried. There's no
downside; just upside.'

And with that last Squib-ism, Brad climbed
into his car and drove away.

You have to give Brad credit: no matter
how bad things get, he always *tries* to look
on the bright side.

Nobody could ever replace you, Dad, but I
admit it: I might actually miss him a little.

'This is so heinous,' said Leah, leaning back in her chair
and peering up at Gilda with disbelief. 'I mean, I've
heard all the rumours about Danielle, Nikki and
Priscilla getting in big trouble for some reason – but
are you sure *this* is what happened?'

'I'm completely sure. I've been investigating this
case since the beginning of the school year.'

Leah's carefully groomed eyebrows arched. 'Since
the beginning of the school year?! Why didn't you say
anything about this before?'

'I tried, but a *certain individual* who works on the
school paper wasn't too keen about having me
investigate the story, if you know what I mean.'

'Oh. I forgot you've been working with Danielle.'

'I knew I'd need to uncover all the evidence before
anyone would believe me.'

Leah frowned as a she re-read a passage of Gilda's
article. 'It's still hard to imagine Danielle being

involved in something like this.' She looked up and squinted into the distance, as if trying to see an image in her mind more clearly. 'Although, now that I really think about it, those three did act very cliquish back in freshman year.'

Gilda nodded, eager to hear some firsthand recollection of the Ladies of the Lake.

'They were always whispering in this annoying way that made me feel like they were probably talking behind my back. And I remember seeing Dolores sitting at their lunch able, but they never seemed to talk to her. I just assumed Dolores was too clueless to take a hint and sit somewhere else.' Leah thought for a moment, then shivered as if suddenly chilled. 'Wow. It's weird to realize they were keeping such a huge secret.'

'It's a pretty weird story.'

Leah looked at Gilda very seriously. 'Gilda, this might be the first real investigative reporting anyone on *The Petunia* has ever done.'

Gilda couldn't help but break into a goofy smile at the compliment.

Leah didn't smile. 'Unfortunately, there's no way Mrs McCracken is going to let us print this, so there's not much point in including it.'

'But that's censorship!'

'I know, but Mrs McCracken has the final say in whatever we print. She hates seeing negative, depressing stories in *The Petunia*.'

'That's dumb. The more sordid the story, the more people love it.'

'Gilda, it's senior year, and I can't afford to get on McCracken's bad side right now. You wrote a good article, but it's just not the sort of thing we cover in the school paper.' She held out the typed pages of Gilda's article.

Gilda merely stared at Leah, refusing to reclaim her work. 'A newspaper is supposed to cover *news*.'

Leah tossed Gilda's article on the chair next to her. 'Ah, to be a freshman. So promising, and yet so very naïve.'

'So you're saying we should just bury this story and replace it with another lip gloss article?'

Leah sighed. 'Gilda, what *good* will really come of publishing this story? Don't you think Danielle, Nikki and Priscilla already feel bad enough about the situation they're in? This would just be so embarrassing for them.'

Gilda felt divided. Was Leah right? Was her urge to publish the story of the Ladies of the Lake merely insensitive? 'But what about Dolores Lambert?' Gilda heard herself saying.

'What about her?'

'Doesn't she have a right to the truth? Ever since I first came to this school, I've been hearing that this place is haunted, and I bet part of the reason is that Dolores wants people to know what really happened to her.'

'How would you know what Dolores wants? She's *dead*.'

'I just have a gut feeling, that's all.'

Leah closed her eyes and rubbed her temples, as if attempting to quell a burgeoning headache.

'Besides, what if some *other* clique starts hazing people just like the Ladies of the Lake did? Maybe people need to know about this so it doesn't happen again.'

Leah stared at Gilda wearily. 'Gilda, I see your point. But it doesn't even matter whether I agree with you or not. The *problem* is what I told you in the first place: there's no way the headmistress will allow this article to run. I'm really sorry.'

Dear Dad,
I can tell the police investigation has started, because I saw a cop car in the school parking lot today. Also, every time Mrs McCracken sees me in the hallway, she looks startled, as if she just spied a rat. Then she makes a big point of not looking at me at all.

My scholarship is supposed to end after Christmas. By then, I'll be *relieved* to get out of here. Mrs McCracken is doing her best to keep things quiet, but soon the news will be out. How, you ask? I just posted my article about the Ladies of the Lake on the school message board. Nasty rumours are already spreading, so I figure people might as well

know what *really* happened. Within a couple
days, Mrs McCracken will discover the story
and delete it, but by then the news will be
out.

A few kids (like Tiara) will be intrigued
with the story, but a bunch of people will
probably be mad at me and wish they had
never heard anything about it at all. That's
one thing I'm learning: some people don't
want to hear the truth. I don't get it. Just
because you decide you don't want to talk
about unpleasant things doesn't mean they
didn't happen!

39

The Apology

Dear Mr Panté:

I'm guessing that by now you've made the acquaintance of a good friend and colleague of mine – Detective Latmos of the West Bloomfield Police Dept. (Don't let his smiling, pretzel-munching demeanour fool you: He means business!)

I'm also guessing that Mrs McCracken has held an emergency staff meeting about the 'little situation' at school that will no doubt become public news very soon. That must have been a little awkward for you, listening to the other teachers whispering in hushed tones about this 'shocking news.' I mean, you must have felt just a teensy bit uncomfortable, knowing that one of your students had alerted you to this very same 'little situation' some time ago. True, this student was less than reliable. Who could blame you for dismissing her ideas? As often

as not, her grammar homework remained
invisible. Her overuse of adjectives was
irksome, irritating, and tedious. As a
dramatist, she was brazenly unsupervised.
Why on earth would you believe that she
would know anything about a secret club
called the Ladies of the Lake?

Still, it must have been a little
embarrassing and even kind of annoying to
discover that this student's 'false accusation'
in question was in fact the TRUTH.

I apologize for rubbing it in, Mr Panté. As
you can probably tell, this is a letter written
by someone who has nothing to lose.

Mr Panté, if you haven't yet tossed this
note into the paper shredder, I also wanted to
apologize for one thing: I know you helped
me get my scholarship in the first place, and
I know I didn't live up to your expectations
in terms of classroom work. I'm truly sorry
about that. It's not that I didn't want to learn
about gerunds and split infinitives and
dactyls and teradactyls! Believe me, Mr
Panté; you know your stuff!! I just got a little
busy with the demands of my career this fall.
(You must know the feeling. I'm sure there
are many evenings when you've just gotten
an inspiration for a sonnet that will blow old
Shakespeare out of the water – but alas! A

fostering pile of adolescent, plagiarized
homework demands your attention. By the
end of the night, you find yourself sobbing
into your handkerchief, and no poems have
been written!) This scenario is just sad, Mr
Panté, and I like to think that in my little
way, I helped you prioritize that epic poem.

Thanks for all the good times, and see you
at the Oscars,

Gilda Joyce

Dear Gilda:

Yes, I was wrong not to take the story you told me
more seriously, and I sincerely apologize for that.

Since you seem to feel that I have been too critical of
you (which I did not intend), I would like to tell you a
couple of things I have appreciated about having you
in class:

1.   So far, you've never asked, 'Do we have to
know this for the test?'

2.   You think for yourself. When something
captures your interest, there's no stopping you.

3.   You're a risk-taker in the best sense of the term,
and I admire that about you.

Indeed, I would have appreciated it if you had spent
more time on your homework, etc. It's hard to strike a
balance between things we have to do and things we
want to do; that's one of the ongoing challenges of life.
I now realize that you have a true passion for

investigative work; because of this, there may be many times when you'll face a conflict between following the rules and breaking the rules. Of course, sometimes the cost for breaking the rules is high.

You'll be missed, Gilda. I have no doubt you'll distinguish yourself no matter where you go. Keep writing.

Fondly,
Mr Dudley Panté

40

Thanksgiving

Gilda and Wendy leaned against the railing of the bridge overlooking Mermaid Lake. Only a few dried leaves remained on the limbs of tree branches, quivering in the cold air. A weak sun shone above, but there was a biting chill in the wind; the first stage of winter was descending fast. Overhead, a group of ducks flew in a V-shaped formation. Something about seeing ducks fly away always made Gilda feel melancholy, as if she were being left behind.

'What's the matter with you?' Wendy asked, noticing Gilda's uncharacteristic silence. 'You're the only person I know who gets sad when she has a half-day of school.'

'Because it's the half-day before *Thanksgiving*.' Holidays always reminded Gilda that her father was not at home – not there to carve the turkey or flip pancakes at breakfast; not there to make his 'secret pumpkin pie recipe'; not there to make jokes about Mrs Joyce's lumpy mashed potatoes; not there to take everyone to the ice skating rink on the day after Thanksgiving.

'I wish I could fly south with the ducks,' said Wendy. 'I'm so sick of winter.'

'It's only November.'

'And I'm already sick of it!' Wendy leaned back and tilted her face towards the sun. 'TAN ME NOW!'

'Sh!'

'Don't shush me.'

'You're supposed to keep your voice down on this bridge.'

'I thought you didn't believe that story any more.'

'Once you hear a story like that, it always stays with you.' Gilda still held her breath when passing the cemetery on Woodward Avenue. When she was five, Stephen had warned her that zombies would get her if she didn't hold her breath when passing a graveyard, and to this day, she never took chances.

Wendy cupped her hands around her mouth. 'HEY! DOLORES!'

A crow sitting in a tree nearby gave a scornful reply. In the chilly sunlight, the lake rippled in shades of blue, green and black.

'That was disrespectful to the dead,' Gilda whispered.

'You sound like my mother. I was trying to explain to her what happened at your school, and she told me we should drop a map of Hawaii into the lake.'

'Why?'

'How else is Dolores's ghost going to find her way to her mom's new house?'

Gilda imagined a girl who wandered the

neighbourhoods surrounding the lake, always lost and alone. She wondered if Dolores's ghost knew that her old bedroom was gone – that her mother was now far, far away. 'Maybe your Mom is right.'

'While we're at it, we should drop an airline ticket and a bikini in the lake, too.'

'Ha ha.'

'And suntan lotion for ghosts. Ghost-tan lotion.'

'OK enough, Wendy.' When Wendy found something funny, she had a way of continuing the joke for several minutes.

'Hey, maybe you and my mom could form a travel agency for ghosts!'

'Sure, Wendy. I'll start working on our business plan.'

A tall figure emerged from the ruins: it was Keith. He carried something over one shoulder – a rake with a piece of pink cloth tied to one end. Spying Gilda and Wendy on the bridge, he waved.

'That's the guy I told you about,' said Gilda, '– the one who says he saw Dolores's ghost.'

Keith disappeared behind one of the crumbling walls and began to rake dried leaves from the interior of the ruins. As he worked, he reflected that it was odd to see three freshman girls sitting on the bridge after school on a half-day. There was something strange about the one with long, tangled blond hair; he didn't recognize her, but she looked eerily familiar. He rubbed his eyes and turned back to his work, grateful that his broken rake still worked pretty well bound together with a pink silk scarf he had found lying at the edge of the lake three years ago.

Dear Dad:

Happy Thanksgiving.

Do you miss having mashed potatoes and gravy up there in Heaven? The turkey was pretty dry this year, so don't feel too bad!

THINGS I'M GRATEFUL FOR:

1. Wendy Choy and I are still friends despite the fact that I've been going to Our Lady of Sorrows.
2. Mom has stopped crying about her break-up with Brad and was actually in a good mood today. (However: I caught her back-sliding and smoking a cigarette. She's also stopped wearing mascara. SITUATION NEEDS MONITORING.)
3. *MYSTERY SOLVED*: My psychic investigation skills are steadily improving!
4. Nikki, Priscilla, and Danielle have not taken revenge on me by egging our house or stalking me on the city bus – YET. Mom doubts that they'll go to jail, but you never know what could happen if charges are pressed. Detective Latmos said: 'they could get a jail sentence, a fine, probation, or just a slap on the wrist. My guess is that

they'll be most concerned about whether the colleges will still accept them after this.' He's probably right: I heard that Danielle has already been 'wait listed' at Georgetown until the investigation is complete. Maybe she'll write another essay to convince them that she's learned something from this experience. (Fingers crossed that I'll survive the rest of the year vendetta free!)

5. 'Kick the Freshmen' day was officially forbidden by Mrs McCracken this year. As you can imagine, the whole sophomore class is devastated.

6. *GOAL ACHIEVED*: Mr Panté's name has been written on the blackboard since the first day of school, and last week, when he finally began to erase his name, he noticed something very strange: the accent on the letter 'É' in his name was actually formed from a piece of material. We all watched as he stared at that letter 'É' for a very long time. Then he slowly peeled it from the blackboard and unfurled the biggest pair of POLKA DOT PANTIES anyone in the room had ever seen. Mr Panté was so surprised, he couldn't help but chuckle. 'I admit it,' he said. 'I have NOT seen this one before.'